Pursued Beyond Treachery

(Harrowed Hearts Book 2)

Teah Kemp Weight

Copyright © 2024 by Teah Kemp Weight

All rights reserved.

No portion of this book may be reproduced in any form without written permission from the publisher or author, except as permitted by U.S. copyright law. For permissions contact: teahthewriter@gmail.com.

This is a work of fiction. Characters, names, and locations are products of the author's imagination. Some locales and public figures are used to set the atmosphere, but resemblances to any other person living or dead, to any business, company, event, institution, or locale is coincidental.

Cover by Karen Thornell

Edited by Julia Allen

ISBN:978-1-959710-13-4

Contents

Preface	V
Dedication	VII
Prologue	1
1. Chapter 1	11
2. Chapter 2	19
3. Chapter 3	25
4. Chapter 4	33
5. Chapter 5	41
6. Chapter 6	49
7. Chapter 7	55
8. Chapter 8	63
9. Chapter 9	69
10. Chapter 10	77
11. Chapter 11	89
12. Chapter 12	97
13. Chapter 13	103

14. Chapter 14 — 111
15. Chapter 15 — 117
16. Chapter 16 — 125
17. Chapter 17 — 133
18. Chapter 18 — 143
19. Chapter 19 — 153
20. Chapter 20 — 159
21. Chapter 21 — 165
22. Chapter 22 — 177
23. Chapter 23 — 183
24. Chapter 24 — 189
25. Chapter 25 — 199
26. Chapter 26 — 209
27. Chapter 27 — 217
28. Chapter 28 — 223
29. Chapter 29 — 231
30. Chapter 30 — 237
31. Chapter 31 — 243
32. Chapter 32 — 249

Epilogue — 255

Also By — 259

Author's Notes — 261

About the Author — 265

Acknowledgements — 267

Preface

Thank you for reading my book. It is a great honor as an author to know that people are enjoying what I worked so hard to create. For this book I'd like to give a content warning.

If you'd rather skip this part, please do so now.

During the editing process both my editor and several ARC readers felt like it was important that readers know there is a miscarriage in this book. The majority happens in chapter 24. As someone who studies psychology in order to both improve my own mental health and those under my care, I understand the importance of taking precautions during times of high stress. However, I also understand that in order to work past certain triggers, one must test them and sit with the discomfort so the amygdala can learn to reduce its violent reactions. Please take this into consideration before you skip significant parts of the story. Above all, though, take care of yourself.

To my youngest son. I love listening to you, no matter how long it takes to get the words out.
And to anyone else who has found it hard to find the words in the moment, I see you.

Prologue

April 1811, Maidstone, Kent, England

The gentle tick of the clock on the mantel sounded more like shots from a rifle in the small parlor. Each reverberating click increased Miss Susannah Wayland's discomfort twofold as she tried to look anywhere but at Aunt Pauline Guthrie and her portly husband.

She hardly knew them after all, and yet Aunt Guthrie acted as if she and her siblings should share their private affairs with her.

"And when again is your father to return?" The rotund little woman asked as she set down her teacup.

Susannah tried unsuccessfully to stop the trembling in her hands. "As I said before, I am unsure. I do not know how long burials take."

"Ah, yes." Aunt Guthrie glanced about the room, her freckled nose scrunching as if she'd smelled something distasteful.

Susannah glanced at her younger sister Amanda who sat completely still on the tattered red settee across from the pair. Her hands were primly clasped in her lap, her shoulders back, and not one light blonde curl out of place. It was unnatural for a thirteen-year-old girl to sit so long without moving, which testified of her sister's terror at being in company with Aunt Guthrie, the woman whom they'd regularly visited when their parents took them to London as small children.

Then one day the visits had stopped. Susannah knew why, but Amanda did not. It was for the best. Knowing the discord between their families would only make her sister more distraught.

The pounding of little feet on the stairs heralded the arrival of her two younger brothers. She stiffened. Glancing at the clock, she realized it was time to teach them their music lesson, but that would not be possible with the present company.

"Nan, we're here," six-year-old Michael said as he rushed in, his brown hair flopping about. Skidding to a stop, he hesitated as he took in the guests.

Ten-year-old Andrew entered at a more sedate pace, being old enough to understand death and the state of the family. The red around his beautiful blue eyes and the droop of his mouth made Susannah wish she could hold him, but such gentleness to the boy would not be deemed acceptable to her stodgy relatives.

"Who are you?" Michael asked without reservation.

"Young man, you should learn that children are to be seen and not heard, but if you must know, I am your Aunt Guthrie, and this is my husband."

Uncle Guthrie, who had said very little before now, put his hand out to shake Michael's. "How do you do?"

Before Michael could take it, Aunt Guthrie batted her husband's hand away. The balding man's brow furrowed, and he blinked at his wife, but accepted her silent reproof without question.

"And who might you be, young man?" Aunt Guthrie peered down her nose at him, her beady eyes quailing Michael's excitement. He stepped back, now nervous to speak to someone as intimidating as their sour-faced aunt.

Andrew stepped forward and bowed. "If I may, this is my brother Michael and I am Andrew."

The words were so grown up, much like Andrew had been forced to become over the last several months. They all had as Mama's sickness had progressed.

"Ah, yes. I had heard my brother had more children."

The entry door opened and Susannah could hear their housekeeper, Mrs. Stone, speaking to her father and brother in the hall.

Terrance entered first, his lanky seventeen-year-old legs eating up the distance between her and the door in five long strides. He stooped and kissed her cheek, but before he rose he whispered, "Are you well?"

She gave a sharp nod, not wanting to speak lest her aunt overhear her.

Terrance straightened and turned to their relatives, but before he could greet them, their father's voice filled the room.

"What are you doing here, Pauline?"

Aunt Guthrie rose from her seat. "I heard the news and have come to visit with you, dear brother."

Susannah scrunched her brow. The buttery smooth way her aunt spoke to her father was so at odds with how she'd treated the boys that she did not know what to think.

"A visit. Why could you not come for a visit a year ago, or even ten? Why now?"

The steel in both her father's voice and his gaze spoke of his anger. Coupled with the fact that he hardly ever raised his voice made his current behavior quite frightening for her little brothers. She did not blame him, though. Years of hurt were buried under that anger and considering he'd just come from burying the love of his life, she would expect no less.

Aunt Guthrie cleared her throat. "Yes, well, you know we have been quite busy—"

"Nonsense." A lock of steel grey hair fell over her father's brow, but he did not swipe it away. His hands balled into fists beside his long legs.

Aunt Guthrie's head jerked back. "I beg your pardon. I have been very busy raising my girls and seeing to my duties in Society."

"Your duties, indeed. It must be so taxing to attend parties and balls."

"One must do what is necessary to make the right connections. I have two daughters to find husbands for and that can only be done if we know the right people."

His eyes narrowed. "I see. And that is your excuse for not coming to visit years ago when they were but eight and ten? Also, if I recall, you sent them away to girls' school, and yet you still did not come."

"I do not know why you are so cross. We are here now, are we not? And I have come with a proposition. I thought it might help if I took your eldest daughter back with me for the rest of the season. She could be a companion to my girls and have her time in Society."

Susannah stared and her father snorted in derision. "A companion, as if she is so poor she needs employment?"

"Well, from the looks of your home she could probably use it." Aunt Guthrie's hand swept out, indicating the outdated furniture in the room.

"Did it ever occur to you, Pauline, that money is not everything? If my wife had wanted to change the furniture in this room at any time in the last twenty years she could have, but we like these pieces. They are comfortable and familiar."

Uncle Guthrie, who had remained seated for most of the confrontation, finally made it to his feet, his wide girth making it more difficult to stand.

"My wife is only trying to be helpful, Wayland."

Her father glared at the man. They were a study in opposites, her father tall and lean compared to Uncle Guthrie's short, fat frame.

Uncle Guthrie cowered.

"How would Pauline even know how to be helpful? She has not been around to know what we might stand in need of."

Aunt Guthrie puffed out her chest. "You do not have to be so cruel."

"Cruel! Would you like to know what cruelty is? Cruel is not visiting your own ancestral home in nearly twenty years because you disagree with your brother's choice in wife. Then showing up on the day he buries said wife, the wife that you treated abominably even though she did everything in her power to pander to all of your whims. Cruel is asking him to give up his oldest child so your pampered daughters can have someone to order about. If you think my anger is cruel, you do not know the definition well enough."

Aunt Guthrie's pudgy face twisted into a scowl. "At least I am here, am I not?"

Her father stilled, his lips compressing and his hands clenching. His brown eyes held her aunt's gaze. "Too late Pauline, too late." His flat tone chilled the room. "You were unwilling to come while Leah was alive, so you are not welcome now that she is gone. Now, get out."

"You would throw out your own sister?" she sputtered.

"Come, man. Do be reasonable," Uncle Guthrie said.

"I *am* being reasonable. Your treatment of my wife, and by extension all of my children, was despicable—I still do not understand how Leah put up with it for so long—but now that she is gone, the best thing I can do to honor her memory is to never let either of you taint my children's memories of her."

Aunt Guthrie opened her mouth to protest, but Father cut her off. "Do not deny it, Pauline. I have heard the rumors you spread in London and here in the countryside. So take your deceitful tongue and be gone."

The awful tick of the clock on the mantel again filled the room in the wake of her father's anger. Susannah hated the sound and vowed to silence it once everyone left.

Aunt Guthrie looked at each of them. Was she trying to gather her words or seek an ally? If the latter, she would find none.

She and Terrance were old enough to remember their last visit to London when Aunt Guthrie had pulled them aside to tell them their mother would probably die birthing Andrew, but it would be for the best for all of them. She'd never been a good match for their father anyway.

The fear and pain of those heartless words had remained with Susannah and her brother ever since. When they had told their father, he vowed never to send them to London again.

Their mother had been far more forgiving, sending letters and trying to make amends. It never ceased to amaze Susannah how her mother could show kindness to a woman who treated her so badly. Even more perplexing was why Aunt Guthrie held such dislike.

Perhaps in the beginning, before the shock of her parents' sudden marriage had worn off, she could understand, but not after decades of concessions and overtures of good will. There had to be something more.

"Fine," Aunt Guthrie snapped. "But mark my words, brother. You will regret this day. Do not expect me or Mr. Guthrie to put forth one farthing to help you or your brood of sniveling brats. You are all dead to me now."

"So be it!"

If Susannah had thought the tick of the clock abrasive, the boom of her father's pronouncement was like a cannon blast in her ears.

"Guthrie," Aunt Guthrie barked at her husband, then stormed out. The quieter man glanced about the room, true regret in his eyes, but when his wife called him again, he jumped at her bidding.

It was sad, really. He seemed a decent sort of man if a little browbeaten. Perhaps if circumstances had been different Susannah could have even come to like him. But if he continued to allow his wife to lead him around by the nose like a bull on a chain, he would only add to the problem.

When the front door closed, her father's stiff shoulders slumped. Michael, who had been glued to the floor the whole time, burst into tears. Susannah scooped him up and set him on her lap.

Andrew too began to cry, but silently. Amanda placed a sisterly arm about his shoulders.

Terrance took their father's elbow and led him to a chair where he gratefully sat.

"I am deeply sorry, children. That is the last thing I wished for you to witness on such a difficult day." The lines about her father's eyes had deepened this last month as Mama's health had faded. They had all known the cancerous growth would take her eventually, but it still did not make the experience any easier.

One look at her siblings and Susannah knew they could not bear any more sadness for the day. "Terrance, will you ring the bell for Mrs. Crabtree?"

"But I do not want to go back to the nursery," Michael said through his tears. "It is music lesson time."

"What if I have Cook send up some of your favorite ginger biscuits?"

This perked the little boy up. "And raspberry tarts?"

"I do not know about that. It will depend on what she has in the larder."

He bounced on her lap. "It has raspberry tarts. I know, Andrew and I checked."

Susannah smoothed his hair back, thankful for the simplicity of youth when biscuits and tarts could take away the sting of death. If only it were that easy for the rest of them.

"What do you say, Andrew? Would you like some raspberry tarts?"

Andrew's enthusiasm was not quite that of Michael's, but he gave a weak smile and a nod.

When the nurse arrived, Susannah gave her instructions, asking Amanda to accompany them. Her sister's dubious expression spoke of her displeasure at being dismissed with her little brothers, but what Susannah had to say was a discussion best left to the adults.

"Did everything go smoothly with the burial?" she asked as soon as the children were gone.

"As well as can be expected." Her father sighed, his shoulders slouching even farther.

Terrance leaned an elbow against the mantel. "The vicar said many pretty words, and there were a good many men in attendance."

Her brother continued to describe the proceedings, but Susannah heard very little. That women were not allowed to attend funerals had never bothered her before, but when she'd been barred from attending her own mother's burial, the tradition had become excessively unfair. Who had cared for her mother? It was not men.

Some might have argued the local physician counted against that assessment, but the man had hardly even lifted a finger to help Mama. He would come, glance at the growth on her chest and then leave. The most he had ever done was identify her condition and suggest she see their butcher of a surgeon. That, and send them exorbitant bills.

The physician had not even been decent enough to leave them laudanum for Mama's pain. Thank heavens for the apothecaries' remedies, otherwise Susannah and the housekeeper would have had little to help her through the last stages of her disease.

Terrance's words broke into her irritated thoughts. "Lord Newhurst should be by soon."

"John is coming?"

Her father frowned. "You are fully grown, Susannah; I think it time you address him properly."

"Oh, I do when I am out, but it is hard to break old habits."

They had grown up together after all. Well, of a sort. She still remembered the first time she'd seen Johnathan Newhurst. She'd been seven when her father finally deemed her old enough to sit through services. For the entire week she'd been excited to do something so grown up, but the experience had been far more tedious than she'd expected. The only distraction had been the white-blond hair of the young man sitting in front of her.

She'd never seen such light hair and without thinking, had reached out to touch it. Her father had snatched her hand back, but not before John had turned and smiled at her.

After services, her father had talked to Lord and Lady Newhurst for what seemed like forever. John had taken pity on her and kept her entertained with a piece of grass that he made into a whistle. She did not have an older brother, but that day she'd found herself wishing she did. One who resembled the lanky youth who had been happy to entertain a restless little girl.

For the next eight years he'd never failed to bring her a treat or some other trinket whenever he was home from Harrow or later Cambridge, and she'd adored him for it. But when he'd returned from his tour of the continent two years ago, something had changed. He'd grown more reserved and a bit distant. It perplexed her.

As did her altered view of him. Something had changed between them in the year and a half they'd been apart, a shift she worried was more the imaginations of her fanciful mind than founded in actual fact.

John had still been attentive to her family, as was evidenced by the amount of time and effort he'd spent these last two weeks entertaining her siblings or bringing baskets of food from his kitchens. But he no longer spent time solely with her. And when they were together, he seemed to guard his words like a treasure he feared would run out.

Three taps from the knocker on the front door interrupted her father and brother's quiet conversation.

"I suppose that must be Lord Newhurst now." Her father rose to his feet. Before he made it to the door, the housekeeper ushered John in.

His hair had darkened since his youth to a very distinct yellow. The shoulders and arms that had once been thin had filled out, but still held a slender and athletic appearance. She and Terrance rose to greet their guest.

When John's blue eyes flicked to her, she gave a soft smile. He did not. Instead he clasped his hands behind his back and shuffled from one foot to the other.

"Newhurst." Her father reached out his hand and the man took it. "Could you come with me to the study? I have some business to discuss with you."

John nodded.

"Terrance, you too. It is time you start learning the ways of the estate."

Her brother glanced at her before following the other men. It was strange seeing him take on such a grown-up role, but with his education at Harrow complete this was the next logical step.

With the click of the door behind the men, Susannah sunk back into her chair. Alone.

It was unfair, really. She had been alone when Aunt Guthrie had arrived and she was alone again now. The click of the infernal clock mocked her as if to say, "Alone, alone, always alone."

She shot to her feet, picked up the clock, and stopped its small pendulum from swinging. For hours the piece of wood and gears had stood silent after her mother's death, but with the dawning of the day her beloved mama was buried, the clocks had been started again.

It was too soon. Far too soon.

PROLOGUE

Susannah needed more time. More time in silence, more time to grieve... more time with her mother. But time had been stolen from her. From all of them.

Chapter 1

NOVEMBER 1811, MAIDSTONE, KENT, ENGLAND

Lord Johnathan Newhurst entered the Waylands' home and handed his hat to Mrs. Stone. The routine was familiar. He'd been coming to Wayland Lodge most of his adult life, but the visits had become far more regular after Mrs. Wayland's passing. How much comfort he brought the family these last six months, he did not know, but he liked to think they drew as much enjoyment at his coming as he did from being there.

Michael appeared at the top of the stairs and, spying him, bolted down, nearly falling in the process. "Lord Newhurst," he called out. "Are you come to play with us?"

At the bottom of the stairs, he flung his arms about John's legs almost toppling him with the force of his little body.

"Whoa there, careful."

"Do have a care, Michael," Andrew said from the top of the stairs, then slowly descended as a man of one and twenty might rather than a boy of only ten. He'd become so serious these last few months that John hardly recognized him.

"Have you heard?" Michael asked untangling himself from John's legs and hopping from one foot to the other.

"Heard what?" Johnathan smiled at the boy's exuberance.

"Nan is going to London so she can get a husband."

John's smile faltered.

"You were supposed to let Susannah tell him herself, Michael." Andrew frowned.

Susannah was going to London? But how, when, why? He supposed he knew the why, but what reason should she have to go in search of a husband so soon? His chest tightened.

"Where is your sister?"

"In the sitting room with Lady Stanford."

As if to punctuate Michael's words, giggles floated down the hall from the small sitting room he knew Susannah loved. She'd taken a liking to the room and could be found there nearly all hours of the day, instead of in the front parlor where most of her family gathered. It was odd, but when he'd questioned her, she'd mumbled something about an infernal clock.

Having taken him an entire ten minutes to formulate the words to ask about her curious behavior, he opted not to question the answer.

When had talking to Susannah become so hard? Ah, yes. When he'd returned from his tour of the continent years ago to find that she had transformed from a sweet schoolgirl into a ravishing beauty.

Her golden blonde hair had grown longer, allowing for all those intricate curls that always seemed to kiss her cheeks, and somehow her big brown eyes had gotten larger in her perfectly oval face.

And her curves...

Johnathan swallowed hard and gave his head a shake. It was hard enough gathering the courage to speak to Susannah without remembering she had a handsome figure. He needed to rein in his thoughts if he wanted to have the wherewithal to inquire why, after all this time, she would ever want to go to London for a season.

It was a dirty, ugly city, but most of all it was full of people. Lots of people who talked incessantly about the most inane topics.

Then again, Susannah loved to talk, and she was good at it. Unlike him. He only had three subjects he conversed decently on: painting, uncommon words, and inventions. Much beyond that and he turned into a stuttering mess—especially with ladies.

The pretty ones were the worst. Hence his ineptitude with Susannah.

Unlike most ladies, however, Susannah did not mind his propensity toward silence. She simply filled in the words he could not find, and that talent was exactly why he'd not let their awkward friendship fall to the wayside.

That and her parents' kindness after his own parents' passing.

The Waylands had been like family to him ever since he'd inherited Gimly Hall as a lad of eighteen. He'd not been ready, and his knowledge of how to run an estate had been minimal at best.

Mr. Wayland had taken him under his wing, training him during his breaks from Cambridge, and caring for the property when he was away. The arrangement had been mutually beneficial as the gentleman had not wanted others to know how dismal his family's finances had become, nor that he'd needed to take up work as an estate manager to bring his own property back into prosperity.

Thankfully, Society only saw his generosity as he tutored a young man in finance and supported him through his grief.

And Mrs. Wayland... thoughts of the sweet lady pulled at his heart and pushed his feet into motion.

"Don't you want to hear the rest of my story about the toad?" Michael whined.

Johnathan stopped. He'd been so preoccupied thinking about Susannah that he'd not heard one word in ten of Michael's monologue.

"My apologies Michael. Might I hear the story when I'm done speaking with your sister?"

The boy's shoulders sagged and the corners of his mouth turned down. "Oh, all right. But I might not be able to tell it to you once Mrs. Crabtree has her tea."

Michael walked away, dragging his feet.

"Why not?" Johnathan called after him.

Andrew answered for him, "Because Michael will get more lines to write when it hops out of her teacup."

While Andrew's mouth stayed placid, the corners of his eyes crinkled as if he were fighting the urge to smile. Neither boy cared for their nursemaid, and Johnathan could only imagine the enjoyment they would get from seeing the cranky old lady dance about like a cat who'd stumbled onto hot coals. But it would not do for Michael to be in the suds again.

"Would you be a good lad, Andrew, and go remove it? I would very much like to hear the end of your brother's story."

"But that would spoil the ending," Michael said, hanging over the banister. "Don't you want to know what Mrs. *Crabby* does?"

Johnathan hid his smile, knowing if he encouraged the lad in his mischief, it would only distress Susannah more. She was already at her wits' end keeping them out of trouble.

Clasping his hands behind his back, Johnathan said, "I think a gentleman would be more considerate of older ladies, especially ones as elderly as Mrs. Crabtree."

A devilish smile lit Michael's face, and Johnathan knew he'd misspoke. Heaven help him if the boy quoted verbatim what he'd just said about Mrs. Crabtree. She'd be livid at being called elderly.

"John—I mean, Lord Newhurst," a light feminine voice exclaimed from behind him.

He did not need to turn to know who spoke. That voice was etched in his mind and planted deep in his heart. And even on the days he did not have the opportunity to hear it in person, it managed to fill his dreams.

"G-g-good morning, Miss Wayland." Blasted stutter, why did it have to emerge when he needed to sound the most composed?

"I did not know you were coming today." Without a moment's hesitation she slipped up beside him, and, taking his arm, led him into her sitting room. "Lady Stanford, look who has come to visit."

Lady Stanford rose gracefully to her feet, her brilliant blue eyes dancing with delight. "*Lord Newhurst*, it is always a pleasure to see you."

What was with all this Lord Newhurst business? It had been months since Lady Stanford had begun calling him by his given name, an intimacy afforded her by her marriage to one of his closest friends. Miss Wayland also called him John—although he had noticed she'd become more formal after her mother's death. There was something afoot.

"Good morning, Lady Stanford. I—" Johnathan paused. In all the months she'd been calling him John he'd not once addressed her so informally even though she'd insisted on it. Was this a commentary on his own behavior? Were the ladies upset that he'd not dropped his formality?

He glanced between their far too sunny faces and his already paralyzed tongue tied itself into knots. One pretty woman was bad enough, but when two looked at him with such expectation, every clear thought flew from his head.

CHAPTER 1

"Proclivity means an inclination or predisposition toward something, most often toward something objectionable."

They both stared at him. Lady Stanford—nay, Melior's—brow furrowed, and Susannah cocked her head to the side.

If only the floor would open up and swallow him whole.

It had been weeks since he'd spouted random definitions of words and he'd been sure he was making headway toward ridding himself of the nervous habit. If only they were men. His mouth obeyed his will far better in the presence of his own sex.

"That is an interesting word," Susannah finally said. "Tell me, did you land on that one in particular because you feel Lady Stanford and I are up to something objectionable?"

His cheeks burned. "No, I-I best be going." Spinning around, he started for the door.

"Lord Newhurst, wait." Susannah rushed after him. "I had not meant to make you uncomfortable. Please forgive me."

He glanced at her. Why should she be sorry? He was the buffoon.

"I do have some news for you," she rushed to say. "Lady Stanford has offered to sponsor me for the season. Is that not wonderful?"

No, but Johnathan did not wish to offend any more than he already had, so he merely nodded.

"You will be attending Parliament this year, will you not?" she asked.

Another nod seemed the only appropriate response.

Susannah smiled. "Then we shall see each other in Town."

Her words were so hopeful that he did not want to inform her how little he went about in Society. However, if Susannah was to be in town, perhaps he'd find the pleasures of London more... well, pleasurable.

His attention caught on a blonde curl that brushed against her neck, the light shimmering off its golden surface. He itched to paint it. Could he catch the essence of such beauty?

Slowly he let his gaze traverse her cheek and then her face, memorizing the details. He'd painted Susannah dozens of times but had yet to adequately capture her vibrance.

When their eyes met, he stilled. That familiar energy pulsed through him in the most discomfiting way, but he saw none of the same in Susannah. She appeared as happy and peaceful as he'd ever seen her. With an iron clad fist, he pushed his attraction back down, stuffing it in the dark closet he'd fashioned for it.

She only saw him as an honorary brother. And at seven years her senior he could understand why. She'd been a little girl when they'd met, not much older than Michael. Eyes bright with childhood admiration, she'd always come to him with her little problems like a sister would. Stepping over that line now seemed like a betrayal of trust.

"Michael asked me to come see him before I leave," he blurted out.

"I see." The brightness in her eyes dimmed.

"Good day, Miss Wayland, Lady Stanford," he said and rushed out of the room without looking back.

CHAPTER 1

Johnathan swirled a dab of white and just a touch of red into the yellow paint until it finally resembled the golden glint he'd seen in Susannah's hair. Choosing a fine tipped brush, he gently layered the color onto the darker shape of the curl on the canvas. With each stroke he berated himself for how foolish he'd acted.

In a little over two months Susannah would be presented to the whole of London Society, which meant he only had that much time to enjoy her company without the complication of other suitors. And what had he done? He'd run away to listen to her little brother's detailed description of a toad.

A chill crept up his back. He'd have blamed it on the cold, but the roaring fire in the hearth chased away any that might seep in through the cracks around the window. No, the discomfort came from knowing Susannah's purpose for going to London. Could she not wait a few more years to find a husband? She'd not yet reached her majority. Why rush? There were plenty of other experiences to have in life.

He should know. At six and twenty he'd had seven more years to explore the sights and sounds of life. She could perhaps take a tour of the continent as he had.

"That is ridiculous," he muttered to himself. If finances did not keep her home, her sex most definitely would. Young women could not gallivant about like men could. Plus, the war with Bonaparte had ruined a good deal of travel for everyone. Sad, really. Susannah would have loved Italy and Spain.

Setting down his flat edge brush, he reached for one with a fine tip. He'd not painted enough curls. Perhaps a few small ones settled about the back or her neck would fix it? Slowly he painted another curl with chestnut brown, then layered it with the darker yellow. The latter color brightened his thoughts.

It reminded him of the flowers Susannah had picked one Sunday after services when she'd been eleven and so full of life. He'd studied her as she'd skipped from one group of cowslip to another until she'd gathered a bouquet full. Her cheerfulness had been contagious, and he'd actually smiled. A rarity that day.

When she'd finished, she presented him with them. Her little offering had done more to heal his hurting heart than any of the empty words of condolences from the rest of the parishioners.

That had been his first Sunday back from Harrow after word had come of his parents' death. And even though he'd had two weeks to adjust to being an orphan, it had felt like the first day. Up until then, he'd been able to pretend they were still waiting for him at Gimly Hall. But a whole night in the gigantic pile of stones he called home had brought reality crashing down on him. They would never return. Instead, they lay in the cold sepulcher where his ancestors had been buried for decades.

Guilt at not being home when they'd both fallen ill mixed with the logic that, if he'd been home, he may have also died. In the end logic won out, as it always did.

As it really should now, but somehow his hands kept painting Susannah's familiar features. The same chin, the same jaw. Only now she'd grown from a compassionate young girl to a vibrant and intelligent woman. Like a flower in the bud, she'd bloomed into the most incredible rose he'd ever seen, one who took his breath away by merely glancing his way. Perhaps his words had also fled with the air that should have filled his lungs, because it had become increasingly difficult to speak with her.

And yet she'd not been put out as others of his acquaintance had when words simply would not flow from his mouth.

Long buried memories from his first days at Harrow fought their way to the surface.

"Spit it out, stupid."

"What a freak."

"Look, it's Addlepate Newhurst. Careful not to fa-fa-fall."

The last had been said before the upper-class boy had tripped him. Johnathan shook his head to dislodge the bad memory. That was the day he'd decided it was better to remain silent than to speak before he had complete control over his tongue—a battle he still fought to this day.

And while other women had become frustrated with his lack of conversation, Susannah had reverted to speaking for him, reading his thoughts and forming them into the words when he could not. Lud, he loved that about her.

Of course, there really wasn't anything he didn't love about Miss Susannah Wayland. Well, almost everything. If only she did not view him as the equivalent of an older brother.

Chapter 2

Susannah's fingers ran over the black and ivory keys with such speed that perspiration beaded on her forehead. Moisture pooled in her eyes but she gritted her teeth and pushed it back, refusing to let emotion take control.

"It is not a race, you know," Lady Stanford said from the doorway of the music room at Havencrest.

Startled, Susannah's fingers came to a crashing halt. Usually the Stanfords left her alone to pour her feelings into their piano, something she appreciated.

Lady Stanford crossed the room to stand by her. "Is not that piece played at a slower tempo?'

Reaching beyond the pain that still lingered at the surface, Susannah managed to find a smile. "Perhaps it was a little rushed, but Beethoven's work is meant to be played with some speed."

"True."

Her Ladyship's blue eyes studied her far too closely and Susannah redirected her gaze to the piano keys. Slowly she played a Scotch ballad from memory, allowing her fingers to float along the keys at an acceptable pace.

The gentle lull of the song did not lend an escape to the turbulent feelings rushing about inside her, but there was no need to worry Lady Stanford with her problems.

Scooting onto the bench next to her, Her Ladyship asked, "Are you excited to go to London?"

A true smile pulled at Susannah's lips. "I am indeed. Tell me, do they really have a lion at the Tower of London?"

"Yes, and a bear or two."

"I should like to see a bear. Can they really stand on their hind legs like people?"

Lady Stanford confirmed they could and went on to explain in great detail her last visit to the menagerie, but Susannah paid little attention to her description. She was not usually so inattentive. On any other day she would relish the details, asking enough questions to keep them talking until supper.

Today, however, her grief had collided with reality and ricocheted off every corner of her heart. It had been Mama's greatest wish for Susannah to have a London season, and now she would have one—but her mama would not be there.

She'd taken solace in knowing that John would be, but he seemed fairly put out with her good fortune. He'd not even congratulated her, only stared at her like she'd lost her senses. Then again, he'd never liked Town all that much, but that did not mean she could not enjoy it.

There were so many places she wished to see, like Vauxhall Gardens, Hyde Park, the opera, even the Royal Academy's Art exhibits. Mostly, she looked forward to finally being acknowledged as a grown woman. She'd been out in Society for nearly two years, although most of that time had been spent at home caring for her mother, but the way John behaved one would think she still scampered about in short dresses, picking flowers and climbing trees.

The steady soft rhythm of the music began to grow in both speed and volume, drowning out Lady Stanford's words.

Her Ladyship's dark eyebrows pinched together as she glanced down at Susannah's hands, then back at her face. "Miss Wayland, is something upsetting you?"

Susannah slowly stopped, curling her fingers and shutting her eyes. Why could she not rein in her emotions? She'd done so well these last few months, limiting her tears and making certain she did not burden those around her.

She let out a slow breath. "I am perhaps a bit fatigued."

It was the excuse she often used. In reality she was sinking into a dark abyss of loneliness that threatened to swallow her whole. But sharing her feelings only brought others down with her, and she could not bear to be the rain in their day.

She'd seen the way her father and siblings had floundered after her mother's passing. It was especially apparent when she did not work to keep up a brave front. They needed her to be the positivity in their lives and she'd much rather be their sunshine, even if it meant a gale of unearthly proportions brewed inside her tired mind.

"You have been playing for quite some time today." Lady Stanford glanced down at the piano. "Let me call for some tea and we can discuss the dresses we need to have fitted for you."

"Dresses?"

"Well, of course. You do not believe I'd take you to London without a town-worthy wardrobe, do you?"

"But I—"

Lady Stanford held up her hand. "Not one more word. I will have my way on this, Miss Wayland, so you best not argue." The right corner of her lips tipped up and she shook a playful finger at her. "And you know how often I get my way."

Susannah chuckled. The beautiful woman did get her way quite often, but only because her way was generous. Who could refuse such kindness?

"Thank you, Lady Stanford," she said as they exited the music room. "I do not know how I can ever repay your generosity."

"You do not. If you repaid me, it would not be generosity. It would be a loan, and I am not the Bank of England."

The moment Susannah entered Wayland Lodge, her siblings inundated her with questions and requests. Such was the case every time she took an afternoon to make use of the Stanfords' music room. If a few hours away could create such chaos, what would happen when she left for several months?

The question followed her all the way to her room that night. They needed her. As much as she loved her father, he did not fill the hole their mother had left. She'd done her best to pick up the pieces, but she feared she was failing them. If she left, it would be a confirmation of her inadequacy. Perhaps she should remain home.

A quiet knock sounded on her door and she fully expected Amanda to come in for her nightly reassurances that all would be well—something Susannah did not think she could give tonight—but Terrance stepped through the door at her bidding.

She sighed. "Is Andrew having another one of his nightmares?"

"No, I came to talk with you."

Susannah tipped her head to the side. "Me?" Of all her siblings Terrance had needed the least amount of comforting, choosing to grieve on his own—if he did at all. He had become the rock of the family as their father floated between good days and bad. But perhaps now that Papa was again taking on the majority of the responsibilities around the estate, Terrance felt at liberty to face the situation.

"Yes, you. You have not been well all day, Nan. What is the matter?"

She tried to protest but he stopped her.

"I am not blind. You interrupted Amanda at breakfast when she was telling you about her latest book. You did not try to interact at all with Andrew even when he patiently waited for Michael to finish his monologue about the injustices of taking tea in the nursery. And you even snipped at Michael a few times. It's not like you. Something is on your mind and I aim to put things to rights."

She leaned back in her chair by the fire. Terrance always had been a fixer. No wonder he'd gone to all the trouble of searching her out.

"Will they hate me?"

Terrance's brow furrowed and his nose scrunched. "Michael, Andrew, and Amanda? I doubt it. A little distractedness and scolding are no cause for hate."

"No, will they hate me for leaving and going to London?"

CHAPTER 2

His expression cleared and he took up the chair across from her. Clasping his hands and resting his elbows on his knees, he looked contemplatively at her. "I don't think so. In time I think they will see how important this step is for you."

"But is it? Many do not take a season and still find themselves happily situated."

"True. But those women do not have a choice. You do. Take this chance, Nan. It may be the only one you get. Mama would have wanted you to go."

"Is it not selfish of me?"

"No," he said with force. "You have given everything for everyone these last eighteen months. And as the selfish siblings that we are, we've let you be our foundation. It's a heavy burden, and, honestly, I have wondered when you would break. It's your turn to think of your own future."

"You're not selfish, Terrance."

"Oh, but I am. Selfish enough to ignore your suffering until today. You need a reprieve, and I am going to make sure you get it."

Her eyes crinkled. "Are you threatening to kick me out if I refuse to go?"

He smirked. "Absolutely. I'll tie you up, gag you, and put you in the Stanfords' carriage myself if you refuse."

An unexpected tear gathered even though she was smiling. "Thank you."

He laughed. "I don't think I have ever been thanked for threatening to bodily throw someone out, but I will take it."

"No. Thank you for seeing my need."

He placed a hand over hers. "It is I who should thank you for always seeing ours. You really do too much. Let us take some of the responsibility for our own problems. Now I order you to go enjoy yourself."

She sniffed as the tear rolled down her cheek but smiled. "I will do my best."

Chapter 3

Johnathan shifted nervously in his seat awaiting his friend's arrival. Glancing at the books on the shelf, he wondered what was keeping him. He and Nate had been friends for as long as he could remember, their mothers having been excessively fond of one another. His earliest memories involved them giving their nursemaids a fright when they'd shimmied up an old log that had fallen across the River Medway.

Sir Nathaniel Stanford finally entered, a grin on his face. "Well, John, have you heard the good news?"

"Perhaps. What news are you referring to?"

He sat down at his desk. "About Miss Wayland traveling with us to London?"

How could he forget? The whole week he'd agonized over thoughts of Susannah surrounded by throngs of men mesmerized by her beauty. Perhaps his imaginings had become a little overdramatic, but she would certainly draw attention.

"I had heard," he said quietly, careful not to let his feelings overwhelm his ability to speak clearly.

"And what do you think of it? Are you not pleased for her?"

He would sound like a complete ogre if he said he was not, especially since the likelihood of Susannah's own father being able to take her to Town was very slim. Too many obligations to attend to.

"It is a great opportunity," he finally said.

"And we shall see you in Town often, I hope."

Johnathan studied Nate's face. The soft brown hair that curled about his ears and neck was styled in the popular Brutus fashion. Starch shirt points nearly touched his straight square jaw as intelligent green eyes gazed back at him.

"I have a lot of responsibilities in Parliament, Nate. While many go to Town for the entertainments, I go to work."

"Work? Do not let the rest of the Ton hear such blasphemy. You know a gentleman is only to have a life of leisure."

John chuckled. "You and I both know neither of us conforms to the dictates of polite Society. If so, I would not have sat on the floor for the better part of the afternoon yesterday playing jacks with a six-year-old."

Nate sobered. "How are the Wayland children doing?"

"Michael is still causing havoc with their nurse, but that is to be expected of one so young. Andrew, on the other hand…"

"Yes?" Nate said when he took too long to continue.

"He has never recovered from Mrs. Wayland's death. I do not believe we will ever see the carefree boy that once played in the fields roundabout Wayland Lodge again."

Nate shook his head. "Such a shame."

"It is. Fortunately Terrance is doing well under his father's tutelage and may be able to help take on some of the estate management." He did not add so Mr. Wayland might have only one estate to keep in line, not having ever shared how much the older man had cared for the Newhurst properties.

"And Miss Amanda?"

"She does not cry as much as she used to, but she is distraught about her sister leaving for so long."

Nate hung his head. "I feared that would be the case, but you must see how much of a help this will be for Miss Wayland. She has taken on the burden of a large family since long before her mother's death. That is a heavy load for a woman not yet twenty years old."

"I-I do understand, and I am not o-opposed, but that does not mean it will not be a stress on the entire family. Mr. Wayland has already begun looking for more help to compensate."

"As he should have months ago."

Johnathan stiffened. "He has done the best he could under the circumstances. How would you feel if you had lost Melior?"

His friend's shoulders slumped. "Terrible."

CHAPTER 3

"Now imagine spending two decades growing close to one another, expecting to spend many more, only for them to be stolen from you."

"I get your point, John; you do not need to belabor me with it."

"Then you will understand if he has not been up to obtaining new staff."

"But the housekeeper—"

"Has had enough on her hands what with Mrs. Wayland's lady's maid retiring and no governess to speak of for Miss Amanda."

Nate must have sensed how much the topic upset him, for he suddenly stood and pulled a book from the shelf. "I forgot to return your book on the Pontcysyllte Aqueduct. Fascinating invention, that."

Johnathan took the book, running a hand over the leather-bound cover. It was not the reason he had come. He had a very important question to ask, but when he tried to form the words in his mouth they faltered.

"Is it—" He stopped, wondering if Nate was the right person to ask. He had, after all, been required to intervene in Nate's own marriage at its very beginning. If he, a veritable novice at interacting with women, had seen what his friend could not, would Nate have the answers he sought?

Then again, seven months had elapsed since he'd tricked Melior and Nate into posing together for a painting at the beginning of their rocky, scandal-riddled marriage. Perhaps his friend had learned a few things since then.

"Nate, what do women like?" he blurted out before he lost his nerve.

"Are you speaking in general or is there a particular female that you wish to impress?"

Heat crept up Johnathan's neck at the insinuation. "In g-general," he choked out. Speaking of his particular interest had never been easy, not even to friends. Nate had shared openly of his attraction to Melior when they were at Harrow, but Johnathan had never found the same amount of comfort in any of his childhood friends.

Feelings crowded his thoughts and jumbled them so much his tongue stopped obeying his will. Stuttering was embarrassing enough, but to do so through a confession of love would be humiliating.

Nate tapped his chin. "Pretty compliments seem to work well, but considering your difficulties…"

Johnathan rubbed the back of his neck. It was no secret among his closest friends that he struggled with his impediment far more when conversing with women. In his early days at Harrow, Nate, Al, and Eddie had been his only defenders, speaking for him and coaching him through simple conversations. But now they were grown men; he could not hide behind their words forever. He needed to take action, but how?

The fire crackled in the hearth and the clock ticked on the mantel. Suddenly Nate snapped his fingers.

"I have got it. Flowers. A lady always likes a bouquet of her favorite flowers. What does she like?"

He frowned. Nate thought himself subtle in his question, but he would not fall for it. The answer was cowslip, but he would never tell Nate that. How was he to find cowslip in November? Perhaps a different flower, one that could be found in hothouses.

"We *are* speaking in generalities, Nate. What sort of flowers do women like *in general*?"

His friend smirked. "Of course, because there is no lady in *particular* that you have in mind."

He stood, trying to escape his friend's probing gaze. Crossing to the window, he said, "Perhaps they are for your wife."

"You want to get Melior flowers?"

"No, but if it will get you to leave off teasing me, we will go with that assumption."

Nate barked out a laugh. "All right." He drummed his fingers on his desk. "How about roses? They seem to be popular."

He shook his head. "That is what lovers give to one another."

"Is that not what you wish to be?"

"Nate, just tell me what small token one might start with."

The smile slipped from Nate's face and he steepled his fingers, bringing them to his lips in contemplation. "Forget-me-nots. They are given after most dances in London, something you would know if you danced much."

"I dance."

"Twice a season is not much. You do realize you will be forced to the floor more if you ever wish to take a wife."

He did and it terrified him. Not that he was a bad dancer, only that making conversation with beautiful women he hardly knew seemed worse than having the blacksmith pull an aching tooth.

"I *will* dance, but perhaps not as much as you wish."

"As long as you lead Miss Wayland to the floor whenever you are both present I will be appeased. We would not want her to be a wallflower all season."

The idea that any man would allow Susannah to take up a spot along the wall for any amount of time was ludicrous. No man that saw her beauty and witnessed her sweet, cheerful disposition would ever leave her to herself.

"I shall do my best. Now if you will excuse me, I need to ride into Maidstone to get... ah... s-some new cravats." That sounded reasonable enough, didn't it?

Nate's eyebrows inched up. "Cravats?"

"Yes, so I might have plenty for the season." The season? Was that the best he could come up with? Whatever the case, there was no way he would admit his intent to get said flowers right away. If he wanted to change Susannah's view of him, he needed to start now.

"You have several weeks until we leave."

"I know, but it never hurts to be prepared."

Nate sighed. "Well, good luck obtaining your *cravats* then."

The laughter in his eyes indicated he was not fooled, but Johnathan refused to discuss it. "Please convey my well wishes to Melior." He gave a short bow.

"That I will."

Riding a horse while holding a paper-wrapped bouquet of forget-me-nots proved difficult, especially with the wind that had chosen that moment to whip down through the trees and right at Johnathan's hand.

He tucked the flowers close to his chest, but the breeze still pelted them, ripping off several petals. By the time he reached the door of Wayland Lodge the flowers looked sad indeed. After plucking off a few bare stocks to improve their appearance, he approached the two-story home.

The housekeeper answered the door, a cheery smile on her face when her gaze lit upon him.

"Come in, Lord Newhurst. Master Michael has been asking if you might come again today."

"Thank you, Mrs. Stone, but I wonder if Miss Wayland might be about?"

The middle-aged lady's eyes went to the flowers, a smile pulling at her lips. "I am sure she is in her favorite parlor. Last I saw, she and Miss Amanda were studying multiplication."

"A fine skill to have."

"Yes, especially in housekeeping." She gestured with her hand and he made his own way to the room, but before he could enter, the door flung open and Miss Amanda rushed right into his chest, crushing the last stems of his offering.

A sob escaped her. "I am so sorry, Lord Newhurst." Her hand came to her mouth and she rushed away.

Johnathan glanced at the mangled flowers. Steps grew closer, no doubt Susannah coming to check on her sister. He glanced around, knowing he could not give such a paltry gift. She would think him daft if not rude all together.

Without another thought he tossed the destroyed flowers into a large open-mouthed vase moments before she rounded the corner.

"Oh, Jo—Lord Newhurst. I had not realized you were here."

He glanced over his shoulder in the direction Amanda had run.

"Yes, she is quite distressed over the new concept. Poor thing, but she must learn even if it is hard. Do come in and have some tea. Mrs. Stone just bought a fresh pot and I have no wish to eat all the sandwiches myself."

Susannah's chatter continued on as they entered the little room set with a sofa and two chairs, a carved wood coffee table in the center. She swiped away the slate and chalk, storing it in a drawer on the table.

CHAPTER 3

She relayed to him the boys' activities, her father's whereabouts, and even a bit of gossip a neighbor had brought. Not once, however, had she talked of her own pursuits.

"And h-how are you, Miss Wayland?"

She glanced up from pouring him another cup of tea. "Me?" She added a dash of milk, the way he liked it, and then picked up her own cup. "No need to burden you with my troubles when you have plenty of your own. Did I tell you Lady Stanford has asked that we leave a few days early? Something about her brother wishing to see us before the season truly begins."

Johnathan smiled at the mention of Eddie, his and Nate's common childhood friend and Melior's older brother. The two of them, plus Mr. Algenon Roberts, who they all referred to as Al, had met Edwin Kendall at Harrow. Having grown up near one another their whole lives, it was strange to accept another friend into their tight-knit group—one with such noble connections as a duke. But Eddie had fit right in, often filling the place of their friend Miss Javenia Harris who obviously was not allowed at a boys' school.

Susannah took a sip of her tea, then tipped her head to the side. "That's right, you are well acquainted with Lady Stanford's brother." The way she'd read his thoughts sent a chill down his spine. He loved that she knew him so well... and yet not.

Or did she see the interest he was certainly doing a terrible job of hiding?

She set her cup down moments before Michael burst into the room and launched himself at Johnathan, knocking the tea right into his lap.

Thank heavens the brew was not as fresh as Susannah had claimed or his legs would have received a scalding. As it was, the heat of his trousers and the wetness of his legs added to his increasing discomfort in the already awkward situation.

"Michael," she scolded.

"Sorry, sorry, sorry," the little boy repeated as he scrambled out of Johnathan's lap and backed away.

"My sincerest apologies, Lord Newhurst, I—" her voice cracked and moisture gathered in her eyes, but no tears fell. "Let me get you something to dry off."

She rang the bell on the tea tray and their maid of all work bustled in. When the towel was procured he dabbed at his lap until he was certain he'd not drip. The wet cloth still clung to him in a most disconcerting way.

"D-do excuse me." He stopped, trying to gather his words. "In light of... the situation."

"Don't go," Michael begged.

"I believe I must."

He gave a slight bow and hurried from the room, heat rushing to his cheeks. How was he ever to recover from such an embarrassment?

Chapter 4

The fabric of the new gown felt divine against Susannah's skin as she waited for the dressmaker to measure and pin the bottom in order to sew a proper hem. To think they would be leaving in a little over a month.

"Do you like it?" Lady Stanford asked.

"I do, very much. Thank you."

Lady Stanford lifted a handkerchief to her nose. "No need to thank me," she said as she dabbed.

Did the shop smell bad to her? Susannah peered down at the dressmaker. The woman did not seem to have any peculiar odor. Whatever the reason, Lady Stanford had been holding the piece of linen to her face quite often during this trip into town. Perhaps she had a cold.

"There ya are, miss." The middle-aged seamstress stood. "Now if you'll step over here, we'll remove it and I can begin the hemmin'."

Susannah did as she was instructed. This was the last of the clothes being prepared for her trip to Town and the thought excited her. Just one more month.

Slipping back into her old brown traveling dress, her gaze strayed to the pretty blue one also awaiting its hem. It had been over a year since she'd gotten anything new, long before Mama grew so ill. Tiny sparks of excitement danced in her chest when she imagined how well she would look, especially if a certain tall, blond gentleman were to take note.

Her smile faltered.

After donning her pelisse, she thanked the seamstress and followed Lady Stanford out the door. Down the street, several young ladies stood outside the milliners admiring a bonnet, while several more seemed to be swarming two gentlemen.

Their hats hid most of their features but the height of one and the gathering of various girls about the other made their identities very clear.

"Oh dear," Lady Stanford said. "Shall we go save John from Algenon's many sisters?"

Susannah giggled. Mr. Roberts had the most sisters of any person she'd ever met, ten to be exact. It had been several weeks since she'd last seen Mr. Roberts, but they often crossed paths in Maidstone when the future baron brought his many sisters to shop.

As one of John's close friends, she had grown up hearing stories about his larks with Mr. Roberts and their mutual friend Miss Harris. That is, until the stories had stopped.

Her gaze wandered to John. He appeared positively frightened. In his hand he held a bouquet of flowers, from which each girl plucked a stem. Poor man had probably tried to do something nice and now had no idea what to do with their thanks.

He'd once admitted that crowds of people made him nervous. She'd seen less of his unease these last few years, but Mr. Roberts's sisters had apparently brought it back to the surface.

When they reached the gathered group, only one cluster of flowers with a broken stem remained of the ones John had been holding. He looked down on it much like a boy observing a crushed toy.

"Good afternoon Roberts family, Lord Newhurst," Lady Stanford said to the gathered group. Several ladies rushed to greet her.

Susannah smiled and nodded to each one, trying to recall all their names.

Mr. Roberts clapped his hands and six faces turned to him. "Sisters, might I have a word with Her Ladyship and Miss Wayland?"

A chorus of 'of course' and 'absolutelys' met his request, but no one moved.

"Alone," he added.

Several girls groaned.

"Georgette, Phillipa, will you lead the younger girls to the mercantile? Get them each a sweet and tell the proprietor to add it to my bill."

Excited chatter began between the two youngest who were no more than ten and twelve. When they all were removed, Mr. Roberts turned to John.

"I *am* sorry about the flowers. It was kind of you to offer them to my sisters even though I am certain that is not for whom they were meant."

John's eyes flicked to her for a brief instant before he said, "No matter. At least it appeased them."

"Like a sacrifice on an altar to pagan gods?" Mr. Roberts grinned.

"More like a sacrifice to stay away from the altar," Lady Stanford said.

Mr. Roberts laughed and John even cast the lady a smile.

"It must have worked," he said.

It had been quite some time since she'd heard a bit of John's dry humor. She'd forgotten how much she enjoyed it.

"And where have you two lovely ladies come from?" Mr. Roberts asked with a healthy dose of his customary charm.

"Miss Wayland is being fitted for a new wardrobe for our trip to London."

"Ah. I had heard you would be joining us in the parade of singles this season."

"Parade of singles?"

"Yes, it is my own name for the marriage mart. Men and women without a match are like single stockings thrown into a basket where everyone hopes one might become useful and find a mate. We, on the other hand, simply hope not to be paired with a smelly one."

They all laughed, John giving his customary quiet chuckle.

"And will Javenia be joining us this season?" Lady Stanford asked.

"How should I know?" Mr. Roberts said. "We are on the outs again and she has not spoken to me for nigh unto two weeks."

Mr. Roberts and Miss Harris had the most peculiar relationship. One minute they were friends and the next... well, exactly as Mr. Roberts had indicated. It seemed they were back to being partial enemies again.

Lady Stanford adjusted her bonnet. "I shall write to her then. Is she still visiting her cousin?"

"No, I believe she returned the night before last."

The man might not be speaking to Miss Harris but he missed nothing that went on at her neighboring estate. Susannah grinned.

John cleared his throat and she glanced his way. He peered down at his broken flower stem again before tossing it in the dirt. The battered forget-me-nots looked so forlorn.

"And how are you this afternoon, Lord Newhurst?" she asked softly as Lady Stanford and Mr. Roberts entered into a conversation discussing which activities they liked best in Town.

"I-I am well." He glanced at his empty hands. "And you?"

"Everything seems to be going well with preparations. Andrew, as you know, will finally be attending Harrow after Christmastide and Amanda is coming along in her education."

She continued outlining each of her siblings' accomplishments, as it always made her nervous when people asked directly about her. As the oldest daughter it was her duty to care for others, not burden them with her own problems. No one need know how much she worried about leaving her siblings or what would happen to her father when he had no one to confide in about his grief.

The feel of John's hand on her sleeve stopped her.

"But how are you?"

She bit her lip and glanced at Lady Stanford. That sweet woman must have seen her distress for she suddenly declared it time to leave.

"I am well," she said quickly. "Good day, Lord Newhurst."

His lips turned down and his eyes followed her as she left, much like the protective older brother he'd always played in her life. But the warmth he'd left on her arm made her feel anything but sisterly.

In truth, she'd wanted to burrow into his arms and cry on his shirtfront. She missed her mother; she was overwhelmed with her duties as a stand-in parent, and as excited as she was for her season, she worried that John would never recognize her as more than a sister and she'd be forced to find someone else.

CHAPTER 4

Johnathan dipped his paintbrush in white and with a steady hand, added a stroke to the side of Susannah's neck, trying to mirror the way the light had danced off her skin. Leaning back, he peered at it.

Why could he not get it exactly right? A growl escaped him.

His deficiencies in painting echoed his ability to deliver a simple bouquet of flowers. He shook his head. When he'd set out yesterday to procure more forget-me-nots, he never even considered what might happen if any acquaintances came upon him. But the moment Al appeared with his sisters, he knew he'd either have to admit his errand or relinquish the blue gems.

Since sharing his objective with Al was out of the question, let alone his sisters, he'd opted for a falsehood, claiming the flowers were for the giggling Roberts sisters. Better to share with the whole gathering than create an expectation that may never come to fruition.

However, he'd not expected Susannah to witness the whole debacle. What must she think of him?

If only the last stem of flowers had not been so bedraggled, he'd have offered it to her. But such a paltry gift did not seem fit for the woman who held his heart.

Cleaning off his brush and putting it back in its place, he pondered on how one delivered flowers successfully. Maybe tomorrow he'd try again. Or maybe not. As it was, it had taken an entire week of licking his wounds the first time to gain enough courage to try again.

"My lord," his butler said from the doorway.

Johnathan spun on the stool to face him.

"Miss Harris has come for a visit."

He smiled. "Tell her I will be down in a moment."

Wiping his hands on a rag, he rose. Javenia would not care if he were less than presentable. Her presence at Gimly Hall intrigued him.

Since they'd entered adulthood, her visits to his home had become rare, as Society disapproved of a single lady visiting a single gentleman with no family, no matter how long the acquaintance. It must be something very pressing if she felt the need to throw off propriety.

Not that propriety really mattered much to Javenia. Only that she had too many siblings and too large a family to foolishly put her reputation and theirs in danger. The oldest of five children, four of them being girls, she had the burden of setting precedent for the family.

Javenia stood by the window as he entered, her normally pleasant expression completely absent. Her maid sat inconspicuously by the door; head bent as she awaited her mistress.

"Good afternoon." His voice seemed to pull her out of her reverie for she turned and cast him a smile that did not quite reach her eyes.

"And to you."

"Is something out of sorts, Javenia? You do not usually come all this way to visit me."

She crossed to the sofa and sat. "Other than my father's usual pressure to find a husband?"

He took up the chair next to her. "That never put you out of sorts before."

She smirked. "Very true, but what makes you think I am out of sorts?"

His lips pulled to the side and he tipped his head at her. "Really?"

She chuckled. "You always could read my mood better than any of the others. Well, John, I am to be congratulated."

He leaned back, not sure what to expect.

"It seems I have achieved spinsterhood."

Johnathan chuckled. "And how does one achieve that at only five and twenty?"

"Her younger sister goes off and gets herself engaged. It seems her baronet came up to scratch after all." Javenia grinned.

He smiled back. "Sounds like news to be celebrated."

"Oh, indeed."

"And you are very proud of the accomplishment by my estimations. Your expression is too jubilant to be anything otherwise."

She chuckled. "I admit, I am proud, but you should have heard my father. He went on for a full half hour on the duties of a daughter. Oh well, such is my life."

"And this is why you came all this way to see me? You wished to make the announcement yourself?"

"I have paid a call to Nate and Melior. It was not that much farther to come see you. I hear Miss Wayland will be accompanying them to London this season. What are your thoughts on that?" She not so casually placed a hand on the arm of the sofa, her fingers tracing the damask pattern.

He pursed his lips, trying to decide what to say. Steepling his fingers, he pressed them to his mouth. "It is a f-fine thing for her."

CHAPTER 4

Javenia glanced up, waiting. When he said no more, she said, "Is that all? I know how you detest Town."

"That is all. I hope the h-holiday away from her family will be a welcome rest from responsibility."

"And if she should find a husband in London she'd have a permanent rest, at least until her own children arrive."

His gaze darted to the window, trying to hide his grimace. Why was everyone so set on Susannah finding a husband? Javenia had been to London for multiple seasons and never married. Why not Susannah?

"By the by, have you heard the rumor?" Javenia blessedly changed the subject.

His focus returned to her. "There are many rumors about Maidstone. You will have to be more specific."

"Georgette came by to relay several bits of news, some of which I cannot share yet, but she mentioned Al has taken a special interest in some girl in London."

So this was why she and Al were at odds again, and if the downward pull of Javenia's lips were any indication, also the cause of her distress. It was an idle tell at best, but Algenon lavished enough compliments on the ladies to make half of London believe he had a preference for them. Yet the only woman he did not pamper with frivolous words seemed not to see the little glances cast her way.

It was a shame neither of them could see what everyone else already knew. And they were so hardheaded they'd probably not believe it if anyone risked telling them.

"Does this girl have a name?"

"Not one that his sister could give me."

"Then it is another idle report. No use fretting over it."

She stood and tossed her head. "I am not fretting, simply asking if you'd heard of it. The man can go chase any tittering, featherbrained woman he chooses."

He smirked. "What makes you think this one is anything like the other silly women he's been involved with?"

She laughed. "History, my friend. Lots of history."

Chapter 5

Susannah had not so patiently waited the last six weeks to begin packing her trunks. If only time would move faster. Two weeks still remained between her and the London season, but that did not mean she needed to wait around like a bump on a log. Time would pass far quicker if she kept herself busy.

Leaning back, she tried to pull the hefty trunk down the hall away from the attic stairs. She'd made it this far; she could do the rest.

"What the devil?" Someone muttered, catching her so off guard that she let go of the handle and fell right onto her backside. Pain ricocheted up from the point of contact and she winced.

Feet pounded and John sunk down next to her. "Are you injured?"

She fought the urge to rub her abused tailbone. "I will be alright."

"M-my apologies. I'd not meant to startle you. May I?" He extended his hand to help her rise.

Without thought she slipped her hand into his—an action she'd done a thousand times over the course of her lifetime—and allowed him to help her to her feet. Unfortunately the trunk had fallen in such a way to pin her hem. The restraint at her feet pitched her forward with an ominous ripping sound.

John let go of her hand and his arms encircled her as she fell into his chest. A grunt escaped him, but thankfully his footing was secure and he held her upright.

It took a moment for Susannah's mind to catch up with her position, but when it did, something warm and exciting washed through her limbs.

Her gaze traveled up from John's snowy white cravat until her brown eyes locked with his soft blue ones. Heat from his breath puffed against the ringlets on her brow, and she realized how quickly his chest rose and fell. Was he alright? Had she hurt him?

Unconsciously her fingers curled in his shirtfront. John shuddered, then abruptly pushed her away from his person, the action almost sending her back to her previous position on the floor. At the last second, his hands steadied her.

"Please forgive me." He turned to leave.

Susannah was completely confused. He'd saved her multiple times from a tumble and now he asked her forgiveness?

"Jo—Lord Newhurst, wait."

He stopped, but did not turn.

"Could you assist me?" It was a desperate bid to get him to stay, but it worked.

One glance over his shoulder at the heavy trunk and he retraced his steps. "What are you... that is, w-why not,"—he hefted the trunk up with ease—"your butler could h-have h-helped."

John had not spoken with such disjointed sentences before his tour of the continent, but since his return it had become his usual form of address. Either that or not respond at all. Oh, he'd always had a bit of a stutter, but it never really bothered her. Today, however, it did.

Why could he not just spit it out? He was questioning her choices. It was evident in his cool demeanor and the way he would not meet her gaze.

He marched toward her bedroom door, not even asking where she meant to take her luggage. What if she'd wanted it somewhere else? She didn't of course, but how would he know where she wanted it?

Because that is the only logical place to take it.

She was being ridiculous. Taking her rushing thoughts firmly in hand, she scurried in to open the door. Frustration only brought her discontent. John did not mean to hurt her. No need to be so sensitive.

He was being his usual helpful self. It was one of the many things she liked about him. That, and his attentiveness to her family. He'd been the only one who had remained a constant support through her mother's illness and after during their period of mourning. More than once he'd been a listening ear when she'd had none, even if she talked of nothing but her siblings' struggles.

"I did not want to be a bother to the staff," she finally said. "They are overworked as it is, especially since Mrs. Crabtree took her leave two days ago."

He stopped midway through the door and stared at her. "Mrs. Crabtree left?"

"She did. Said taking care of boys as devious as my brothers was only meant for saints, and she did not pretend to any such delusions of grandeur."

The corner of John's mouth tipped up, but he said nothing as he deposited the trunk at the foot of her bed. Retracing his steps, he passed her still holding the sturdy wood door.

"For London?" He tipped his head toward her room.

She followed his line of thought seamlessly, knowing he'd question her need for the trunk. To anyone else, his short two-word sentences would probably seem completely disjointed, but she was used to filling in the blanks.

If only she didn't have to. If only he'd talk to her like he used to before she left the schoolroom. Then perhaps she could share with him her joy at finally having a season, one her father probably could never have afforded—not after he'd spent so much on doctors for Mama.

Or perhaps they could discuss how torn she was at leaving her siblings when they looked up to her almost as a mother figure. She tried to convince herself that going to London would help her family, but deep in her heart she worried Michael would never understand. Already he'd started to fuss when conversation turned to her intended trip, his earlier excitement vanishing when he realized how long she'd be gone.

But what she really wished to discuss with John was the sensations she'd experienced in his embrace. Had he felt them too? He certainly did not seem quite as affected, at least not now. His breath had been unsteady. Was that a good or bad sign?

John rubbed his left hand along his trouser leg. Impatience? Ah yes, she'd forgotten to answer his question.

"I know we will not set out for another three weeks, but it is better to be prepared."

He nodded. "And you are... excited."

It was a statement, not a question. Perhaps he understood her as much as she did him.

"I am. Aren't you?"

His nose scrunched as if the question smelled distasteful. One hand rubbed the back of his neck as he smoothed his expression.

So he did not hold her same enthusiasm.

"I am late for my meeting with your father."

Embarrassment colored her cheeks. She'd not meant to keep him from his appointment. "My apologies."

"Do not apologize. I am… that is… it was my p-pleasure to h-help." A small smile pulled at his lips.

She smiled broadly back.

He cleared his throat and made his way to her father's study.

As his long legs strode down the hall, she took stock of his fine form. The season lay in front of her; an opportunity to meet and marry the man of her dreams, but over the last two years John had begun to fill the role of long-hoped-for suitor.

As a little girl she'd looked up to him as one did a brother. Their relationship had naturally moved to a friendship of mutual comfort as they spent many of his holidays from Harrow playing as youth did. But the strain between them now pulled at her heart.

It was her fault. If only she could take hold of her attraction to him, but his embrace had sent her dancing onto a ballroom of puffy white clouds, her heart as light as air.

Like a large foot in her way, reality sent her tumbling from her dance floor in the sky. John viewed her like he would a beloved little sister, not a woman full grown approaching her twentieth year.

Besides, he was a viscount, the highest-ranking man of her acquaintance—well, except the Duke of Bedford whom she'd met once last spring. Society expected him to marry well.

And who was she? A nobody. Daughter of a country gentleman who'd married a woman below his station. And while her grandfather had eventually achieved the life of a gentleman, he was new money and looked down on for his lack of education.

Even with Lady Stanford's sponsorship, Susannah had little more to recommend her than passably pretty looks and a measly dowry.

"What are you staring at?"

CHAPTER 5

Michael's voice startled her. John had long since entered her father's study and her eyes were trained on nothing in particular, but she refused to divulge her thoughts to a six-year-old boy.

"I am thinking you should be in the nursery."

"Why?" he whined. "It's boring in there, and Mrs. Stone says she's too busy to play games with us."

As she should be. The poor housekeeper now had two posts with Mrs. Crabtree's resignation. How did she do it? They needed a new nurse, at least for Michael. Andrew would be headed to Harrow. In truth, he should have already been there, but Mama had insisted they keep him home as long as possible. Poor Michael would be heartbroken when Andrew left after the day of Epiphany. She herself would be gone several days before that. The house would be quite empty.

"I'll tell you what, Michael. If you will go find a book I shall read to you, but first you must find Andrew, and you must agree upon the story, no squabbling."

That alone would keep him busy for at least a half an hour. Perhaps it would be enough time to wipe out her trunk and begin the tedious task of deciding what to take and what must stay.

Her eyes strayed to her father's study as Michael happily ran off to find Andrew. If only…

Those two words held so much in their torturous clutches. If only she had more consequence in the world. If only she had a bigger dowry. If only John saw her differently, maybe then she'd not need to go to London at all.

Even so, she was determined to enjoy herself. And if the end of the season came with nothing more than the ability to see the many wonders of the city, then she'd have to be content.

But what if this season John found his match… and it wasn't her?

Three weeks passed far quicker than Susannah could have imagined. On the morning of her departure, she wondered why she'd wished the time away. Sir Nathaniel was busy giving orders to the footmen while Lady Stanford waited inside the carriage, giving Susannah the space to say goodbye to her family in private.

Amanda, bundled in her coat and her eyes rimmed with red, gave her a crushing hug. Regret tugged at Susannah's heart knowing her sister would not have another woman, other than their housekeeper, to confide in over the next few months.

"I will write to you often."

Amanda nodded, then rushed into the house as the tears she'd held back began to spill over on her cheeks.

Michael had refused to come out, upset both at Susannah's leaving and the new nursemaid. The younger woman was far more caring than Mrs. Crabtree had been, but it was one more change her brother had been forced to endure in his young life.

Andrew approached next, his face stoic, but when she wrapped her arms about him, his shoulders shook.

"Are you frightened to go to Harrow?" she whispered.

"A little," he admitted. "The stories I hear, Nan." His big blue eyes, so much like their mother's, rose to meet hers and she wished for a few more years to protect him from the harsh life of becoming a man.

"Do you have the three things Mama said you would need to take when the time came?"

"I hope so. But how will I know if I have bravery, compassion, and a sense of humor?"

She ruffled his dusty blond hair. "You do, Andrew. Hold tight to those, and you will do fine."

Turning to Terrance, she gave a tremulous smile.

"Enjoy yourself, Nan. And try not to worry about all of us here. We will be fine."

"Even Michael?"

"I shall make certain of it."

After a brief embrace, it was her father's turn. Deep lines marred his face, worry clearly written across his brow. "I wish I were the one accompanying you."

CHAPTER 5

His words pulled tears to the surface. "Me too, Papa."

He gathered her hands in his. "Be careful, Nan. Not every man in London is honorable. And if it comes to choosing between status and true affection, I beg you to choose love like your mother and I did. It may not bring you fine furs and fancy dresses, but it will fill your heart with more wealth than any rich man could ever give."

The tears trickled down her cheeks and she threw her arms about him. "Oh Papa, I shall miss you."

"And I you, my girl."

"Are you ready, Miss Wayland?" Sir Nathaniel asked as he rounded the back of the post chaise.

Her father kissed the top of her head and released her. Susannah wiped away any trace of her tears, then turned with a smile.

"I am."

She glanced one more time at her family, then made her way toward the carriage. Sir Nathaniel took her hand to help her in, but before she could set foot on the step, a little brown-clad bullet rushed toward her from the steps of the house and wrapped his arms about her legs.

"Don't go, Nan. You can find a husband here. Terry has lots of friends or maybe Lord Newhurst will have you. You don't need to go to London."

Michael's cheeks were wet and his grip fierce. She lowered her hands to hold him against her. If only his words were true. She'd stay in a heartbeat if she thought John would ever consider her, but two years had proven his disinterest.

Her father came forward to pry her little brother off her, but before he reached them she said, "I will miss you, Michael. And if you are very good I shall bring you some candy and a trinket when I return."

The promise did little to calm him, but when her father picked him up, he released her willingly. She placed a hand to one cheek and kissed the other. He gave her a tight squeeze around the neck.

"I will miss you too, Nan," he said in a tiny broken voice.

Quickly she entered the carriage, trying not to lose her composure again. She needed this trip to London. For her family… and for herself.

Chapter 6

Weeks had come and gone, and Johnathan had done nothing, a whole lot of nothing. Why was he such a coward?

Well, maybe not nothing. He *had* tried one more time to obtain flowers for Susannah, only to run into Nate and Melior before he'd even reached the hothouse. Not wanting to explain himself, he'd turned about to walk with them, taking it as a sign that he was not meant to give Susannah flowers, not from Maidstone anyway.

He'd spent so many days over the last three months in the Waylands' house with very little to show for it. His painting of her was complete and another one begun, and yet he still had not found the courage to speak more than the plainest pleasantries. In return she'd smiled and chattered on about the future season with all the delight he'd come to expect from her. He'd found peace in those moments, enjoying her cheer as they'd sat by the fire with all her family and welcomed in the new year, but today all that peace was gone.

Today she would leave for London. He would follow soon after, but it still did not comfort him.

Why had Melior insisted on giving Susannah a season?

It was the one question that had plagued him over and over again, and yet he'd not been able to bring himself to ask. Fear of her answer mixed with his stumbling tongue—not that he feared Melior herself, but she read him too well. As the sister of one of his friends, and the wife of another, she knew him better than most. Had she deduced his secret affection? If so, why take Susannah away?

It seemed cruel. But Melior was not cruel, not by nature.

His butler entered the library where Johnathan had taken to sulking, the heavy door complaining loudly at having to be moved. "Sir Nathaniel Stanford to see you, my lord."

The baronet strode in without waiting for Johnathan's acceptance.

Shutting the book of poetry he'd not even had the presence of mind to read, he placed the leather-bound copy of Milton's *Paradise Lost* on the round end table near his favorite leather chair. Removing his reading glasses, he blinked up at his friend. Wasn't Nate supposed to be on the road to Town by now?

"There you are. We have come to take our leave."

"We?" Johnathan asked.

"Yes, the ladies are waiting in the parlor. I know you are to follow in a few days, but Mel insisted we make our visits."

Of course she would; she'd been raised to the highest standards. The question that had burned within him came to the surface.

"Why, Nate?"

"Probably because she cannot stand going against expectations."

"No, why did Melior offer to give Miss Wayland a season?"

Nate rocked back on his heels; his attention suddenly drawn to the bookshelves that graced every wall of the large room. He locked his hands behind his back and hummed. "Like I said before, she simply wanted to be generous. Miss Wayland has had a difficult year and we both know Mr. Wayland probably doesn't have the funds or time to take her to London. Plus, with one less mouth to feed it will ease some of the family's burden."

Johnathan had first-hand knowledge to refute several of his friend's claims, but the way Nate would not make eye contact set him on edge. He observed him closely. The tell-tale tuck of Nate's lip as he bit on the corner, a twitch under his eye, the way he rocked forward and back. The details were all there. Nate was lying. Well, perhaps not outright, but he told only half the truth.

He wanted to press him, but he would not keep the ladies waiting. Far be it from him to be rude after Melior had given him the opportunity to see Susannah one last time before all of London beheld her beauty.

Slowly he rose to his full height. Looking down at Nathaniel, he said, "Lead the way."

CHAPTER 6

A tiny sigh slipped past his friend's lips, but he'd not escaped questioning. No, Johnathan planned on thoroughly interrogating him once they were all settled in London.

In the splendor of his visiting parlor, he found Susannah dressed in brand-new traveling attire. He should not have been surprised; Melior would not allow her to go to town ill fitted for the fashionable world, but the fine cut of the light blue garment trimmed in black made the whole experience far more real.

Susannah really was going to London to find a husband. His tongue froze in his mouth as his mind screamed in protest.

"Lord Newhurst." She curtsied.

She even sounded more cultured. Had Melior given her lessons on diction?

Her name escaped him in a whisper. "Susannah." When his mind caught up with what he had done, he straightened. It had been years since he'd allowed himself the pleasure of her given name.

Her cheeks pinked and he cursed himself for embarrassing her. "My apologies, Miss Wayland. You are for London, then?"

His words were so blessedly clear of his usual stutter that he gave himself a mental pat on the back.

"I am. And when do you follow?"

Had her father not told her? They'd spoken of it just yesterday. "Day after tomorrow."

Out of the corner of his eye he saw Melior's hand briefly flutter near her midsection, a suspicious smile on her lips. But the moment his head turned she wiped it away, coming forward to offer her goodbyes as well. It was all so awkward and unnecessary.

He studied her as she invited him to spend his first evening in Town with them, claiming he'd need a good meal after such a long journey. Flitting eyes, fidgeting fingers. It seemed Nate was not the only one withholding information. He tipped his head to the side in contemplation.

Melior stopped, then added, "You will not be the only one in attendance as I have invited several families to Kendall House that evening to celebrate our arrival."

Kendall House? Why not Nate's townhouse? His gaze flicked to his friend.

Nate stepped forward. "We thought it would make more of an impression on Society if we stayed in Melior's family home. With Eddie being the only occupant at present, there is plenty of room."

Johnathan nodded. "And Eddie does not mind you interrupting his peace?"

"He's the one who begged us to come and relieve him from his solitude. Claimed he would go mad before the opening of Parliament if we did not come early."

Eddie always had liked company far more than he or Nate. His love of Society could only be rivaled by Al who simpered about, plying ladies with his overly sweet compliments and winning their undying affection.

"Heaven help us if we were responsible for my brother's deterioration into bedlam." The smirk on Melior's face matched that of her husband's. They made the perfect pair, their banter and absurdity running together like a bubbling brook bringing smiles to both his and Susannah's faces.

"I suppose dinner at Kendall House would be nice." He shifted from one foot to the other, realizing he should have offered to have everyone sit, but the way Susannah glanced at the door stopped the words from forming. "I should not keep you. Do you have any other stops before you depart?"

"No, this is the last," Melior supplied, her gaze wandering to Susannah.

"Yes," Susannah added. "I... that is...Will you be attending the Prince Regent's ball at Carlton House in a fortnight?"

The Prince's ball? How in the world had his friend come by an invitation to his Majesty's ball?

Nate cringed and Melior stepped forward, wringing her hands. "My uncle, you see..."

He filled in her meaning when she trailed off. Her uncle was the Duke of Bedford. Of course he would be invited to the most opulent balls London had to offer, and by extension his family.

"I am afraid I will not be at His Majesty's ball, but I wish you a most wonderful time."

There, that had come out both fluent and benevolent. But inside a riot of emotion pounded at his chest. He'd not be at Susannah's first ball of the season. How was that possible?

He'd hoped to be the first to lead her to the floor. Not that his dancing could be called elegant, or even proficient, but the idea that someone else would stand up with her in front of all of Society and he'd not be there to protect her, to

CHAPTER 6

support her... who was he fooling? He would not be there to quail the attempts of all the eligible bachelors.

Susannah's expression fell, and he wondered if he'd allowed his frustration to show. "I see." Then she brightened. "Well, I look forward to our dinner Monday evening."

And like that, the cloud of gloom that had settled over him lifted. She looked forward to seeing him? Dare he hope that those words meant more than in a brotherly fashion?

Gathering all the courage he had, he reached out and took her gloved hand. "Safe travels, Miss Wayland." Then he bent and placed a kiss on her wrist, just above the edge of her kid gloves.

It was the boldest thing he'd ever done, but the smile she graced him with when he rose compensated for his discomfort tenfold. His mind danced forward on wings of hope, desperate for a chance at winning Miss Susannah Wayland's affections.

Then she left, and reality sunk in. How was he ever to gain the courage to declare himself? What if she did not feel the same? Could she ever see him as more than a brother?

Somewhere inside he needed to find the courage to speak, and he needed to find it soon or he'd lose her. But how would he find the words?

Chapter 7

London was not quite what Susannah had imagined. To begin, it smelled horrendous.

She'd taken to carrying a handkerchief doused in perfume everywhere she went. The strong scent counterbalanced some of the worst areas of the city, but it did not dissipate the depravity she witnessed.

Dirty children seemed to beg at every corner, their sunken eyes pulling at her soul. Lady Stanford had supplied her with a small purse for such occasions but warned her to be careful and only give out small amounts—and *only* when they were in Sir Nathaniel's company. No need to excite thieves and pickpockets.

Only a few streets seemed clear of the poverty, one of which being where Kendall House was situated in Mayfair. The tall stone home flanked by its companions stood four stories high, a multitude of windows boasting its size.

It intimidated Susannah to think of how much splendor her hostess had grown up in. But Lady Stanford paid little attention to the elegance around them and simply smiled at Susannah's awe.

Three days in residence had done little to stifle her amazement as she slowly made her way down the stairs to the beautiful gold and cream drawing room on the second floor.

Sir Nathaniel and Lady Stanford were already present as were a few other ladies and gentlemen she did not know. Introductions were made and Susannah hoped she'd be able to remember all of the guests' names. Mr. Kendall came to stand by her, a cheery smile on his face.

"It is a bit overwhelming, is it not?"

"Indeed." She clasped her hands in front of her hoping he did not see how they shook.

She liked Lady Stanford's brother. Easygoing and affable, he put her in mind of her younger brother Terrance. Both had ready conversation and seemed to find enjoyment in being helpful to others. However, at nearly a decade older than her brother, Mr. Kendall's mannerisms were more polished as he led her from circle to circle, blessedly repeating the names of people she'd met as he conversed with them.

The door opened, and the butler announced the final guest. Her gaze flew to the door, hungry for the sight of John in all this chaos.

Her eyes widened as she took in his evening blacks. In the country he rarely dressed so impressively, generally sticking to drab colors with little ornamentation. But tonight a sapphire stick pin was nestled in the folds of his cravat and a silver chain peeked out of his pocket which no doubt held his timepiece.

As he entered, several of the young ladies took note. As a viscount, he commanded the highest rank in the room for this evening. Ladies leaned together behind fans, their eyes dancing with delight.

Something hot and sticky sank into Susannah's middle. She wanted to poke their eyes out. The feeling caught her off guard and she quickly adjusted her face, hoping no one had seen her jealousy.

"Welcome, Newhurst," Sir Nathaniel greeted, using John's title in the company of those who were not close to them.

The realization that they called each other by given names in her presence suddenly struck her. But it had always been so. From her earliest memories they had used abbreviated names for one another. A name she had taken to using for John.

She knew his full name to be Johnathan, but none of his friends called him that, so neither had she. That is, until her father had insisted she be more formal. It was odd calling him Lord Newhurst but it was probably for the best.

As he approached her, though, the only name that came to mind was John. Her John. No, she could not think of him that way. She had no right, but, oh, how she wished she did.

And he had called her Susannah back in Maidstone. Did he still think of her by her Christian name?

"Good... evening." He swallowed so hard his throat bobbed.

CHAPTER 7

Had the room full of strangers made him nervous? He'd never liked big groups.

"Good evening, Lord Newhurst. How was your journey?"

She did not expect him to give more than a one-word answer, but he surprised her.

"It would have been more pleasant had my man not become ill along the way. I was obliged to stop multiple times for him to cast up his accounts, but we managed to make it here without ruining my rig's upholstery."

Susannah grinned when John's face suddenly colored. While she did not mind hearing about his ill servant, a woman who had approached them covered her mouth and quickly chose a different course. Good. She had hoped for a little more undivided attention before she was forced to share him with all the ladies who kept glancing their way.

"D-do excuse me, Miss Wayland. I'd not meant... I mean, that sort of information"—he swallowed again—"is p-probably not suitable for a drawing room."

Instinctively she reached out and placed a hand on his sleeve, much as she'd done all their years growing up. "Do not apologize. I asked for the information. I am sorry Fernley is ill. Does he often struggle with carriage rides? Many people do. Lady Stanford had a terrible time of it on our way to town."

John confirmed that he did, but they were interrupted when the butler announced dinner. She'd hoped to ask a few more questions about his valet in an effort to keep him talking, but she supposed the conversation would have to wait.

Dinner proved to be fairly uneventful, John leading Lady Stanford into dinner and Susannah being paired with the elderly father of one of the ladies. The same lady who seemed determined to catch John's attention when the men joined them in the drawing room after their port.

Lady Stanford had informed Susannah that Miss Eleanor Wallace with her golden-brown curls and her perfectly formed nose was cousin to the Viscount Ansley. Her father, Mr. Wallace, held a seat in the House of Commons. The information brought no comfort to Susannah's already flailing hopes. How could she compete with women of such connections? No doubt the woman's dowry was ten times the size of hers.

But when the men joined them, John took up the seat next to hers and all thoughts of competition fled. He placed his hand on the cream armrest embroidered with yellow and red flowers, his fingers slowly moving over the stitches as he glanced at each of the room's occupants. She waited for him to speak, but her wait was in vain.

The rest of the night he remained silent, eventually leaving early, something Miss Wallace complained extensively to her companions about. Susannah had to agree. She'd not wished him to leave so soon, but he'd traveled most of the day with a sick servant. After such a journey, who could deny him a good night's rest for their own selfish comforts?

CHAPTER 7

To Susannah's delight, she found John the next morning at the breakfast table talking with Mr. Kendall and Mr. Roberts. All three gentlemen rose when she entered.

"Good morning Miss Wayland," Mr. Roberts said with a dip of his head. "So nice to see you again."

Susannah greeted him equally as warm, doing the same with John and Mr. Kendall who stood waiting for her to collect her plate. Quickly she crossed to the sideboard and chose a piece of toast, preserves, and a boiled egg. When she returned to the table all three men sat.

"How are you enjoying Town, Miss Wayland?" Mr. Roberts asked.

The footman came forward and poured her a cup of tea. "I have not seen much of it yet, but it is... different than I thought it would be."

She'd wanted to say dirtier, but at the last moment decided on a more diplomatic answer. So many people had touted the superiority of Town, who was she to point out the obvious?

"Yes, London can come as quite the surprise after the fresh air of the country. And what sort of pleasantries do you have planned for your day?"

She looked to Mr. Kendall who merely shrugged. "I am uncertain. Lady Stanford is in charge of our scheduling. The only activity I am aware of is a card party this evening at the Duke of Bedford's home."

"Ah yes, I shall also be in attendance," Mr. Roberts said. "You are in for a treat as the duke likes to keep his parties far more intimate and so you will not be overwhelmed with new acquaintances at every turn."

What a relief. After the dinner last evening, she did not know how many more names her poor head could hold.

"I believe your definition of small is quite different than the rest of ours." John speared a piece of meat as he eyed his friend. "You will have to excuse him, M-miss Wayland. Al thinks anything less than a h-hundred people is small."

"I cannot help it. You've seen the size of my family. My sisters alone would take up a tenth of the party."

Susannah smiled as she spread preserves onto her toast.

Mr. Kendall smirked. "Yes, and it is likely to be an eleventh by Easter."

"Do not remind me." Mr. Roberts shook his head.

It was not polite to speak of women being in the family way if unrelated to oneself, but she deduced by the conversation that the newest Lady Roberts was indeed with child. The fifth of Lord Roberts's wives, Susannah hoped she'd be far more fortunate than the four that had come before, each one birthing several daughters before dying of childbed fever.

"Perhaps this time luck will be on your side and you will gain a brother." Mr. Kendall smiled over his coffee cup as if he'd told a grand joke.

"I lost hope of my father gaining my replacement long ago."

"Replacement, never. He only wishes to make certain the title is secure."

"Because he thinks I will either *die* or not do my duty and provide him an heir. I consider either of those a replacement. It is certainly not me he is focused on."

John, who had been silently eating his breakfast, put down his fork and cleared his throat. "Perhaps we might speak on s-something other than your father's hoped for o-olive branch." His head tilted toward Susannah and she frowned.

Did he consider her too young and naive to participate in a conversation about children? The thought stung. She was nearly twenty years old, two or three years older than many women taking their first season.

At thirteen she'd even taken part in Michael's birth, the midwife having taken too long to arrive so she'd assisted the housekeeper. Maybe other ladies of his acquaintance were not aware of the facts of life, but she was not one of them.

Her hopes of appearing as more than a younger sister plummeted at his insistence on changing the subject. The kiss at Gimly Hall had given her hope that he'd begun to see her as more, but his need to protect her from reality proved he still viewed her as he always had.

Susannah fumed as she put all her focus into eating her breakfast. She was a little girl no longer. The sooner John realized that the better things would be for the both of them.

Mr. Roberts glanced over his teacup. "Nonsense, John. Women do not hold as tender of sensibilities as you might think. I am sure Miss Wayland is much more acquainted with life than you suppose."

Bless him. At least someone at the table realized she was a woman full grown.

Mr. Kendall's fork paused midair. "All I can say is I pity the child if it is another girl. What sort of masculine name will your father feminize next?"

Susannah's hand stilled, a piece of toast midway to her mouth as she reviewed the few names she could remember. Henrietta, Paulette, Georgette, Phillipa. "Charlotte is feminine."

"Oh they are all feminine now, but Charlotte is the female of Charles." Mr. Kendall smiled as he speared his eggs.

"I pity the child as well," Mr. Roberts said. "My father's new names of fascination are Robert and Richard. Can you imagine? Boy or girl, Robert is a complete disaster. Robert Roberts? What is the man thinking?"

A laugh bubbled out of Susannah even though her mouth was full of toast. It took all her efforts to keep crumbs from escaping through her lips.

Mr. Kendall, on the other hand, gave a hearty guffaw. "And how shall he fit Richard to suit a little girl? Richette, Richia, Richarda?"

Even John laughed at the names, breaking through the silence he'd kept. "Richarda? Even your father cannot be that cruel."

"I certainly hope not." Mr. Roberts dabbed at his lips. "Maybe if I suggest something so absurd he'll finally come to his senses."

The right side of Mr. Kendall's mouth pulled as he tried to contain his mirth. "Either that, or you will end up defending yourself from the poor girl's reproofs her entire life since she'll have you to blame for such an abomination of a name."

Mr. Roberts's lips twitched.

John leaned forward to look at Mr. Kendall. "Do not give him ideas, Eddie. This is the same man who finds an odd sense of pleasure in Javenia's insults. A little girl's ire would be nothing compared to his own lifelong amusement."

Susannah cracked the top of her boiled egg and scooped out a spoonful.

"I am not so cruel," Mr. Roberts protested. "It would be my father, after all, saddling her with such a monstrosity of a name. But now I am of the same mind, Eddie. I believe it is high time another Roberts boy enter the world, for Robert Roberts is far better than my poor little sister Richarda."

The spoonful of egg Susannah had just placed in her mouth sputtered out, dotting the tablecloth as she tried to cover her laugh, only succeeding at inhaling bits of egg which sent her into a coughing fit.

John quickly shoved his handkerchief into the free hand not covering her mouth, giving her back a couple firm pats. She waved him away. When her coughing eased, she used the piece of linen to wipe the moisture the fit had brought to her eyes. With her vision cleared, she noted all three men staring at her with matching looks of concern.

Her cheeks pinked. "Forgive me."

"There is nothing to forgive," Mr. Kendall said. "It is Al's fault for his incredibly poor timing and even poorer drollery." Turning to his friend, he said,

"Try not to kill the ladies by humor this season. Stick to disgusting flattery, it suits you better and is far less likely to get you hanged."

Chapter 8

The Duke of Bedford's card party was indeed small, only encompassing family and close friends. John placed his whist cards face down, waiting for the others to organize the hands they had been dealt.

Across the parlor, Susannah sat with the Duchess of Bedford on a plush red settee. The middle-aged woman was far younger than the duke, having only married the older man last spring after he'd lost his first wife the year before. The duke had no children from his first marriage, but from the looks of Her Grace, it seemed they would soon welcome a possible heir.

The way Susannah kept the obviously uncomfortable woman company while the rest of the guests enjoyed cards warmed his heart. She had always been particularly attentive to the needs of others.

Bids were called and John pulled his attention back to the game. Javenia had been invited to even up the numbers and he'd been relieved when they drew the lowest cards which paired them for the game. Al sat to his right, and on the other side Al's partner was a Miss Guthrie, who apparently was related to Her Grace through some means.

John covertly took stock of the young woman's appearance. Oddly she reminded him of Susannah. Same golden hair and medium build, but where Susannah's eyes were a warm brown, Miss Guthrie's were a nondescript blue. They both possessed full cheeks and a small smattering of freckles, but the effect did not herald the same emotions in John that Susannah's well placed sunspots did.

For starters, Miss Guthrie's freckles were large and obtrusive rather than blending with her features. In addition, she quite clearly viewed herself as a person of importance calling out orders in the game as if she were the dealer, her competitiveness evident in the set of her shoulders and the focus of her eyes.

Not that he minded a woman of competition, but her muttered complaints when she lost a trick proved her a poor sport. After some time, he wondered how he could ever have compared her to Susannah. Their personalities were completely different.

Javenia tossed in a trump card and Al groaned. "Do you always have to win?"

She grinned at his complaint. "Only when I play against you."

John covered his smile with his hand.

Al tossed his card down. "Someday a hard lesson in humility will come your way, *Miss Harris*. I only hope I am the one to give it to you."

"Keep dreaming, *Mr. Roberts*."

They had resorted to emphasis on titles, a sure sign that they were still at odds, otherwise they'd have referred to each other by given names, company or not.

Miss Guthrie grumbled something, but then requested another game.

"I am afraid not," Javenia said. "I am going to quit while I have the upper hand on *Mr. Roberts*."

"Coward," Al mumbled under his breath.

Javenia grinned and sauntered away.

"Perhaps my sister will join us," Miss Guthrie offered, motioning to a taller version of herself. Miss Martha Guthrie echoed her sister in appearances except for her greater height and an absence of the large freckles.

She too seemed quite competitive and after a second game, John decided he was done with cards for the night, choosing instead to find his way to Susannah's side.

Other card tables were beginning to break up, the occupants of the room finding their way to a refreshment table where tea and cakes were being served. That was where he found Susannah, a plate in each hand.

Teasing words escaped his lips before he'd had time to think better of it. "Did you miss supper?"

She smiled at him. "No, I had plenty, but lest you think both these plates are for me, I am on an errand for Her Grace."

Of course she was; her kindness knew no ends.

CHAPTER 8

"So you have found a better position than the one I offered. No wonder your father refused." A familiar rotund woman with dark hair liberally peppered with grey approached them.

Susannah's brow furrowed and one of the plates in her hand trembled. John quickly relieved her of it, confused by Mrs. Guthrie's words.

The woman tsked. "And to think I could have presented you as family. Well, that is all ruined now. Tell me, how long have you been a companion to the Duchess of Bedford? She did not mention a need to employ anyone."

John gripped the plate he held so tightly his knuckles turned white. How dare the woman imply that Susannah was not here of her own right?

He straightened, his tall frame towering over the much shorter woman, but before he could speak, Susannah cleared the air.

"You are mistaken, Aunt Guthrie. I am only showing her a kindness. I am the guest of Sir Nathaniel and his wife, who you must know is the niece of His Grace."

Her aunt? On further inspection he recognized several features in the woman that were reminiscent of Mr. Wayland. The man did have an older sister, but John had never had the pleasure of meeting her—or rather, the displeasure by her current sour expression.

Mrs. Guthrie sniffed. "I see. Well, that is not much better. Such a scandalous marriage, you must know."

The reminder of Nate and Melior's rough beginning needled at his nerves. The rake Mr. Fairchild held the majority of blame for their forced marriage. How dare this woman bring up such matters, and at the duke's house no less?

"And why are you here, Mrs. Guthrie?" he asked through barely parted lips.

"I beg your pardon. Have we been introduced?"

They had, two seasons ago. Who did not know the Guthries? They seemed to be everywhere, invited to everything, and connected with everyone.

John usually kept to the back of most gatherings, speaking mainly to the men. Their introduction had been a mere coincidence, even so, this woman certainly thought highly of herself to slight him. "Lord Newhurst," he said shortly.

Her bluster faded and a saccharine smile bloomed on her face. "Ah yes, my apologies, Your Lordship. My memory is not what it once was." She made no pretense of hiding her thorough examination of his person. "It has been some time since we have spoken. You have, of course, noticed my two daughters are here as well."

Was the woman daft? He'd played at cards with both her girls. How had it slipped her notice? Then again, without his title he was probably of little importance to such a self-serving woman.

"I have." He pressed his lips together, biting back the insults he wished to hurl at her.

"Splendid." She rubbed her pudgy hands together. "Is this not a fine party? And does not my husband's cousin look splendid in her role as the new duchess? I dare say she will fulfill her duty much better than her predecessor."

John's free hand curled into a fist. Perhaps a few choice words would help put this woman back in her place. How dare she insult the Duke of Bedford's first wife? Lucinda Kendall had been everything that was kind and gracious. Just because she'd never been able to give the duke a child did not mean she had been remiss in her duties.

A small hand brushed against his fist, and his attention shot to Susannah. The pleading in her eyes mixed with a subtle shake of her head. Slowly, he allowed the tension in his fingers to relax. She was right. No amount of force would change a woman such as Mrs. Guthrie. It was better to pay her no mind and allow her to ruin her own reputation.

"You will excuse us, Mrs. Guthrie, but your cousin is awaiting her refreshments." He offered his free arm to Susannah and she hesitantly took it.

"Your Lordship," Mrs. Guthrie rushed to say. "Might I have a word alone with my niece?"

"Perhaps later." Or never, he wished to say. Leaving Susannah to suffer by this woman's acrid tongue went against every instinct. "Her Grace is awaiting Miss Wayland's return. I bid you a good evening."

The woman gave a tight, close-mouthed smile, but he was not fooled. Anger burned in her eyes at being so summarily dismissed.

He did not care. No one spoke to Susannah in such condescending tones. No one.

"Thank you," Susannah whispered when they were far enough away from her aunt.

"No need. That woman is... is..."

"Unpleasant," she supplied.

"Abhorrent is more accurate, or reprehensible."

CHAPTER 8

"Obnoxious, distasteful, disagreeable."

"Retched, loathsome, and deplorable."

She smiled up at him. "How many words are there that mean unlikeable?"

"Not enough."

She laughed softly and for the first time he realized how easily their conversation had flowed. Of course it had centered around one of the three topics he excelled at, but it was a success. If only he could show such self-possession in every encounter he had with her.

"Forgive my impudence, b-but—" He paused, his mind throwing out several questions about the odd interaction.

Susannah waited, a strange occurrence as she usually knew what he wanted to ask and would often fill the void where he'd left off.

He gathered his courage. "Your aunt, am I right in a-assuming she offered you a p-position as a companion?"

"She did."

"And your father refused."

"Most vehemently."

He smiled at her word choice. "But why?" She tipped her head and he elaborated. "Why would your aunt not s-sponsor your s-season as the Stanfords have?"

Susannah peered at the ground. "My mother. She was not what Aunt Guthrie wished for in a relation."

John could hardly believe it. Mrs. Wayland, composed, patient, thoughtful, and brave woman that she was, did not measure up to Mrs. Guthrie's expectations. How could anyone have one unkind word to say about the woman?

"Mama's father was not always a gentleman. He only recently left his position in trade."

So naturally Mrs. Guthrie had disliked Mrs. Wayland on principle. It made sense, especially for a woman who stooped so low as to insult a deceased duchess—in her own home, no less.

Susannah's chin crept toward her chest as her resolute stance faltered. "I believe my aunt felt she was being magnanimous. As a companion to her girls I would have been able to experience London in much the same way I am now, and I would have been given an allowance that could have helped my family."

"But you'd have been forced to serve your own cousins."

She nodded. "Service is not a bad thing. I serve my siblings daily."

"It is not the same."

"No, but they are still family and as such I choose to keep the peace."

He had to respect her decision. It showed a strength of character he doubted her aunt possessed.

Silence settled between them as Susannah delivered the duchess's refreshments and took up a seat across from her. The spindly legs of the gold and green chairs gave him pause. He was not a large man, but his height added a significant amount of weight. Carefully he lowered himself into one, praying the delicate piece would hold.

Her Grace accepted the refreshment with many words of thanks, further attesting to her discomfort and reticence to rise with such an encumbered body. The duke joined them, his smile holding a subtle intimacy as he sat beside his wife.

"Newhurst, I am glad I caught you before you left. I have something for you."

John's curiosity piqued.

"My niece mentioned an oversight that, thanks to my connections at the palace, I was able to remedy." Reaching into the pocket of his dinner jacket, the duke extracted a square of canary yellow paper. John's eyes widened. Could it be?

Carefully, he took it. There, in beautifully penned script, was an invitation to the Prince Regent's ball.

John glanced at Susannah. She smiled back. Perhaps he would stand up with Susannah for her first dance after all.

Chapter 9

The next week flew by in a whirlwind of shopping, visiting, a trip to the opera, and many other pleasant pursuits. Susannah relished each experience, making sure to write in detail to her younger siblings as often as she found time.

The luxury of having clean paper so readily accessible still left her in awe. If her brothers and sister were distinct in their writing, they might be able to send the sheets back to her written crosswise. The cost of paper aside would save them enough to write to her almost as often as she did them.

She especially took time to write to Andrew, knowing he'd feel less lonely at school if he had a cheerful account. Perhaps she'd even get a chance to visit him at Harrow, it being nearer to London than Maidstone.

Many people came to welcome the Stanfords back to London, increasing Susannah's circle of acquaintances so much that she'd begun to keep a list of names to memorize in her free time. Today would be no different, for Lady Stanford had already summoned her for more visitors.

Susannah took one more glance in the mirror, adjusting her fichu and pushing a pin back in place. A loose hair clung to her pink and white day dress. With two fingers she plucked the golden strand off the little embroidered rosebud.

Perfect.

In the sitting room she found Lady Stanford already deep in conversation with three women. Her gaze flitted to the eldest of the three and she stopped.

What was her aunt doing here?

"Miss Wayland, come." Lady Stanford motioned to her, a bright smile gracing her pink lips. "Why did you not tell me the Guthries are close kin to you?"

Susannah did not know how to answer. Not only had her aunt been terribly condescending to her last they met, but Aunt Guthrie's threat that she'd have nothing to do with any of them still haunted her memories. Why was she now claiming the association?

Her vengeful side wished to break ties. If her mother had not been good enough for Aunt Guthrie, then the self-serving woman would certainly hold no amount of love in her heart for her. But Society would not look kindly on either of them for breaking expectations. Best to do as her mother had; be kind and hope for the best.

Still the questions swirled in the back of Susannah's mind. Why had her aunt disliked her mother so, especially after all the overtures Mama had made?

"It has been quite some time since we last saw one another," Aunt Guthrie supplied. "Other than His Grace's card party, that is."

"Yes, come cousin." Miss Guthrie motioned to Susannah to sit next to her on the plush blue settee. "It has been quite some time since we last met. You must tell us how you are enjoying Town."

Was the offer sincere? She did not see anything false in her cousin's wide-set eyes.

Lady Stanford's smile slipped as she glanced between Susannah and Mrs. Guthrie. Did she see her hesitancy?

In the end, Susannah chose to keep the peace, taking up the seat offered and doing her best to show her own good breeding—even if her aunt was less than pleasant.

Miss Guthrie asked where she had been and conversation turned to the fine lace that was to be had in the shops on Piccadilly street. The quarter hour visit gave Susannah great insight into her cousins whom she'd not seen since she was eight. Miss Martha Guthrie was the quieter of the two, choosing instead to sip her tea and watch the happenings around her rather than participate in full.

Miss Guthrie, however, made up for her sister's silence by commanding most of the attention and rarely letting anyone other than her mother get a word in edgewise. She declared herself a great study of laces and believed she knew the best to be had.

The clock chimed indicating a quarter hour had passed and Susannah nearly breathed an audible sigh of relief. But instead of rising as they ought, Miss

CHAPTER 9

Guthrie began extolling upon her many virtues with Aunt Guthrie seconding her words.

"She is quite accomplished you must know, Lady Stanford."

Lady Stanford's head had begun to nod, eyes heavy, but at being called upon to give her attention, she gave a slight dip of her chin.

The encouragement set the two ladies to talking again, this time however they unabashedly boasted of their many connections. They recited at which tables they'd dined and whose private parties they'd been invited. Susannah began to wonder if there was a single person in London's lavish society that did not know the Guthries. From her limited experience, she'd witnessed how well they were received. Perhaps a connection would not be so terrible.

When John's name crossed Miss Guthrie's lips in reference to her latest trip to the shops, Susannah sat forward.

"And then Lord Newhurst picked up my wayward bonnet and handed it to me. I must say he has very fine eyes." Miss Guthrie and her sister shared a conspiratorial smile. "He even asked me if I intended to be at the Fortescue's soiree this evening, which of course I shall, especially if a handsome and well-connected man such as His Lordship will be present."

John had spoken to her, had actually strung several sentences together in order to ask after her plans for the evening? Did that mean he found her cousin attractive?

Heat filled her chest and she picked up her teacup in an effort to hide the frown that marred her lips. He must have found Miss Guthrie quite appealing to make the effort of speaking so much.

What did that say about her?

The only gloom over the last few days was John's absence. She'd not seen him since Parliament had opened. Knowing he'd been at the same shops she'd frequented this week, perhaps even on the same days, pricked at her happiness. If he was not otherwise engaged, why had he not visited?

As if her mind had conjured him into existence, the subject of her thoughts walked through the door and all conversation ceased. Hands behind his back, he paused, eyes widening.

"Lord Newhurst," Lady Stanford said as she rose to her feet. "What a pleasant surprise. Please come have some tea with us."

"I—" His eyes flicked from each of the ladies and eventually landed on Susannah. Wrinkles formed in the space between his eyebrows and his gaze shot back to her aunt.

His concern for her well-being soothed the hurt at knowing he'd spoken with her cousins these last three days but not her. When his attention returned to her, she gave a subtle dip of her head toward the chair across from her. He nodded.

"Thank you, Lady Stanford. Tea would be lovely." He inched forward a step, then another.

"Cream as usual?" Lady Stanford asked.

He blinked at her, shifting his position so Susannah caught sight of something behind his back. When he confirmed his preference, Lady Stanford poured him a cup and extended the plate to him with a generous slice of lavender cake.

He winced. "I... ah." Quickly taking the last few steps, he handed a bouquet to Lady Stanford and took the cup and saucer with the other hand.

She stared blankly at the posy of tiny blue flowers.

"As a thank you," John finally said. "For holding the dinner for me."

Lady Stanford's mouth formed an oh and she bent to the side to hand the flowers to a maid standing behind him. Pain creased her brow and she stopped, her hand coming to rest at her middle.

Susannah had seen her mother favor her middle like that, but only when she was increasing. Come to think of it, Lady Stanford had missed breakfast every morning this week. Was it possible?

The maid ducked around John and took the flowers, allowing Lady Stanford to remain seated.

"Please have them placed in water."

The maid dipped her head and left with the blooms.

Susannah opened her mouth to ask after Lady Stanford's condition and whether she was well, but then bit back the words. It was not her place nor the time to be asking such personal questions, especially in the present company. If Lady Stanford wanted her to know, she would tell her.

"Now," Lady Stanford said as if nothing unusual had happened. "I know you cannot have come to simply sit and listen to Town gossip from a bunch of ladies. Tell me, Lord Newhurst, have you come to steal my husband away for the afternoon?"

CHAPTER 9

John smiled. "Only if Your Ladyship will allow it."

"I am not my husband's keeper."

Susannah nearly snickered, covering her mouth at the last second to keep the expression of mirth from disrupting the room. While laughter was not expressly forbidden in company, Lady Stanford had made it clear that it was not as acceptable in Town as in the country.

When her aunt's dour expression turned to her, she was grateful for the warning. Aunt Guthrie seemed like the type of person prone to adhere strictly to societal dictates purely for the satisfaction of being able to look down on those who did not conform.

"Then I am free to go?" Sir Nathaniel asked from the doorway with a smirk. Everyone moved to rise, but he bid them stay. "I have only come to collect my friend, but I see he has found a better offer. I too would choose the company of so many eligible young ladies if I was not so happily situated."

Miss Guthrie tittered and Miss Martha smiled, but Susannah's attention was drawn to Lady Stanford. Her company smile had slipped and a look of horror entered her eyes as her hand came to her mouth.

Sir Nathaniel rushed to her side, helping her to her feet and ushering her out of the room. It was not fast enough, however, for they all heard her cast up her accounts in the hallway. Susannah grimaced at the sound.

She'd grown quite certain Lady Stanford was in the family way and this episode confirmed her suspicions.

Moments later, Sir Nathaniel entered again. "Please forgive my wife, she is unwell."

"No forgiveness is necessary," Aunt Guthrie said, a smug smile playing on her lips. "I remember those early days quite clearly, but we will say no more of this. Please do not let us keep you, Sir Nathaniel. I know you and Lord Newhurst have business to attend to."

Miss Guthrie cast her mother a look of alarm, motioning with her head to Lord Newhurst, but Aunt Guthrie ignored her. Susannah on the other hand, noticed everything. Her cousin obviously had decided to pursue John and it aggravated her.

"Thank you, we did have plans for this afternoon, but in light of my wife's current condition I am not inclined to keep our fencing engagement."

John set his cup down. "I completely understand. In that case, perhaps I should go. I have several papers to look over before next week's meetings, and I'd like to be more informed on the naturalizations for this year."

"You are not leaving already?" Miss Guthrie asked.

"I am afraid I must, but I shall see you all this evening at the Fortescues'."

So her cousin's information had been correct. The knowledge rankled, but not as much as John's smooth speech. How had he managed to speak so evenly to her cousin, and yet could hardly put two sentences together when in her presence?

Aunt Guthrie rose, her expression grim. "I had not noticed the time. We should also be leaving, for our quarter hour is up."

Half hour to be exact, but there was no point in bringing the time to her aunt's attention. Instead, she would rejoice in their departure.

Miss Guthrie quickly crossed to John's side. "Might we walk out with you, Your Lordship?"

John hesitated, then nodded, offering his arm to the young woman. Susannah frowned. Perhaps she was not happy they were leaving so soon.

To add salt to her wounds, that evening Sir Nathaniel informed her they would not be attending the soiree, Lady Stanford still being kept to her bed by illness.

Susannah went to bed trying not to think of what John might be doing, but it was no use. Her thoughts continually returned to him as she tried to sleep. Was he even now sitting with her cousin, discussing some interesting word or describing his latest painting?

Those had been things they had spoken freely of before his tour of the continent.

What if her cousin found those subjects as interesting as she did? What if she found John as interesting?

Susannah grit her teeth. How could anyone not find him interesting? He was talented in a way she'd never be, well read, and ever thirsting after new knowledge.

She did not know much about Miss Guthrie—Harriet, if memory served—but from the little she'd seen, she seemed far more concerned with her self-importance than with the acquisition of knowledge. Interest in painting, words, or inventions would be the last subjects she'd want to converse on. She probably was not even interested in John himself, but his title.

Her aunt's family was very well connected. Not that they had a large amount of family in the peerage, but rather they were well liked because her uncle was talented in investing. More than once in the last few weeks she'd overheard gentlemen sing his praises because of an extremely profitable investment he'd suggested to them. That set her cousin far above her in both wealth and connection. Add Miss Guthrie's pleasant appearance and it was all most men needed to create a union.

But would her cousin ever love John? Highly unlikely. Oh, she might feign a connection in order to secure him, but it would dwindle and die the moment their vows were said. The notion of John trapped in a loveless marriage did not sit well with her, but what could she do about it?

How could she simply stand back and allow Miss Guthrie to dupe the man she loved?

The man she loved?

Susannah snuggled deeper under her blankets. Did she truly *love* John? Her heart thumped back a resounding yes. Then the fear set in. What if he never loved her in return?

Chapter 10

Susannah watched the other young ladies in the room, pulling out her fan and trying to mimic their movements. Lady Stanford had tried to teach her the language of the fan, but she'd yet to master it.

The evening's celebration for a Miss Giles's presentation into Society was a lavish affair complete with an ice sculpture in the shape of a swan. People milled about the rooms, chatting and enjoying refreshment.

Susannah took note of how the ladies flirted with the gentlemen. Perhaps if she became more adept at the practice she'd be able to gain John's attention. It seemed to entail a great deal of lashes and fan fluttering. The tap of a fan on a gentleman's arm also seemed to gain ladies a great deal of attention.

"Are you well, Miss Wayland?" Miss Harris leaned close to her.

"I am, why do you ask?"

"You are beating that fan so fast it is making poor Mr. Cartright's toupee lift off his head."

She glanced at the older man who stood several feet in front of them. "I am not."

A smirk pulled at Miss Harris's lips. "Only because you have stopped."

"Do be serious. Was I really lifting it?"

"Only a little. Are you nervous?"

"More like uneducated. Lady Stanford has tried to teach me how to use fans in Town, but I am afraid I am a poor student."

Miss Harris took pity on her and repeated the rules. Susannah listened so intently that she did not see Mr. Roberts approach until he stood directly behind Miss Harris.

"I see you are corrupting another young lady, and for all Society to see. For shame, Miss Harris."

The hand that had been demonstrating paused midair. Slowly Miss Harris turned, switching the fan to her right hand and fluttering it gently below her nose.

"Just because you are incapable of understanding fan movements does not signify that all ladies who know it are corrupt. It only proves your ineptitude."

He leaned forward scandalously close and dropped his voice to a low hum. "Come, we both know I understand ladies far better than any other gentleman."

Miss Harris blinked at him, her fan coming to a complete stop and resting on her right cheek. It moved forward a fraction. He straightened and smiled, triumph gleaming in his amber colored eyes.

She let out a huff. "Come, Miss Wayland. It is time to practice what you have learned."

"I would not attempt to apply anything Javenia has taught you, Miss Wayland. It might lead you to commit an unforgivable social faux pas."

Miss Harris rolled her eyes, pulling Susannah away. "Do not listen to him. *Algenon* is simply jealous of what he will never be able to understand."

"And what is that, pray tell?" Mr. Roberts trailed after them.

She cast him a dazzling smile over her shoulder. "If you have to ask, you are more obtuse than I thought."

He stopped, eyes narrowed and mouth firm. His hands clasped behind his back as he watched them walk away. Susannah did not know if she should feel sorry for him or laugh at the obvious win Miss Harris had enacted. Even in her small knowledge, she'd read something in the movement of the fan that would probably have surprised the tall gentleman.

"Ah, there they are," Miss Harris said as they spied Mr. Kendall and the rest of the party from Kendall House in the next room. "We will practice with people who I know are safe and will not be offended if you make a mistake."

When they arrived, the gathered circle opened to admit them and it was then that Susannah caught sight of John holding a glass of champagne in his left hand. Could she really practice with him in the circle?

CHAPTER 10

"Miss Wayland," Mr. Kendall said when he saw her. "Are you enjoying the evening?"

She let her fan rest on her right cheek, but also followed the movement with her words. "Yes. It has been lovely."

He smiled. "And Miss Harris, are you as pleased with the party as Miss Wayland?"

She closed her fan. "Of course. Except when I meet daft men who claim to know more about the female sex than they actually do."

Susannah had caught the movement of Miss Harris's fan, which from her memory meant she wished to speak to him. Turning her attention to Mr. Kendall, she wondered how he might respond, then saw Mr. Roberts, his eyebrows raised, ready to argue his point. Before he reached them, Mr. Kendall spoke up.

"I see. Would you care to accompany me to the refreshment table? Perhaps we can discuss my incompetent friend along the way?"

Her mouth fell open at how masterfully Miss Harris had spoken to Mr. Kendall without ever uttering a word.

"Traitor," Mr. Roberts muttered.

Mr. Kendall smirked and led Miss Harris away.

Susannah glanced about the room as a new understanding opened to her. There was far more flirtation happening than she'd originally thought, but not every man seemed to notice or care. Or perhaps they did notice, but simply did not return the sentiment.

Lady Stanford spoke up. "For all your flattery, *Mr. Roberts*, one would think you could spare a little for your childhood friend."

He spun one of the two gold rings he always wore about his finger. "And cause her self-importance to puff up like bread dough, I think not."

Sir Nathaniel offered his arm to his wife. "I do not believe Javenia is the one we should worry about becoming puffed up." He tipped his head to the side, indicating Mr. Roberts.

His actions were met with a scowl. "I know where I'm not wanted. I shall find company who appreciates me." With two hands he straightened his waistcoat, then turned with a flounce. The action was done too comically to signify true upset, especially when he cast them a dashing smile as he approached Miss Giles.

"Well my dear, I believe we should find you a seat," Sir Nathaniel said. "You have been on your feet too long."

Lady Stanford rolled her eyes but did not object. Since Susannah had not been invited to follow them, she chose to stay. Only she and John now remained. Normally she'd move closer to converse easier, but a bout of swirling butterflies chose that moment to take up residence in her stomach. Could she really flirt with him? The idea seemed awkward, given their years as friends. But how else would she change his mind?

Slowly she lifted her fan to just under her nose and began to flutter it. John glanced at her, his brow creasing before he returned his attention to his champagne.

Glancing down, she paused. Was it the left or right hand that meant come closer? Not sure she switched the fan from her left to her right to see if the results would be different then cleared her throat to gain his attention. He did not move. She cleared it again but louder.

John glanced at her. "Are you in need of refreshment, Miss Wayland?"

She batted her eyelashes at him. "I am indeed."

He tipped his head to the side. "D-do you have s-something caught in your eye?"

Mortification swept through her. She must have done it wrong. When all the other ladies had displayed the coquettish action, the gentlemen had drawn closer.

Quickly she lifted a hand to her eye and swept it across her lashes. "Yes. Forgive me. There, that is better."

"Good. Might I fetch you something to drink?"

"Or I could go with you."

He nodded and offered his arm. A footman passed with a half-full tray of empty glasses and he placed his on it. Slowly they made their way through the gathered crowd.

"It is quite the crush, wouldn't you agree. I do not believe I have seen so many people. And look at the ladies' dresses. So exquisite. Of course the gentlemen look fine too, but I do not believe they desire compliments as ladies do. Or do they? As a lady I would not know." She was rambling and she knew it, but she could not stop herself. "What do you say, Lord Newhurst? Do you wish for compliments on your appearance?"

Now why had she asked that?

She stared up at his face. A polite smile graced his lips and for the first time she noted how full they were. Not that they puffed out, but they appeared healthy

CHAPTER 10

and moist, not thin and chapped like other men's. What would it be like to kiss lips as soft and warm as his?

John stepped to the side, his arm suddenly pulling her off balance, but not before she collided with someone, her teeth clinking with the impact. John's arms came up to right her.

A man with dark hair spun to face them. She blinked a time or two trying to clear her foggy head. When she did, her cheeks flamed. She'd been so occupied with looking at John that she'd walked right into someone. A handsome someone, no less.

"My apologies, miss. I had not meant to back into you."

"No, it is my fault for not paying attention to my surroundings. Do forgive me." Susannah took note of his broad shoulders and fine figure. Perfectly styled dark hair curled about his ears.

His smile grew. She smiled and dropped her gaze.

John gave a little tug on her arm to indicate he wished to continue on. The stranger apologized again, but she had no time to answer as they were already walking away. She wanted to ask who the man was, but when she turned to look at John, his face was set in a deep frown.

A tiny shard of shame pricked her heart. Had she embarrassed him?

When they reached the table, he spoke slowly. "P-please forgive me... for not being a better escort."

Relief washed over her. "It is not your fault that I am so unobservant. Without you, I would have come to much more harm. I believe your tug pulled me out of the way of the greatest impact."

His serious expression lightened and his shoulders relaxed. "What drink might I get you?"

She glanced down at the table's contents. There was a questionable punch at the end of the table with small cakes and pastries laid out next to it. At the other end were glasses of negus and orgeat. She chose the latter, preferring the orange and almond flavored drink to the others. When he handed it to her, however, she realized she no longer held her fan. She glanced about herself, wondering where it had gone.

John leaned into her line of sight. "Is something the matter?"

"I seemed to have misplaced my fan."

Lifting her gaze from the floor around them, she peered about the room. An idea settled in her mind. "I think I may have dropped it when I bumped into that gentleman."

She placed her half-consumed drink back on the table, a servant eyeing her as she did so, but there was no help for it. She needed to locate her fan. Lady Stanford had gifted her the intricately painted piece and it would be an insult to have lost it so soon.

John walked slowly next to her as they returned the way they'd come, their eyes sweeping the floor. When they reached the spot where the mishap had happened, they stopped, combing the area carefully. Still no fan.

"Could someone have picked it up?" she asked.

"Perhaps. Either that or all the moving feet may have displaced it."

They agreed to go in separate directions from the spot in hopes they'd find it faster. In the center of the large room Susannah saw it peeking out from under a matronly woman's skirts. She paused, her gaze traveling up lavishly adorned lavender silk to a pinched face. The woman bent to the side, holding her own fan to her mouth, speaking softly to a taller, angular lady.

Not knowing who they were, Susannah dared not approach, but hovered nearby to see if she could catch one of their names. Perhaps she could find someone to introduce them. Otherwise it would be exceedingly rude for her to interrupt them by reaching under the shorter lady's skirts.

"I did not s-see it near the wall," John whispered.

Susannah startled at the warmth of his breath on her ear, her head bumping into his nose as she straightened. He reeled back and she grimaced.

He rubbed the offended appendage. "M-m-my a-apologies."

A sudden urge to laugh so overcame her that she had to cup a hand over her mouth to keep it from spilling out. The reaction was illogical, but she could not help herself. How many mistakes could she make in one evening?

"I do not know why you are apologizing when it was I who hit you. It seems I am doomed this evening to beg forgiveness of everyone."

A large group of people entered and Susannah's gaze shot to where her fan lay on the floor. It would be even more difficult to retrieve it with all the ladies and gentlemen now joining them.

John must have followed her gaze. "I will f-fetch it."

CHAPTER 10

Stepping in front of her, he approached the two ladies. "Lady Plum, Mrs. Cline, do excuse me, but my friend h-has dropped her fan and I believe that is it there on the floor." He pointed to the fan painted with pink roses.

Mrs. Cline stepped back so her skirts no longer obscured it. "Dear me. That was a mite clumsy of her, don't you think?"

"Not at all. She was bumped by a gentleman who did not take the time to watch where he was going. If you will excuse me." He bent and carefully retrieved the fan.

Lady Plum looked him up and down. "It is a surprise to see you here, Lord Newhurst. We are not often graced with the opportunity to view your fine figure at parties."

John stepped back, the pink on his cheeks appearing to match the rosy hue of his hurt nose. "I—that is… t-thank you." Then under his breath, he said, "I think."

Again the woman ogled him. "No need to thank me. But should you find yourself without someone to keep you company, do find me. I would be happy to *chat* with you for a while."

He backed away, brows raised, then spun as if he wished to escape the room all together. The laugh that Susannah had been holding burst out, causing several people to cast her looks of disdain.

It seemed her embarrassment for this night was complete.

Johnathan gripped the fan tightly. The blatant way Lady Plum had admired him was disconcerting. Of all the ladies he wished to catch the attention of tonight, she was the very last. Second would be her friend Mrs. Cline. The two women were the biggest busybodies London had to offer and over twice his age—not to mention married.

He would have left the event entirely if Susannah's laugh had not reminded him of his cause. Her hand slapped over her mouth and her eyes widened at her outburst. She looked so cute that his feet stopped. He extended the fan to her and she took it without saying anything, her head dipping to hide her face.

Several couples scooted around them, censure on their faces. No wonder she was embarrassed.

"Come, let us find the others."

She glanced up, her soft brown eyes filled with something. Was it relief? It was unusual for him not to be able to read her, but he found this expression different than most. Then again, she'd been acting odd all evening.

Her hand found his forearm and he steeled himself for the fire he knew her touch would ignite. The warmth of her hand spread up his arm as she offered her thanks and then chattered nervously about the beauty of the rooms. He loved the sound of her voice. It was neither too high, nor too low. The sing-song way she spoke soothed his own embarrassment at Lady Plum's attentions.

If only Susannah showed as blatant an interest in him as the old matron had, then it might be easier to pursue a possible courtship with her. Or it might not. What would he do if she looked him up and down like she wanted to eat him for supper? His hands began to sweat in his gloves at the mental picture. Perhaps he ought not to think about such things in a full ballroom. He'd likely need to borrow Susannah's wayward fan to cool himself.

It took several minutes to locate Nate and Melior, they having found a quieter part of the house. Eddie and Javenia were also there, plates of refreshments in their laps.

"What can he possibly see in her?" Javenia was asking as they approached.

Melior's eyes flicked over her friend's shoulder and Javenia immediately stuffed cake in her mouth, her attention completely on her food. He had no doubt what they were speaking of, but it seemed the ladies were not comfortable voicing their concerns about Al in front of Miss Wayland.

CHAPTER 10

There were only two seats left on the sofa next to Javenia, Eddie having taken up the seat on the opposite side next to his sister. The arrangement did not disappoint in the least.

If he'd been more of a gentleman he might have stayed standing to give Susannah space, but the opportunity to sit next to her was too tempting. They sat so close to one another that their arms touched and the hem of her skirt brushed the tops of his shoes.

Conversation turned to the newest fabrics, and his mind wandered. Was Susannah at all affected by his closeness? Did she feel the warmth they shared? He stole a glance at her. She sat perfectly still, only adding to the conversation when called to do so. Was she uncomfortable?

Not wanting to discomfit her more, he let his gaze travel about the room. In a chair at the other end, a familiar gentleman with dark hair stared blatantly at Susannah. Johnathan's eyes narrowed. He had a passing acquaintance with Mr. Wallace, the man that had bumped into Susannah, but it had been some time since the gentleman had joined them for the season in London. His sister, however, had been a constant these last three years, seeking Johnathan out whenever they attended the same gathering.

Finally Mr. Wallace's gaze found Johnathan's, but instead of looking chagrined, he only smiled and returned to speaking to the man next to him.

Johnathan shook his head. Some men were a bit too bold.

"I believe we have bored poor John to distraction," Eddie said.

Pulling his attention back to the group, he noted all their eyes were on him. Had no one else noticed the people in the other chairs watching them? Probably not. The other guests had paid little attention to their group either, except of course Mr. Wallace.

"I am s-simply tired," he lied. Why had he given such an excuse? His starched posture and clenched muscles were sure to dissuade them from such a notion.

Melior covered a yawn. "It is getting late."

"Maybe for country hours," Eddie argued, "but not in town. You have grown soft, Mel. It's time we toughen you up a bit."

Nate shook his head. "I like my wife the way she is, thank you. There will be no brotherly intervention this season. If she is tired, then I believe it best that we make our excuses to the hostess and retire for the evening."

Eddie peered at them in confusion. Johnathan did not blame him. Melior was a woman of Society; she bloomed in large groups usually floating about the room impressing everyone. Why would she want to leave early?

More to the point, why would she take Susannah away so soon? He enjoyed sitting next to her even if Mr. Wallace's eyes were again upon her. There was no help for it, though. They declared they would leave and no convincing could change Nate's mind.

Deciding to make the best of the last few moments, Johnathan offered his arm to Susannah who was surprisingly quiet. Was she as fatigued as Melior? He escorted her to the front entry where a footman retrieved their coats.

The group shifted toward the door, but Susannah held back, her grip on his arm keeping him there. He did not mind. It gave him a few more moments to enjoy her company.

"I forgot to thank you for retrieving my fan."

She blinked in that odd way again, the one that made him wonder if she had something caught in her eye. He searched for a wayward eyelash but saw nothing. Even so, he did not mind her gaze on him. If only he could rein in his nerves enough to respond to her.

Several sentences formed in his mind, but all of them sounded ridiculous.

You're welcome. Retrieving fans from under lady's dresses is my specialty. He cringed at the implication. *It was my pleasure* was even worse, especially considering Lady Plum's reaction to him.

He peered down into her doe-like eyes and the words slipped out. "It was nothing."

"Perhaps to you, but it meant a lot to me."

Instinctively he covered her hand. The blinking had stopped and she held his gaze with an intensity that made his knees week. She was so beautiful, especially with the candlelight dancing off her rosy cheeks and giving her hair an ethereal glow.

A throat cleared so close that he jerked back, not realizing he'd leaned toward Susannah.

Eddie's unrepentant smile met his gaze. He held Susannah's pelisse open and looked at them both expectantly.

Susannah blushed and stepped into her coat. "Thank you, Mr. Kendall."

When all her outerwear was in place, she turned back to Johnathan. "I suppose we shall see you tomorrow at the Prince's ball."

CHAPTER 10

He nodded, anticipation filling his gut and stealing words from his mind.

She reached a hand out to him and he bowed over it. "Good night, Lord Newhurst."

"Good night..." he managed to choke out.

She took hold of Eddie's arm and they turned to walk out the large double doors.

"Susannah," he whispered before it closed behind them.

Chapter 11

Lady Stanford's lady's maid tucked tiny white blossoms in the twists at the crown of Susannah's head. Like pearls in spun gold, they accented the white gown she had donned to perfection.

In an effort to add some color, she added her mother's gold chain and matching bracelet. The maid finished her ministrations and Susannah stared at herself in the full-length mirror. Who was that woman staring back at her?

It had been years since she'd considered herself a child, but the person in the mirror was taller than she remembered, her curves more pronounced, and her cheeks less round.

Lady Stanford knocked on the door before entering. "Oh, Miss Wayland!" she exclaimed. "You look absolutely stunning. I am sure you will catch the attention of half the gentlemen in London."

Susannah's cheeks warmed. "Thank you, but I would settle for just one." She peered down at her dress and whispered, "The right one, that is."

"And who would that be?" A mischievous glint sparkled in Lady Stanford's eyes.

"I do not know," she lied. Was it truly a lie, though? She cared for John deeply, but what if fate was not on her side? What if she never won his regard?

The memory of the way he'd come to her over a week ago when Aunt Guthrie had been so condescending floated across her mind. He'd been so angry she'd worried he might give her aunt a thorough set down. In all the years she'd known John, he'd been the most even tempered, patient man of her acquaintance. She'd hardly known him in that moment, but it had warmed her heart to know he would jump to her defense.

That did not mean he had any regard for her, though. Brothers defended their sisters after all.

Lady Stanford patted her arm. "Well, when you find such a gentleman, I beg you will let me know. Perhaps there is something Nathaniel and I might do to bring him up to scratch."

She followed her statement with a cheeky grin.

Susannah laughed. "I shall do that."

At the bottom of the stairs, Sir Nathaniel waited for them, his wife's pelisse in hand. Lady Stanford smiled and slipped her arms into it, then winced, her hand settling over her midsection.

"Are you alright?" Susannah asked.

Lady Stanford inhaled deeply. "I am. Only a slight twinge. Perhaps I stepped wrong."

Suspicion clouded Susannah's mind, but she chose to push it away. Any woman could suffer abdominal pains.

The short drive left little time for conversation, even so Susannah doubted she'd have been able to string enough words together to sound intelligible. Excitement pulsed through her, keeping her warm even in the cold winter air.

When the pillars of Carlton House came into view, she gasped. Kendall House, or even the Duke of Bedford's home, were tiny in comparison to the grandeur before her. Inside, the staircase split into two, both paths reuniting at the top where people filed through a narrow space only to turn and continue up more stairs.

Susannah's feet froze to the floor as she looked around in wonder. She'd attended plenty of country dances, but this was like nothing she'd ever seen before.

The ball was to be held in the main court with other smaller rooms also readied for guests, the furniture having been moved for the occasion. But the crowd that filled the space left little room for dancing. Only half a dozen couples could possibly find room right in the center.

Unlike most balls, their host had not been at the door to greet them. Instead they were directed to enjoy some refreshment until His Majesty and the royal party arrived. Susannah glanced around at all the people milling about as the orchestra played.

CHAPTER 11

A flash of yellow hair above the crowd caught her attention as it drew closer to them. Her heart pounded and her palms began to sweat. This was her moment. She prayed her preparations had been enough.

"Miss Wayland," a female voice said from behind her. She turned in confusion.

The face of the lady was familiar but try as she might, she could not recall a name. She'd met so many people these last few days that her mind could not hold onto more than a few names at a time, then she'd meet others and the first names disappeared without a trace. A vague memory of the young woman at Kendall House floated in the back of Susannah's mind.

"What a fine thing that we should meet again." The woman motioned to the man next to her. "Do allow me to introduce my brother, Mr. Wallace."

The gentleman gave a slight bow, his brown eyes dancing as they took her in. Dark brown hair curled around evenly set ears and at the temples of his wide brow. Susannah's eyes widened. The man she'd collided with last evening.

He smiled at her. "Miss Wayland, it is a pleasure to finally make your acquaintance—this time with much less pain involved."

Susannah battled the urge to hold her burning cheeks. "Again, I am so sorry for my clumsiness."

"Do not trouble yourself. I was at fault. If I'd been more attentive, we could have avoided such a collision. But you can imagine my delight when I found you share an acquaintance with my sister. She has told me a great deal about you."

She had? Susannah had hardly spoken to Miss Wallace at the Stanfords' dinner party, but she had not forgotten the way the woman's attention had been focused on John. Was this some sort of jest?

"I hope they were all good things." She tried to add a smile to give her words a note of teasing, but she really did wonder about Miss Wallace's intent.

The brother and sister glanced at one another. "Of course," he said. "And I now can declare that her description of your beauty was completely accurate."

Susannah blushed at his pointed attention.

"Tell me, are you engaged for the first set?" he asked.

"I am not."

"Might I have the honor then of leading you to the floor?"

She smiled. "That would be lovely."

Out of the corner of her eye, John stopped. He stared at her, and she turned to greet him hoping his look of shock meant he approved of her appearance. But before she uttered a single word, he turned and left.

Her heart plummeted into the toes of her dancing slippers. What had she done wrong?

CHAPTER 11

John cursed himself for a fool. He'd been in company with Susannah days ago, had intended to ask her for the first dance, but Mrs. Guthrie and her daughters had been present. He could not very well ask for a dance from one lady and not promise to dance with the rest. Only now did he realize that the Guthries had probably not been invited.

Blast his cowardly heart.

He'd even seen her last evening at the Giles' soiree. If he'd asked her yesterday, he would not have lost his place to Mr. Wallace. Not that he had anything against the man. Other than his pointed stare at Susannah last evening, he seemed decent enough.

But the dream of partnering Susannah for her first dance of the season had been stolen out from under him, and like a rug suddenly yanked away, he felt unsteady on his feet.

"Lord Newhurst," Miss Wallace called after him.

He turned.

She wove her way through several people. "I am so delighted to see you here this evening." She clasped her hands behind her back and did that weird thing with her dark lashes that he'd noticed Susannah do.

John swallowed. He needed to speak, but all he could summon was a nod.

"Do you like to dance, Your Lordship?"

Another nod.

She waited expectantly.

Algenon sidled up to him. "The correct answer is 'would you like to dance?'" he whispered.

John glared at his amused smile. Al received far too much enjoyment from teasing him.

When he continued on in his silence, Al turned to Miss Wallace. "Good evening, Miss Wallace. You are looking resplendent in that jonquil dress. Is that stunning lace from Mrs. Barclay's establishment?"

Leave it to Al to save the situation with one of his flowery compliments.

"Why yes it is, Mr. Roberts. You are quite versed on your shops."

"I should be. I have enough sisters to empty most of them."

Miss Wallace giggled.

"Now, if you do not mind, my friend and I would like to ask for your next two sets."

Her face scrunched up and motioned between them with her hand. "Together?"

John nearly snorted a laugh. While she might be pretty, Miss Wallace was a bit lacking in sense.

"No, Newhurst shall take the first and I shall take the second."

She flashed them a brilliant smile and leaned in. "Of course. I would be honored to dance with you both."

"Very good. We shall be sure to find you when the dancing finally begins."

She pulled out her fan and began fluttering it right below her nose, her lips pursed in such a way to draw attention. Al's left eyebrow hitched up and he gave a slight shake of his head.

With one arm around Johnathan's shoulders, he directed him away from her. Dropping his voice he said, "And that is how you procure a dance partner, though one with more sense would have been more preferable."

Johnathan snorted. "Did it ever occur to you that I may not have wanted to dance with Miss Wallace?"

Al stopped, his mouth hanging open. "Not dance when the chance is right before you? What a travesty. One might assume you do not even like women with how much you avoid them."

The humor faded from Johnathan's face and he instinctively found Susannah in the crowd.

"I see." Al's lips tipped up at the corners. "You know the same method works in asking other young ladies to dance."

"Not when they have already procured a partner."

"Now that is a shame," Al tutted. "But she cannot be engaged for every dance."

"No, only the one that counts."

They were interrupted when the clock struck nine and the doors of the court were thrown wide open. All conversation stopped and Prince George himself walked in, dressed in his favorite military style, complete with gold buttons and faux medals. His sister, Mary, dressed in a fine silk gown of blue, clung to his arm.

Attendees parted like waves of the ocean, bowing deeply as the royal dinner party passed. Likewise Johnathan stepped back, Al following suit.

"My goodness," Melior said from beside him. "His Royal Highness has grown rather thick about the middle since I last laid eyes on him."

CHAPTER 11

Johnathan turned in surprise, not realizing the party from Kendall House had joined him. Al moved back, creating space for Susannah to move to the front in order to have a better view.

His Majesty moved slowly, nodding to those he recognized and every once in a while stopping to speak a word to someone. Those from the royal dinner party, which included the Duke and Duchess of Bedford, waited patiently while he advanced. When he reached them, he stopped, extending his hand out to raise Melior from her deep curtsy.

"Miss Kendall, nay, it is Lady Stanford now, is it not?"

"It is, Your Majesty."

"Always a pleasure to see you." Prince George's eyes traveled liberally over Melior's form before moving to the rest of the group. "And who is this magnificent creature?"

His Majesty placed the tips of his fingers on Susannah's head to raise her from her curtsy. She glanced up in surprise. Johnathan clenched his teeth. No one spoke against the Prince Regent, but he did not like the way the man took such liberties with his eyes.

"Your Majesty," Melior said, "This is Miss Wayland, of Maidstone."

"Lovely. Absolutely lovely. I do hope you enjoy yourself, Miss Wayland."

Johnathan wished the corpulent man would move on and keep his hands and eyes to himself.

When the prince finally left, he turned to Susannah. "Are you well?"

"Absolutely divine." Her eyes were all aglow. "Can you believe the Prince Regent himself called me lovely? How many ladies in England could boast of such a thing? Certainly no one of my acquaintance."

In the wake of her joy, Johnathan relaxed. At least she'd not noticed the prince's ungentlemanly attentions, and from a married man no less. It was no wonder he and Princess Caroline were at odds with each other.

Susannah smoothed the front of her pristine dress, still preening over the compliment. Johnathan's mouth went dry. She was stunning. It was no wonder the prince had noticed her. Candlelight flickered off her locks, making them shimmer like the surface of a golden pool.

"It's now or never, old man," Al whispered from behind him.

He swallowed hard. "Miss Wayland."

"Yes." She clasped her hands behind her back, the picture of innocent beauty.

"May I... that is, would you..." He was butchering this. "Will you dance with me?" There, he had said it.

"My first two sets are taken, but I would be honored to dance the third with you. If there is room, that is. With this crush, I am not certain we will have any."

"If not... a turn about the room will do."

Her face lit up. "I would like that, John."

His heart stuttered to a stop at her use of his Christian name. He'd heard it on her lips dozens of times over the years, but it had been months since she'd used it. With a painful lurch his heart flew back into action, racing as if it were a horse in a steeple race.

His mind rushed through subjects he wished to speak with her on, words to fill the space between them and pull them closer, but the announcement of the first set and subsequent arrival of Mr. Wallace brought his excitement to an abrupt halt.

Susannah placed her hand in Mr. Wallace's, her attention fully on her partner as if he'd been completely forgotten. Of course. Why not? He held the place of an older brother after all. Nothing more.

Chapter 12

Mr. Wallace was an excellent dancer and Susannah hoped he would not notice her deficiencies. One of only six couples in the middle of the room, they danced the minuet to the music of an orchestra, the likes of which Susannah had never heard before. Princess Mary led out the dancers at the head, leaving all others to follow suit.

If Mr. Wallace had any complaints about Susannah's dancing he hid it well, for his attention hardly ever strayed from her. In truth, his attentions were so bold it left her in little doubt of his interest. Never before had any man appeared so awestruck in her presence.

Heat crept up her neck and onto her cheeks. If only John would look at her with such admiration. It had taken the notice of a prince to even get him to ask her for a dance.

The thought was lowering. Was he the sort of man who only saw value in a woman if she attracted attention from his peers? She'd never seen him as the competitive sort. Then again, he did fence regularly. Perhaps it was a side of him he kept hidden behind the doors of sporting clubs.

Her gaze crept along the edges of the crowd until she found John deep in conversation with Mr. Kendall, Mr. Roberts, and Sir Nathaniel. He did not even look her way.

Fine. Then she would not search him out either. She needed to focus on the moment before her, anyway. But her disobedient mind replayed John's look of shock when he'd first seen her. He had not appeared pleased or angry, but hurt. Could he have been disappointed in her acceptance of Mr. Wallace?

She glanced at her dance partner and he flashed her a brilliant smile. Her chest expanded. It was nice to be appreciated.

The dance brought them together. "You look contemplative. Might I be so bold as to ask what is on your mind?" he asked.

What to say? She could not tell him she had been thinking of another man. That would be rude. "I was admiring your dancing, sir. Not many have such grace and self-possession."

"And I might say the same of you, Miss Wayland. You bestow a great honor on the whole room with your beautiful presence."

His compliment flustered her and she stumbled on her next steps. Mr. Wallace's hand shot out, catching her about the waist and righting her. Back squarely on her feet, John's concerned face was the first she saw in the crowd. Why could he not have noticed her before she made a fool of herself?

"Are you well, Miss Wayland?" Mr. Wallace asked as they resumed the dance.

She could not respond right away as the pattern led them apart, but she reassured him when they again united that she'd suffered no ill effect—at least nothing more than a little embarrassment at John seeing her stumble like a girl still in short dresses—but she need not tell Mr. Wallace that much.

"I enjoyed our time together immensely," he said when the second song ended. "Where can I escort you?"

Susannah scanned the crowd. Halfway down the room near one of the refreshment tables, Lady Stanford was deep in conversation with Miss Harris. She gestured to them and Mr. Wallace began clearing a path through the crowd. It took a great deal of maneuvering to get through all the people, but it gave her time to get to know him better.

They talked of his siblings which she found equaled the same amount as hers, he being the second in order of birth. The subject reminded her to take in all the details of the night so she might write home about the event.

When they reached the women, Mr. Wallace bowed over her hand, his eyes never leaving her face. "I will leave you then, but if it is acceptable to Lady Stanford I should like to call on you."

"Tuesday we shall be at home to our friends," Lady Stanford supplied.

He smiled. "Tuesday then. Enjoy the rest of your evening, Miss Wayland."

"Well," Miss Harris said when Mr. Wallace was out of earshot. "You must have made quite the impression on him, Miss Wayland. He looks absolutely besotted."

Susannah opened her fan to hide the wide smile on her face. "Interested perhaps, but besotted seems a bit intense of a word for one set, don't you think?"

Lady Stanford shook her head. "No, I concur with Javenia. He made a cake of himself over you."

Had he really? Susannah searched him out in the crowd, but instead her eyes landed on a petite young woman not much older than her dressed head to toe in black lace, the underskirt of her dress a vibrant white. Her black turban had a large black ostrich feather poking out of the right side.

When the woman turned in her direction, green eyes on a delicate face stared back at her, the expression not soft in the least. Shoulders back, the lady stood no taller than five feet, but she seemed to command the room around her.

"Who is that?" she asked her companions, gesturing with her chin.

"I do not follow," Lady Stanford said.

"In the black lace, with the carved stone topped cane." The affectation seemed more of an addition to the woman's persona rather than a necessity.

"That is Lady Braithwaite," Miss Harris said. "Widow of the late Earl of Braithwaite."

"And the widow of Mr. Herbert before that," Lady Stanford added.

"But she looks too young to have lost two husbands." Susannah glanced between her companions.

Miss Harris nodded. "Yes. But do not let her innocent exterior fool you. The woman is as tough as they come. And while you may hear a good deal of rumors about her, most are not true."

Lady Stanford snorted, then covered her face with her wafting fan. "Most."

Miss Harris peeked at her friend. "I do not understand why you still hold your distance from her, Melior. She is not as scary as you think."

"Can we talk about this somewhere else, Javenia?" Lady Stanford glanced at the crowd around them, her expression guarded.

Miss Harris looked unconvinced, but she nodded. "I suppose so. Oh look, your husband is come to collect you for a dance, no doubt."

Susannah turned to see Sir Nathaniel approaching.

"Not so. Miss Wayland is his partner for the next set." Lady Stanford retrieved a glass from a servant who walked by and took a sip. Her nose wrinkled. "The lemonade is a bit tepid."

"As it always is." Miss Harris waved the man away when he tried to offer her one. "I'd rather drink water from a puddle than that sludge."

"Careful, Javenia," Mr. Roberts said, joining their party. "If the prince hears you insulting his drinks he might have you beheaded."

"Catch up with the century, Algenon. He's not Henry the Eighth."

The friends' banter brought a smile to Susannah's face. They must be back on good terms as they were using first names again, something that had been absent often of late.

"Fine, but at least dance with me so I might vouch for your not so reprehensible character when His Majesty comes to have you led away to his dungeons."

"I'd rather John speak for me; he's a far more reliable witness."

"Ah yes, but he is not here right now, so you are stuck with me."

She rolled her eyes. "I suppose I shall have to accept, then." But the little smile pulling at her lips as Mr. Roberts led her away belied her annoyance. Everyone knew they did not detest each other as much as it appeared.

Sir Nathaniel glanced at the center of the room. "That makes eight couples. I'm not sure there is enough room to admit us, Miss Wayland."

"Indeed," she agreed.

"Would you like to try again on the next set or do you have someone else waiting?"

"Lord Newhurst solicited a dance."

Lady Stanford shared a glance with Sir Nathaniel. "Well then, we would not wish to take away his time, would we, my dear?"

"Not in the least. Would you like me to lead you to where he is stationed, Miss Wayland? It might give you both a better chance of dancing if you are the first to the floor after this set ends."

Susannah gave a little bounce on her heels. "I would like that very much, Sir Nathaniel." Had that been too enthusiastic? She'd not meant to show her excitement quite so openly.

He offered an arm to each lady and they slowly made their way through the crowd. When the back of John's head appeared above everyone, Susannah's hands began to sweat in her gloves. She hadn't danced with John since before his tour.

The memory tickled her mind. She'd been nearly sixteen and so excited about her first dance at the assembly in Maidstone. John had worn a green coat, tan britches, and a smile that had melted her insides like hot butter. Looking back, it was probably the moment she'd started to see him more as a man and less as the youth she'd idolized.

When they reached John, Sir Nathaniel gave his shoulder a tap. He turned and his gaze settled on Susannah. Little sparks kindled in her chest and she gave him a shy smile hoping to appear alluring.

"I have brought your dancing partner, Newhurst. I know it's a bit early, but there was no room for us on the floor."

"I thank you. It would have been hard to find you at all in this crowd, even with my added height. Too many feathers and head adornments to see clearly."

"No doubt. Well, we shall leave Miss Wayland in your care while we greet my wife's uncle."

Susannah took note of His Grace across the room, his very pregnant wife on his arm. "Her Grace does not appear very comfortable." In truth, she looked miserable.

"No, she does not." Lady Stanford pulled her husband in the direction of her uncle.

John silently stared after them for a moment. Susannah waited. Normally she would fill the silence, but the loud ballroom did not need any more noise.

He finally turned to her. "You do not have to dance with me if you do not wish it, Miss Wayland."

Her head jerked back in surprise. Where had he gotten the idea that she did not want to dance with him? "I very much want to dance with you, only I worry there will not be room for us."

He nodded. "Let us find a quieter parlor then. I know there have been several set aside for guests."

John wanted to spend time alone... with her. Well not completely alone. There would be guests milling about. The idea appealed to her. At least she'd not embarrass herself again in front of all the esteemed guests.

Chapter 13

The light touch of Susannah's hand on his arm did strange things to Johnathan's mind. Like butterflies dancing along his skin, each brush of her fingers seeped through his sleeves and left the hair on his arm standing on end.

"This way." He directed them toward the closest sitting room. Inside there were several people socializing in small groups, but at least the music was not so loud. A table in the corner was laid out with tea, coffee, and tiny sandwiches. "Will this do? There are others."

"No, no this will do nicely." She smiled up at him and turned the butterflies on his skin to fire pulsing through his veins. He swallowed hard. If he did not get control of his feelings he'd not be able to carry on any sort of conversation tonight.

After collecting some refreshments, they sat in matching mahogany chairs. Johnathan searched his mind for a topic of discussion when he noticed that every few seconds Susannah glanced down at her dress.

"Is something amiss?"

She shook her head. "I am not used to wearing white and I worry I will stain my dress. How do gentlemen wear such white cravats and not stain them?"

"W-we do. All the time. But a good valet knows exactly how to launder them correctly."

Her mouth formed an oh but she said nothing more. He searched for another topic, but nothing came to mind that did not include his three specialties, and he would not bore her with those. There was always the weather. That seemed to work for many people.

"Dreary weather we've been having."

She nodded in agreement.

That had gotten him nowhere. Susannah was not the normal London miss who talked on end about useless subjects. He needed something to draw her out.

"W-what is your f-favorite flower?" he blurted out before he lost his nerve.

She paused, setting the sandwich she'd been nibbling back on the plate. He felt ridiculous. He knew it was cowslip. Why had he asked such an inane question?

"Roses." She ducked her head. "Pink ones are my particular favorite, but all of them are beautiful."

His fingers curled tight around his plate. All this time he'd assumed it was a common field flower. Why? Just because she picked them often did not equate to her adoring them.

"I especially love the ones that have a strong fragrance. They smell like how love should feel." Her eyes slowly rose to meet his, and his mind stopped working.

Just having the word love floating between them was enough to stop his tongue, but the intent way her eyes trapped his made it impossible to even swallow, much less speak. He wanted to ask how a rose's smell resembled the feel of love. Why she'd even say such a thing? If she had ever been in love? Was she in love? With whom?

But nothing came out.

She set down her plate on the beautifully carved coffee table in front of them. "Have you painted anything interesting lately?"

So much for staying away from his fallback discussions. "I have. H-have you s-seen the w-wedding portrait"—he stopped and took a deep breath, composing his thoughts so he could control the words— "I did for the Stanfords?"

She leaned forward. "Yes. The way you mixed the cobalt to highlight Lady Stanford's eyes is magnificent, and the detail." She let out a happy sigh. "Each hair seemed to have a life of its own."

His chest puffed out with pride. She'd noticed the painstaking work he'd put into the gift.

"But what have you done recently?" she asked.

He opened his mouth then realized what his last project had been. No, he could not tell her he'd painted her without permission. He needed another project to relay, but none came to mind. He'd been so obsessed with getting the light on the side of her neck and hair just right that he'd worked on nothing else for months.

"I—" His teacup rattled and he focused on subduing his trembling. "A portrait."

"Really? Is it someone I know?"

He nodded and took a sip from his tea.

"Who?"

When it became apparent that he'd drop his cup and saucer if he did not put them down, he bent forward and slowly arranged them on the table, taking time to come up with a plausible answer.

"I am afraid the p-person who commissioned the painting might be u-upset if I share that information with you. Perhaps once it is delivered, I can... that is... I might ascertain if it would be permissible."

"Now you have me intrigued. Tell me, is the subject male or female?"

He glanced at the other occupants of the room to see if anyone was listening in.

"Female," he said softly.

"Really?"

A myriad of emotions played across Susannah's face and he wished for a little window into her mind to see what she was thinking. Since no such convenience existed he had to rely on what he knew of her expressions. A furrowed brow could mean several things, but the way she sat back led him to believe she was disappointed. Why would a painting of her be upsetting?

But she did not know it was about her. Dare he hope a bit of jealousy might be involved?

"The subject is quite l-lovely with the most *fascinating curls*."

"I see." She picked up her cup and her arms pinched close to her sides.

It could not be. The small glimmer of hope led him to be a bit reckless. "The line of her jaw was hard to mimic, but her cheek is the most captivating color of pink."

Susannah's lips compressed and his heart cheered. Now how to go about finding out the depth of her feelings. The thought of talking about such sensitive subjects set his hands to shaking again. A lump formed in his throat and the ease with which he'd spoken fled.

Light blue skirts swished in his periphery.

"Miss Wayland," Miss Wallace said as she approached them. "It seems you have found the exact spot to be this evening. Is not this a fantastic crush?"

He would have called it ghastly or abhorrent. No person needed to be pressed as much as he had been all evening.

Susannah cast her a tight smile. "It is. I have not seen its equal."

"This is nothing compared to the ball he held last June," Mr. Wallace said from behind them.

Johnathan turned to see the man approaching with his own refreshments. Susannah's expression brightened and he wanted to groan. Did Mr. Wallace have to appear right at this moment? Or at all, for that matter?

"I heard there were nearly five thousand people in attendance," Susannah said. "Is that true?"

"I would not doubt it. Unfortunately we did not attend as we had to remove to the country for our mother's health. Family comes first, you see."

The way Susannah smiled at his declaration did not bode well. He knew how much she valued family. Hers was the center of her life, and her loyalty ran deep. Any man who declared the same sentiment would certainly win a portion of her heart.

But Johnathan had no family. No parents or grandparents, and no surviving aunts or uncles. He'd heard tell that a second cousin lived somewhere in the north of England, but he'd never met the man. So how could he declare the importance of family when he had none to speak of?

Conversation fell into a natural rhythm between the others as they shared similar family experiences leaving Johnathan with nothing to contribute. His mind spun around Mr. Wallace's statement about needing to leave London. That he knew of, the man had not been in Town. Then again, perhaps he'd come to collect his mother and sister so his father might stay to take part in the House of Commons.

At a lull in the discussion Miss Wallace said, "Lord Newhurst, I tried to find you in the crowd when the dancing began but failed, so instead I gave Mr. Roberts my first set. I hope you are not offended."

CHAPTER 13

He hoped his face did not appear as horrified as he felt. His thoughts had been so consumed with Susannah all night that he'd forgotten he'd promised Miss Wallace a dance. "Yes... well..."

"I believe he was looking for you when I came upon him." Susannah's rescue was a godsend. "And since he'd also promised me a dance he was too polite to turn down my request that we find some refreshment. The floor, as you probably witnessed, is very full."

"It is." Miss Wallace's lip jutted out, then her expression switched to a sweet smile. "But we have found each other now. Perhaps we might return to the court and see if there is room to admit us."

There was nothing for it. He'd promised Miss Wallace a dance and he must see through as a gentleman. "If that is what you wish."

"Absolutely." She rose to her feet and he stood. "Oh, and Miss Wayland, Sir Nathaniel has been looking for you. Something about Lady Stanford not feeling well."

Johnathan frowned. They'd been in the room a full ten minutes at least and she was just now delivering the message?

"I will help you locate them." Mr. Wallace offered Susannah his arm and she took it with a smile.

Blast the man. First he had ruined the one dance Johnathan had set his heart on, and now he was leading Susannah away, probably to leave the ball if Melior felt particularly puny.

"Are you ready?" Miss Wallace asked as he watched Susannah walk away.

No. This was supposed to be Susannah's dance. But he was a gentleman and so he led Miss Wallace back to the court room.

Only a few steps into the main room, Mr. Kendall approached Susannah, his lips turned down.

"There you are. I am sorry to be the bearer of bad news but we need to cut our evening short."

"Lady Stanford?"

He gave a curt nod, his blue eyes not quite meeting her gaze. "Mr. Wallace, forgive me for taking Miss Wayland from your company, but my sister is already waiting for us in the carriage."

"By all means. And I wish Lady Stanford a speedy recovery."

"Thank you."

Mr. Kendall put a hand to Susannah's back and propelled her out the doors she'd just entered.

"Is it that bad?" she whispered.

"Nate has already sent for a doctor to meet us at the house."

She asked no more questions, putting her focus into making sure she did not fall down the many steps on their way out.

Susannah did not know what she had expected when entering the conveyance, but it was not a very calm and collected Lady Stanford—a wince every now and then was the only sign she was unwell.

No one spoke on the ride. The silence suited her. Consumed with John's revelation about his painting, she'd not have been up to conversation anyway. Who was this woman that had brought so much light to his countenance? She'd never seen him so proud of a painting, nor heard him so complimentary of another woman.

At the house Lady Stanford refused Sir Nathaniel's offer to carry her and walked slowly up the steps. Susannah carried on to the parlor with Mr. Kendall, but after a quarter hour of stilted conversation they both lapsed into silence.

What was happening upstairs? Was Lady Stanford's condition serious? Only the ticking of the infernal clock met her questions. After the physician had come and gone, nearly an hour after they'd returned home, she realized she may never know. Lady Stanford had not confided in her about her pregnancy and it was not her place to ask.

When the clock struck one, she decided she might as well get some rest. Bidding Mr. Kendall a goodnight, she climbed the stairs to her room.

Maybe the problem had not been a serious one and tomorrow Lady Stanford would inform her of the situation. Thoughts of her own mother's travail when Michael came into the world chased her into bed.

It had been a hard labor and she'd been confined to bed for months afterward. Memories of Mama's insistence that even with all the pain she would have done it again if it meant bringing such wonderful children into the world made Susannah's heart ache. She wished for one more conversation, one more hug, one more word of wisdom from her beloved mother, and for the first time in weeks she cried herself to sleep.

Chapter 14

To Susannah's complete surprise, Lady Stanford was in the breakfast parlor the next morning.

"Are you well?" she asked hesitantly, glancing at the men in the room.

Sir Nathaniel frowned, but Lady Stanford smiled. "The physician tells me it is normal to have a bit of discomfort and other symptoms when one is increasing."

Since Mr. Kendall did not appear surprised, she assumed he already knew.

"Congratulations. I must say that I've suspected all week."

"I knew I'd not be able to hide it from you much longer. My symptoms have been far too obvious and have lasted a great deal longer than my mother-in-law says hers did, but the physician says it is normal to still be ill."

Susannah nodded. Not having any experience of her own, she would have to take Lady Stanford's word.

"When do you expect the joyous occasion?"

"Spring."

Her eyes widened. So soon? Was it truly normal for a woman to be ill that long?

"I see I have shocked you." Lady Stanford appeared amused.

"But your confinement. Are we leaving earlier than expected?"

"No. I can complete my lying-in as comfortably here as in Kent. Some even claim Town doctors are quite superior to those in the country. Unfortunately it will mean you may not have a chaperone for the last few weeks of the season."

"By then I will relish the break, I assure you."

Her Ladyship smiled brightly at her husband. "See, I knew she would be understanding."

"Indeed," he grumbled. "Even so, I still think you should take several days off from the bustle of entertainments."

Lady Stanford's smile turned to a frown. "I am not made of glass, Nathaniel."

"No, but I'd feel more comfortable if you'd take more care… please."

Her expression softened. "All right. You do not mind, do you, Miss Wayland? We will need to cancel our visit to the theatre and send our regrets for Lady Lincolnhurst's soirée next Friday, but we can still have our at home on Tuesday."

"Whatever is needed for your health, Lady Stanford. I would never want you to suffer on my behalf."

"It is not as desperate a situation as that. Nathaniel is simply being overly cautious."

Sir Nathaniel captured his wife's gaze. "It's my duty to protect my family; would you deny me my responsibility?"

A fond look passed between them and Susannah ducked her head, feeling oddly caught between the couple during an intimate moment.

"Can we cool the flirting? Poor Miss Wayland is not used to your overt gestures." Mr. Kendall's lips twitched.

"Overt? I hate to know what you consider subtle," Sir Nathaniel said.

Lady Stanford leaned forward and looked around her husband at her brother. "I believe we are interrupting your intimate moment right now."

Mr. Kendall's brow furrowed. "I do not follow."

"By your definition, Eddie, subtlety would be simply thinking about the person. Tell me, brother, do you have a certain someone on your mind?"

Sir Nathaniel snickered. "Yes, do you? I noticed your eyes straying toward a certain petite blonde last night."

Mr. Kendall pointed his fork at his friend. "Shut up, Nate."

"So there is someone." Lady Stanford's dark eyebrows inched up.

Crumpling his napkin, Mr. Kendall stood. "I believe I am finished. Do excuse me."

Both Stanfords laughed.

Susannah would have thought it rude if Mr. Kendall had not flashed her a bright smile, his eyes full of amusement.

CHAPTER 14

They ate silently for a few minutes. Lost in her thoughts, Susannah was surprised when Lady Stanford suddenly ran from the room. Sir Nathaniel glanced up in alarm, his gaze flitting to the door before they heard retching. He hung his head.

"If I'd known she would be so ill…"

He slowly rose to his feet without finishing his sentence, but Susannah completed it for him. "You would not have come to London."

Glancing over his shoulder, he gave a quick nod. "She needs rest."

"I truly do not mind staying in. Tell her to rest all she needs."

"I shall do that, but it is not you that pushes her. It is the voice inside her head. I have no doubt it sounds a lot like her mother telling her if she stays in bed instead of doing her duty in Society she is not living up to her name. If only I could send that awful woman's influence to the North of England with the lady herself."

Susannah blinked at him, not quite sure what to say. In the end she said nothing. As uncharitable a thought as it was, she realized that having a good mother for a short time was so much better than having one who tormented her for her entire life. Perhaps time with some people was not quite as important as the influence they left.

Johnathan pulled the flowers he'd procured after Sunday services close to his chest as the strong cold breeze threatened to steal petals from the buds. He probably should have had the flowers delivered instead of taking on the responsibility himself, but he wanted to be there to see Susannah's face. Their conversation about her favorite flowers had led him to the hothouse early this morning for their best pink roses.

A little street urchin ran by so close that he bumped Johnathan's leg which sent him sprawling onto the ground.

The boy, no more than six, let out a curse usually reserved for grown men. Then he glanced up. His eyes grew wide when he realized the station of the man he'd accosted.

"Sorry, sir. I meant nothin' by it. I ain't no pick pocket. Please don't—"

"Rollins!" Someone yelled from down the street. A big man jogged down the sidewalk waving a large chimney broom. "Get back here, boy!"

The little lad's eyes widened and he scrambled to his feet, wincing as he did so. His first few steps were a little unsteady and Johnathan wondered if the boy was sincerely hurt.

"Rollins, you worthless scrap. Get back here." The man was getting closer.

The boy bolted down a nearby alley.

The angry chimney sweep closed in. Johnathan was not sure why he did it, perhaps it was because the boy reminded him so much of Michael, but instead of stepping out of his way and allowing him to chase after his apprentice, he stepped in front of him. His intent was to bring the man up short but he did not stop, bowling him over and crushing the precious flowers in the process.

A string of curse words flowed from the man's mouth as they both tumbled into the street. *So that was where the boy had learned such crass language,* Johnathan thought as he picked himself up off the ground and dusted off his trousers.

"What do you think you're doin—" The man stopped, taking in Johnathan much the same way the boy did. "My apologies, sir."

Normally he'd have let the incident go and accepted the man's apology, but the boy needed time to make an escape. Doing his best to summon the indignation Al would have had at having his clothes rumpled, he said, "I should think so." He retrieved his dirty hat. "Do you know how much this topper costs? Perhaps I should charge you for it."

"No, sir. It were an accident. The boy, he—" The big man glanced around, his eyes narrowing when he did not spy his apprentice. "I just needed to catch the boy that knocked into you. We got a chimney to clean and he's too much a coward to do it. If anyone is to blame it's that boy for runnin' off."

The thought of the little lad being shoved down a dirty chimney sent a shiver down Johnathan's spine. Wasn't there a law against using someone so young? If there was not, there should be. Perhaps he'd pursue it in Parliament next session, but that would not help this lad now.

"Even so, you are a grown man. Have a care and take some responsibility for your own actions."

The chimney sweep's jaw flexed, his eyes narrowing. "Of course, sir."

Johnathan thought about correcting him, but what was the use in telling the angry man he was speaking to a peer? It would only bring more anger down on his poor assistant. Hopefully the boy had found a good place to hide.

"I shall let this incident go for now, but perhaps you should think about employing an older boy as your son is so opposed to the work and is a mite young for the occupation."

"He ain't my son. He ain't nobody's son. Just another no account that needed work for a scrap of food. But if he ain't gonna work, I ain't gonna feed him."

Not willing to give this heartless man any clues, Johnathan stopped himself from looking the way the boy had gone, his heart pinching. He did not have parents anymore either. If he'd not had money, would people feel this way about him as well?

"But you're right. I might as well get me a new boy." The man touched his hat, Johnathan nodded, and they both walked their separate ways.

Ten steps away, Johnathan remembered the flowers. He retrieved the bundle only to find most of them had been broken beyond repair. How could it be so hard to give flowers to one lady?

One rose in the middle stood out and he carefully pulled it from the others, hoping the stem was whole. A petal drooped, but that seemed to be the only detectable defect. One flower wasn't much, but it was better than nothing. Hopefully it was enough.

Two streets down and one street away from Kendall House he came upon Al as he strode in the same direction.

"On your way to see how Melior fairs?" He asked as Johnathan came abreast of him.

"I—" He looked down at the flower in his hand. "Is she still ill?"

"According to the messy note I received this morning from Javenia, the doctor was called. I suspect she is already there."

They turned the corner. Halfway down the street a hack stopped in front of Kendall House and a swirl of light-yellow skirts exited before the driver could even get down to open the door. With quick steps she ascended the stairs.

"It is uncanny how well I know that woman," Al said, the right side of his mouth lifting. "Well, shall we go join the drama?" He picked up his pace, catching up with Javenia at the top of the stairs.

Johnathan smiled. Al would adamantly deny his interest in Javenia's sort of drama, but they all knew better. One day those two would stop circling each other and it would end in fireworks. Whether the sparks would pull them together or blow them completely apart was yet to be seen.

If the argument that erupted on how best to enter the house was any indication, it would be the latter.

Chapter 15

Susannah turned the page on her book, having made her way to the library after breakfast. Lady Stanford had gone to bed to recover and Susannah had been happy to lose herself in a gothic novel.

The butler entered. "Mr. Kendall asks that you join him in the east sitting room."

She rose, placing the book on the table next to the sofa. Before she could ask why he needed her presence, the butler turned to lead the way. She followed without complaint, deciding to hold her tongue. Perhaps John had come to spend time with Mr. Kendall and had asked after her.

The thought brightened her day until she remembered the painting. Who was the woman that had inspired him so much?

John, however, was not the man awaiting her.

Mr. Wallace and his sister rose to their feet upon her entrance. "Mr. Wallace, Miss Wallace. What a surprise."

"Forgive us," Mr. Wallace said. "I know these are not your visiting hours, but we wanted to inquire after Lady Stanford."

She glanced at Mr. Kendall, the only other occupant of the room. How much should she divulge? It was not her information to share.

"All is well. My sister was ill but is feeling better today."

She sent Mr. Kendall a grateful smile. He subtly nodded in return.

"Shall I ring for tea?" she asked.

"I already have." Mr. Kendall's eyes flitted to the door, but he said nothing more.

Once they were all seated, conversation turned to the close of the ball. Susannah expressed her surprise at their visit after such a late night, but Mr. Wallace assured her it was no bother; he only wished to make certain all was well. His thoughtfulness did him credit and she again found herself drawn in by his attentiveness.

When the tea tray arrived she poured each person a cup.

"Have you ever attended Almack's, Miss Wayland?" Miss Wallace asked.

"I have not, but Lady Stanford has arranged for me to meet with one of the patronesses to see if I might obtain a voucher."

Mr. Wallace lifted his cup as if in salute. "We wish you well then, for not everyone who applies is found worthy. Some of the patronesses are uncommonly picky."

"Very true, brother." Miss Wallace then relayed the ups and downs of her own journey to obtaining a voucher. Ten minutes into the conversation the door to the sitting room flew open.

Miss Harris quickly made eye contact with each person.

"Your hat, Miss Harris," the butler called from the hallway.

She yanked the pin out of it and tossed it to the harried-looking man. "Where is she?"

"Who?" Susannah said at the same moment Mr. Kendall said, "Upstairs."

That seemed to be enough explanation. Miss Harris spun around and bolted for the stairs.

"Wait!" Mr. Kendall rushed after her.

When the pounding of his feet on the stairs died away, Susannah turned to Mr. and Miss Wallace, a bit taken aback by all the commotion. "Well, that was unexpected."

Miss Wallace tittered. "Entirely. What does she mean by coming in here in such a state? She looked positively wild."

Susannah's back stiffened. It was one thing to be surprised and quite another to cast judgement. Miss Harris's worry was understandable. She and Lady Stanford were as thick as thieves and equally as protective of one another.

"I—"

The door opened again, this time far more respectably, and the butler announced Lord Newhurst and Mr. Roberts. The occupants stood and Mr. Roberts sauntered in, John close on his heels, a single pink rose pinched between his fingers. Each gave an abbreviated bow to the room as a whole, but Susannah's gaze was drawn to the flower.

Had John brought her a pink rose?

"I see *Miss Harris* is not here," Mr. Roberts said with a smirk. "I told her not to go running into the house like a hoiden, but I suppose I should not have expected her to listen."

After Miss Wallace's affront, Mr. Roberts's words raised her defenses. Then his eyes twinkled. His was not a rebuke but rather an odd sort of affectionate statement and that knowledge softened the remark.

"Those are exactly my thoughts, Mr. Roberts," Miss Wallace said. "Her arrival was positively scandalous."

The cheer in the gentleman's face swiftly fled. His lips turned down and his cheeks tightened as his jaw worked back and forth. And if it were possible, his already proper posture somehow became straighter and taller.

"It is not at all scandalous to show deep concern for a friend, Miss Wallace." Turning his attention to Susannah, Mr. Roberts said, "Javenia received word this morning that a doctor had been called to the house. Is this true?"

"Yes, but Lady Stanford is fine. She is merely resting from the night. Miss Harris has gone up to see her."

Miss Wallace snickered, obviously oblivious to Mr. Roberts's earlier rebuke. "More like barge in on her peace. Mr. Kendall is trying to stop her as we speak."

In all the time Susannah had known Mr. Roberts she had never seen him look so fierce. "Perhaps you misunderstood my earlier address, Miss Wallace. I will thank you to curb your tongue where Miss Harris is concerned."

"But you—"

"*I* am given the liberties afforded one of a long-standing friendship with the lady in question. We have known each other since our cradles. I may peck at her, but you *will not*." Without another word he marched out, calling over his shoulder, "I am going to find Nate."

The strain in the room was palpable after such an exchange. Susannah instinctively searched out John's gaze, unsure how to proceed, but his focus was firmly on Mr. Wallace. Both men appraised each other.

Miss Wallace flounced into her seat and put her hands to her burning cheeks. A tiny sliver of sympathy filled Susannah. Mr. Roberts and Miss Harris's relationship was a complicated one even for those who knew them well, but someone unfamiliar might think Mr. Roberts's comment was an open invitation for unkind discourse.

"Will you join us for tea?" Susannah finally asked John, motioning to the tray.

"I thank you, yes." His jaw clenched as he approached the group.

Resuming her seat, she was surprised when he took up the other end of the settee. Though the distance was still proper, it was the closest he'd sat to her since Lady Lincolnhurst's soiree. He twisted the flower in his hand a time or two before setting it on the small coffee table in front of them. Her eyes caught on it and her hope diminished.

"The weather has been... rather, ah, gloomy," she said, hoping to dissipate the tension.

Miss Wallace pulled herself together quite nicely. "Yes, the misty rain early this morning was positively depressing and wets a body clear through if one does not have the right outerwear."

The conversation, completely ordinary and dull, caught Mr. Wallace's attention. "Let us hope for better weather this week. There are so many pleasant pursuits available in London if only the sun would shine for a few hours."

"Indeed," his sister said.

The room again fell quiet. John did not contribute anything to the conversation. His chilly demeanor began to wear on her nerves. The last few hours had been difficult enough without him adding to her burden with a foul mood.

Not to mention his mystery lady. The knowledge that John's heart might already be taken pinched at her weary nerves.

"Well, I believe it is time for us to go." Miss Wallace rose to her feet and her brother scrambled to stand. His umber-colored eyebrows pulled together as they exchanged a look.

"Yes, um... I suppose it is time. Do send our regards to Lady Stanford and our wishes for a speedy recovery."

"I will." Susannah smiled at him. The discomfort written across his handsome features after his sister had so abruptly ended their visit lifted.

She could not blame her for wanting to leave. John's uncharacteristic glower would have set even the stoutest heart to trembling. What was wrong with him?

Miss Wallace curtsied and Mr. Wallace took hold of Susannah's hand. The pressure of his fingers on hers chased away a bit of the pressure weighing on her chest. At least one man appreciated her. The knowledge soothed her wounded pride and aching heart.

Johnathan clenched his teeth. Blast Mr. Wallace and his nicely sculpted face, for it seemed to be the only thing Susannah had eyes for at the moment. When the man took her hand and kissed it, Johnathan wanted to throttle him.

But the light in Susannah's eyes had a completely different effect, sending his heart into his shoes.

"Until we meet again, Miss Wayland." Mr. Wallace backed away slowly, then turned and followed his sister out.

Susannah's eyes followed him, adding so acutely to Johnathan's pain that he was tempted to leave with the others. It was evident she held some regard for Mr. Wallace, far more than she'd ever shown for him. Who was he to stand in the way of her happiness?

As soon as the doors shut she turned on him. "Could you not have been at least a little more hospitable? The way you glowered at everyone; it is no wonder they left in a hurry."

If she only knew his reasoning. But he could never tell her of his astonishment at finding Mr. Wallace at tea with her. The man who had stolen his dance and, it seemed, was in the process of stealing Susannah's heart.

Regardless of his reasons he could not tell her the source of his upset. With her hands on hips and eyebrows slammed down over flashing brown eyes, she would never accept what he had to say. She might even scold him for such nonsense. Even worse, she might laugh at him.

So he chose a different truth. "His sister insulted Javenia."

"And that gave you permission to stare her brother down like he was the one who uttered the words?" Her arms came down to her side, hands balled in fists.

"He should have kept her in check."

Her voice rose. "Like a recalcitrant puppy. Women speak for themselves, Lord Newhurst. No one can stop that, not in the moment."

His mind caught on the word recalcitrant, loving the way it slipped off her tongue, but her accusation hit deeper. She knew him to be a fair and compassionate man. He'd not speak ill of women, nor expect them not to speak for themselves.

He matched her volume. "Yes, but Javenia has been my friend since as early as I can remember. I will not stand by while someone demeans her and neither should Mr. Wallace. He could have corrected his sister after her first insult, but he did not."

"And what of Mr. Roberts's insult when he arrived?" She stepped closer to him.

"That is different." He leaned forward.

"I understand that, but they did not."

His breath came out quick and short; she too seemed to be struggling for control. They were standing so close he could reach out and pull her to him, and it finally occurred to him that he'd had a whole conversation without once stumbling over his words. Was frustration all it took to loosen his tongue?

One of his hands began to move forward of its own volition, the urge to hold her so strong it verged on desperation. Even in anger she was beautiful; the flash of fire lighting her cheeks and brightening her eyes.

The door opened, drawing their attention.

Eddie, Nate, Al, and Javenia walked in, then stopped. No one seemed to know where to look, their eyes landing on him and Susannah in turns.

"Are we interrupting *something*?" Eddie grinned.

Susannah skittered back.

John wanted to wipe the grin right off of Eddie's face. The man meddled too much in affairs that weren't his own.

"No," he finally said. "I have business to attend to at home." With purposeful steps he strode toward the door in a path that led him around everyone. It was not a lie. After coming across the boy in the street he had a new proposition to put before Parliament.

"John, wait," Eddie said, chasing after him.

He tried to ignore his plea, but when he stopped to collect his coat and hat, Eddie caught up with him.

"Hey, what happened back there?" He gestured with his head to the sitting room.

"You inferred things that do not exist, that is what happened."

"I apologize. I thought—well, it does not matter what I thought. But why would you leave Miss Wayland like that, especially after it appeared you were"—he dropped his voice— "on *very* good terms."

His head jerked back. "We were arguing."

It was Eddie's turn to appear shocked. "That is not what it looked like from the door."

"It does not matter what it looked like. Miss Wayland is angry with me and there is no more to it."

The butler handed him his black beaver and he slammed it down on his head more firmly than was necessary. "Good day, Eddie."

Eddie's shoulders slumped and he put his hands in his pockets. "And a good day to you."

Chapter 16

Susannah pulled the covers up to her nose. Why had she been such a ninny? John had a right to be angry. His friend's character *had* been called into question. His intense emotion had caught her off guard, and she had reacted in kind. Why, she did not know.

Yes, you do, that pesky inner voice chided. She knew exactly why she'd reacted so harshly, and it embarrassed her. Somewhere in the world there was a woman with *fascinating curls* and *captivating pink cheeks*. Whoever the woman was, she hated her already.

How had she managed to draw John's attention with only a painting? Then again, perhaps the woman was married and her husband had commissioned the work. That would be a relief.

But would John talk about someone else's wife like that? Certainly not. No this Venus of a woman had to be of the young unmarried variety, and as such, would be direct competition. Unless, of course, the lady of the painting had already won his heart.

She rolled to her side, yanking the blanket up over her head. Life was unfair. Just when she'd got up the courage to pursue John, he'd gone and fallen in love with someone else. Not that he'd called it love, but she could see it in the way his blue eyes lit with excitement, the ease with which he spoke, and the broad smile that had bloomed on his face the night of the ball, before they were interrupted by the Wallaces.

Was there any hope he'd change his mind? Probably not.

When John found something he liked, he committed himself to it heart and soul, hence the reason he was so good at painting. If this angel of a woman had his heart, she'd hold it forever.

Tears gathered in Susannah's eyes, the futility of her hopes bringing anger with them. She punched her pillow, once, twice. It didn't help.

It was time to look elsewhere. Mr. Wallace had certainly shown her a preference, and she had to admit she enjoyed his company. When she and John had first quarreled she had told herself that her anger came from a desire to get to know Mr. Wallace better. And in truth, some of it had. Perhaps her mind already knew what her heart refused to recognize.

It was time to move on, no matter how much it hurt.

CHAPTER 16

How had he messed things up so thoroughly? Johnathan paced back and forth in front of the hearth the next morning. He'd lost his temper, something that rarely happened but seemed to be increasing in frequency of late.

What better way to display his faults against Mr. Wallace's talents?

The man had recovered nicely from the tension, and what had he done? He'd let his jealousy boil over in anger against the wrong person.

He owed Susannah an apology, one he would have given as soon as the time was acceptable for visiting hours, but she'd not been at home. She and Javenia had gone to the shops and according to Nate would not be home until well into the afternoon.

He had a choice. Brave the shops now or wait another day, for this evening he had plans to meet with Lord Ansley to discuss several bills that would come before Parliament tomorrow afternoon.

Shopping was his least favorite activity. Actually, any activity that involved large numbers of people did not agree with him. Like the time he'd tried spicy Indian cuisine. Idle chatter burned his mouth and shopping left him with an upset stomach.

But he would brave the crowds if it meant any chance at seeing Susannah again.

When he reached the shops on Bond Street, he realized his mistake. How was he ever to find Susannah in this mess of bonnets and parasols?

He slowly made his way down the east side of the street, peeking into windows as he went. Several shops down, a feminine voice called out to him.

"Lord Newhurst!" Miss Guthrie caught up to him nearly out of breath, her younger sister coming up at a more acceptable pace. "I thought I saw you from the window of the haberdashery."

True to its unfaithful nature, his tongue caught in his mouth as his mind began to race. Why did Miss Guthrie and her sister have to carry such similarities with Susannah? What would he say to her? There was a polite way to begin a conversation. What was it again? A yes.

"Did you know that vicissitude comes from the Latin word *vicissim*? It means a change of circumstance or fortune, usually by unpleasant means."

She tipped her head to the side, observing him as one might an odd animal in the menagerie. He wanted to turn and run. That was not what he'd meant to say.

There were so many conclusions one could draw from his choice of words, and while he knew the source of his vicissitude, Miss Guthrie might think she was the unpleasant means.

Miss Martha Guthrie chuckled. "And what has brought on your unpleasant change of fortune, Lord Newhurst?"

"An in-in-inability to find Miss Harris and Miss Wayland in a crowd such as this."

Miss Martha's smile faded and she glanced around at the hordes of people. "I can see your dilemma."

The elder sister took hold of his arm. "Then we shall help you. Best to start in this direction."

"But Harriet—"

Miss Guthrie shushed her sister. "It is no trouble at all, Martha."

Miss Martha glanced over her shoulder, then back, a downturn to her lips.

"Come along," Miss Guthrie said, pulling him with her.

Johnathan did as she ordered, feeling bad for the maid that had come up behind them, her arms full of packages. Miss Guthrie chattered about each of the shops they passed, relaying to him which she liked best and which were not worth a lady's notice. The sound of her voice was so much like Susannah's it almost lulled him into forgetting his quest.

But when, after turning at Piccadilly and coming up the west side of the street, he saw Susannah with Mr. Wallace at her side, his mind stopped working entirely.

Mr. Wallace held two packages as he leaned in to say something to Susannah. She smiled up at him. Johnathan glanced around for Javenia, but she was nowhere in sight.

"Miss Wayland," he called.

Susannah glanced in his direction at the same moment Miss Guthrie's hand tightened on his arm.

"Oh, look at that beautiful piece of silk, Lord Newhurst." She tried to pull him to a stop, but he kept walking.

"In a moment, Miss Guthrie, I need to speak with Miss Wayland."

A frown marred Susannah's face as they approached. "Miss Guthrie." She nodded.

"Cousin." Miss Guthrie gave a similar nod of acknowledgement. "How are you on this fine day?"

CHAPTER 16

"I am well. It is nice to have a sliver of sun, is it not?"

The pleasantries wore on Johnathan's nerves. How was he to apologize with so many people present?

"Where is Ja—Miss Harris?" He opted for formality in view of the company.

"Inside." She motioned to the cafe. Through the window he saw her speaking with Lady Braithwaite.

He never had understood Javenia's friendship with the lady. For his part, he found himself quite frightened of her. She may have been small, but she had a fierce air about her, as if she'd seen battle and walked through thousands of bullets unscathed.

"What brings you to the shops today?" She asked, but Miss Guthrie answered.

"Lord Newhurst is kindly escorting us about."

His nose scrunched. How had a search for Susannah turned into what sounded very much like a courting activity?

"I see." Susannah turned to Mr. Wallace with a smile. "Mr. Wallace has also been kind enough to help us. We met several shops back and he offered to carry my packages for me."

Mr. Wallace returned her smile. "It is the least I can do after you assisted me in finding the perfect gift for my sister."

The same irritation that had plagued him yesterday bubbled to the surface, but he pushed it down. He needed to regain Susannah's trust, and if the only way to do so was by being friendly to his competition, then so be it.

"And what did you decide on, Mr. Wallace?"

"A jade comb carved with lotus flowers." He pulled the small hair piece out of his pocket and showed it to them. "It will look splendid in Eleanor's hair, don't you agree, Lord Newhurst?'

Johnathan tipped his head, recalling Miss Wallace's brown hair flecked with gold. The green would indeed be pretty, but far more stunning against a darker or lighter shade.

"I believe you are right, Mr. Wallace."

The man smiled, flashing far too straight and white teeth.

Miss Guthrie, on the other hand, let out a huff. "Martha and I were just going to show Lord Newhurst a fine piece of silk from India. Are you familiar with Indian silks, Miss Wayland?"

The turn in conversation confused him, but who was he to understand how Miss Guthrie's mind worked?

"I am not. Perhaps we can accompany you all."

The bell on the cafe door tinkled and Javenia exited. Her gaze immediately fell on him and she frowned.

"*John*, I need to speak with you." The way she drew out his name let him know he'd somehow landed himself in her black books.

"Um... excuse me, ladies." He gave a slight bow to the others and stepped to the side of the shop where they would be out of hearing.

"How could you run off like that yesterday? You left Miss Wayland nearly in tears and she is still not the same today."

"I know, that is why I have come to apologize."

"You could have fooled me. Why were you with Miss Guthrie?"

"I visited Kendall House this morning, but they said you had taken Miss Wayland to the shops. I came upon Miss Guthrie by the haberdashery and she offered to help locate the both of you."

"Then she took you the long way around because we met with her in the same shop over half an hour ago."

Had she?

He glanced over his shoulder at Miss Guthrie who now spoke exclusively with Mr. Wallace while Susannah wandered down the street with Miss Martha. The three ladies seemed at ease with one another.

Then again, Susannah's aunt had been absolutely abominable to her. He'd have to watch out for the Guthrie sisters in case they followed the same dissolute bend as their mother.

"Look, John, I do not usually insert myself into your affairs, but you need to be careful in this bid to win Miss Wayland's affections."

He stepped back. "How did you..."

"Anyone close to you can see how much she means to you. What we cannot decide is whether she returns the sentiment. For your sake, I hope she does."

Mr. Wallace and Miss Guthrie must have noticed the others leaving because they rushed to catch up. What if Susannah really did favor Mr. Wallace? Could he let her go?

He sighed. "I have loved her for so long that the thought of losing her nearly suffocates me."

"Then why have you not spoken before now?"

CHAPTER 16

He raised an incredulous brow at her.

"I mean what reason, other than your particular difficulty in speaking."

He had to think about that for a while. Finally he said, "Because if I do, and she does not accept me, I won't only be throwing away a friendship, but I might lose my place in her family. It is the only one I have left."

Javenia placed a hand on his sleeve. "Not the only one, John. Al, Nate, and I are here. We might have families of our own, but you have been like a brother to me since we both learned to walk."

He shook his head. "But that is the crux of all this, for I have been like a brother to Susannah as well. What if I can never be more?"

Chapter 17

The rest of the outing on Bond Street was an awkward affair, but it was the look of pity in Javenia's eyes that followed Johnathan home. She had no answers. No one did. The only person that could answer his questions was Susannah and she seemed completely enthralled with Mr. Wallace.

He'd overheard the man reminding Susannah of a drive they'd apparently planned and she'd asked him if he intended on attending Almack's in a sennight. They'd been entirely too cozy chatting in low tones and ignoring the happenings around them. His stomach clenched at the memory.

Eventually the two parties had parted ways and he'd escorted the Guthries back to their carriage before collecting his horse.

Miss Guthrie had *also* asked him about his intentions to attend the assembly rooms on Wednesday next. He'd never tried to procure admittance. Too many people, especially ladies. But the knowledge that Mr. Wallace would be advancing his suit at every opportunity drove him to answer in the affirmative.

Only, he needed a voucher—and that required him to talk to a lady.

He groaned.

He *would* do it. He just hoped he didn't make as big a fool of himself with Lady Jersey—the only proprietress with whom he was acquainted—as he had with Miss Guthrie.

It was too late in the day to visit the lady today and he needed to ready himself for dinner with Lord Ansley.

Tomorrow, he promised himself. He would visit Lady Jersey during her at home hours in the morning and pray she had pity on him. If not, he did not know what he would do.

Probably go mad sitting at home, wondering if Susannah was losing her heart to Mr. Wallace.

How could he have been so wrong about her supposed jealousy? He'd been certain she held some regard for him, but her obvious attention to Mr. Wallace conveyed a completely different sentiment.

Maybe what he'd seen as envy had been boredom with his conversation. That certainly had happened a time or two with other ladies. The thought was lowering.

Why could women not come with instructions on how to win their hearts? It would make the courtship process infinitely easier. Then he might know how Susannah truly felt.

Then again, did he want to know? What if, as he already suspected, she viewed him only platonically? What if Mr. Wallace fascinated and intrigued her far more than he ever could? What if the man's kisses burrowed straight into her heart?

He stomped up the steps of Newhurst House, wishing he could shut up his overactive brain. He could not, would not give up now.

He'd overheard Susannah speaking to Javenia about remaining at Kendall House for the week, allowing Melior to rest. Perhaps if he stopped by after his dinner meeting, he could finally offer the apology he owed Susannah.

Yes, that was the start he needed. Best to send around a note advising them of his late arrival.

In his study he pulled out a scrap of paper.

Nate,

Would it be permissible for me to call on you, Eddie, and the ladies this evening near nine?

J. N.

He almost added a line about needing to speak with Miss Wayland, but on second thought realized that if Nate did not read too much into it, Eddie would. After Javenia's revelation, he had no doubt they would all unabashedly play the matchmaker if he gave the smallest inkling of his plans. And while the help would be a godsend, they would probably find some way to bumble it so badly he'd never recover.

CHAPTER 17

He'd muddled things enough anyway.

An hour later, a note came back to him.

John,

Miss Wayland and Eddie will be away this evening having been invited by Javenia and her mother to attend the theatre we'd originally planned. You would find only myself and Melior this evening, which I doubt is your purpose. Best take up your box at the theatre.

N.S.

Glancing at the clock, he contemplated sending his regrets to Lord Ansley, but duty won out over desire. The theatre started in one hour, the same hour he was expected to arrive at Berkley Square. He tossed the letter onto the desk. If only he did not hold such strong convictions.

Johnathan sighed as he descended the steps of Lady Jersey's home, patting the pocket that held his voucher safe. How he'd managed to keep from stumbling all over his words he did not know. It helped that the lady also enjoyed painting and even found the definition and etymology of tergiversation highly entertaining.

That he'd jump to the word while trying to evade her questions on any lady he might be particularly interested was no secret.

"And are you trying to tergiversate my questions, Lord Newhurst? For I know there must be at least one young lady to whom you wish to be introduced," she'd said.

He'd been trapped in a corner with no other option than to cease his evasiveness. "There is none, your Ladyship. I am already acquainted with the only lady of interest to me."

If he'd thought the woman's matchmaking interest impertinent before, her insistence on a name became downright invasive. But he had his voucher and a ticket with very little inconvenience to himself, and perhaps an ally in Lady Jersey.

Pulling out his time piece, he noted the hour. The ladies at Kendall House would receive visitors for three quarters of an hour more. If he hurried, he could offer his apology before he needed to ready himself for Parliament.

At the door of the four-story structure, he straightened his coat and adjusted his cravat. Three taps of the knocker brought the butler who took his card to present it to his mistress. The practice seemed odd considering how many times he'd walked about his friends' houses without the staff even noticing his presence, but he wanted to do things right today.

"Lady Stanford will see you now." The butler motioned toward the open door.

When he entered, only Melior and Javenia occupied the room.

"John." Melior rose. "How lovely of you to call on me, but why the card?"

"I..." He looked around the room, somehow hoping Susannah was hiding in the shadows. "That is, I'd hoped to..." He stopped. How could he say he did not wish to see either of them? It would be abominably rude. "I'd hoped to ask after your h-health."

"My health." Melior cast Javenia a wayward glance, amusement pulling at her lips. "I am well. And you?"

"I am well... as well." He sounded like an imbecile.

CHAPTER 17

Silence filled the room until Javenia finally took pity on him. "She is not here, John. She is out driving with Mr. Wallace and his sister, remember?"

The fire of excitement that had burned in him since receiving his voucher for Almack's sputtered and died. He *had* forgotten.

"Please have a seat." Melior gestured to the same blue settee he'd shared with Susannah two days ago. "Would you like some tea?" she asked once they were all situated.

"Yes, please."

"Same as usual?"

"If you please."

Javenia was unusually quiet as Melior poured the tea, her eyes flicking to the door every few seconds.

"Are you well, Javenia?" he asked.

"Have you seen Algenon lately?"

"Not since Sunday, why?"

"No reason." She picked up a biscuit and began to nibble.

There certainly was a reason, but her nonchalance communicated her unwillingness to talk about it. Javenia had always been like that. Even as children, she'd act like nothing was the matter even when her little world was falling apart from the loss of a favorite animal or even worse, her beloved grandmother.

The rumor she'd questioned him about weeks ago came to mind. Had she found cause for alarm?

He held his cup of tea close to his nose, allowing the smell to calm him. Kendall House had one of his favorite blends. His cook had tried to duplicate it, but to no avail. And the Kendall House cook refused to share her secret.

The butler entered again with a card, holding it out to Lady Stanford on a silver salver.

She frowned. "Why have they come?"

"Who?" He and Javenia asked simultaneously.

"The Guthries."

Javenia groaned. "Perhaps you should send word that you are finished with visiting hours already."

Voices in the entry came closer and before any word could be sent, the Guthries followed Susannah into the room.

Her cheeks were pink and the tip of her nose red from her time out of doors, but the brightness in her eyes pulled at his artistic eye. They shimmered in the morning sunlight. Did that mean there were tears? Her expression did not appear distressed. On the contrary, she positively glowed.

There could be only one source for such joy, and it made him want to turn and leave, but he would not. Instead he tried to mask the hurt with a placid expression of indifference as he stood to greet everyone.

She stopped.

"Jo—Lord Newhurst."

"Miss Wayland."

"It is a fine day to see you again, Lord Newhurst," Mrs. Guthrie said, bustling past her niece to greet everyone. "And you, Lady Stanford. I do hope you are feeling better."

Melior's jaw flexed. "I am. Thank you."

The coolness in her voice spoke clearly of her dislike of the woman, but Mrs. Guthrie either did not notice or chose to ignore her tone altogether. When Mrs. Guthrie turned to Javenia, her cheerful countenance fell.

"And a good day to you, Miss Harris."

Was it just him, or had the woman's chin hitched up a notch? He studied her profile. Indeed, she looked like her nose had a decided tilt toward the ceiling. What could have possessed her to think she could assert superiority over Javenia, the daughter of a baron?

The noblest relation Mrs. Guthrie had was the Duchess of Bedford and that was obtained only through her marriage to Mr. Guthrie.

"Come girls, do sit down." Mrs. Guthrie motioned to the settee he now occupied as she sat on the opposite end of the settee from Javenia.

He would have thought she'd choose a chair with her obvious dislike, but after assessing the furniture a second time he realized it would never do. If Mrs. Guthrie tried to squeeze into one of the beautifully embroidered chairs, they'd never get her out of it. Either that, or it would collapse.

Covering his mouth with one hand, he tried to hide his amusement at the ungracious image in his mind of the mean-spirited lady flopping around on the ground like a fish. Then a hand brushed against his sleeve.

"Oh, do forgive me," Miss Guthrie said, batting her eyelashes at him. Why did women do that? It looked ridiculous, like she had something in her eye. She made a pretense of giving him more space but only succeeded in moving the edge of her skirts over his leg.

CHAPTER 17

Did both she and her sister have to sit on the settee? There were two more chairs, other than the one Susannah had taken up.

Talk turned to the weather and his eyes strayed to Susannah. She, however, seemed wholly occupied with observing her hands. Not once did she look up at him.

Miss Guthrie leaned forward, effectively blocking his view. "And how are you enjoying this little bit of sun we have been blessed with the last couple of days, Lord Newhurst?"

"It is lo-lovely." There, he'd spit it out. Goodness, did the woman have to be so close?

"Yes, it has been fine." Mrs. Guthrie agreed. "So enjoyable that one ought not to be indoors during such good weather as this. Even if there is a bit of a nip in the air."

The woman's eyes moved pointedly between him and her daughter several times. He ignored her.

"Miss Martha, how are you enjoying… things?" Why could he think of nothing else?

The corner of the younger woman's mouth inched up as she glanced at him and then her mother. "Quite well. I am especially pleased with the birds that have decided to come out and enjoy this bit of false spring. But the geese in the park have been quite annoying. There is one such that cannot stop honking and pecking at certain gentlemen when they pass."

Was she…? He nearly laughed at the thought. His eyes strayed to Javenia and she'd caught the same implication, if her smile were any indication.

"And does this goose have fine white and black feathers?" Melior asked.

Johnathan glanced at the turban Mrs. Guthrie wore. Poked into the folds were several such feathers. He ducked his head and bit his lips.

"Indeed, Your Ladyship."

"I do believe I know of the bird you are speaking of," Mrs. Guthrie said. "Is it the one that nests near the lower path?"

Miss Martha nodded, but her sister only looked between them all with a furrowed brow and wrinkles around her nose. The only person who did not participate was Susannah.

She'd left off observing her hands to stare out the window. Probably missing Mr. Wallace already. The supposition stung.

He glanced at the room's occupants. With all these ladies there was no chance he'd have the opportunity to speak with her. Perhaps he should try again tomorrow. He'd stayed the requisite quarter hour. He set his cup down, but Susannah suddenly rose.

"If you will excuse me."

She gave no reason, simply left. This was his chance, but Miss Guthrie's hand settled on his sleeve.

"Will you be at Lady Lincolnhurst's soiree on Friday?" Her voice was low and inviting.

The hair on his arm stood on end, as if a specter might jump out at any moment.

"I am unsure." He rose. "I believe my time has come to a close. P-parliament and all."

The ladies began to rise but he bade them stay and with a quick dip of his chin, left them to their conversation. Or lack thereof, as the room had become eerily quiet on his retreat.

Susannah was not in the hall, but Eddie was.

"I see you have chased her off again." Eddie frowned.

"Me? I have done nothing of the sort. The Guthries are here. Blame them."

"Ah. On your way out then?"

"Unless you can point me in Miss Wayland's direction so I might apologize for my behavior two days ago."

"That I cannot do, as she has retired to her room."

Could his luck get any worse? "I see. Well, in that case, I will bid you a good day."

Eddie clapped him on the back. "Enjoy the monotony of Parliament."

John rolled his eyes at him. "I'd rather be an idle gentleman like you, paying no attention to anyone else's interests but my own."

"No you would not, and we both know it. Besides, I have plenty of interest in some things, and as such I will confide in you that I am not below being a messenger boy. If you have anything you wish to send to a certain someone, I will not squeal on you."

Johnathan searched his face, trying to decide if sending his apologies in a note might be worth it. Writing to a woman you were not engaged to was highly improper, but not unheard of. Perhaps if future attempts failed he'd have to resort to such stratagem.

"I will keep that in mind."

Chapter 18

Susannah paced from the hearth of the east sitting room and back to the door, careful not to muss her dress. Lady Stanford had declared herself well enough to attend Lady Lincolnhurst's soiree after all, and no amount of argument from Sir Nathaniel could convince her otherwise. That meant that Susannah would again be forced to watch her cousin's obvious ploys to gain John's attention.

Miss Guthrie had practically snuggled up to him on the settee, fluttering her lashes and extolling her many virtues. It was positively disgusting.

Susannah had entered, excited to tell Lady Stanford of her diverting ride with Mr. Wallace and his sister and the comical way her bonnet had been snatched off by a low-hanging tree branch, only to find John's stern disapproval. He'd whisked it away behind a mask of boredom, but she had not been fooled.

She owed him an apology, but they'd been in company. And the last people she'd ever want to admit fault in front of were her aunt and cousins. While her aunt put up a front of familial felicity, she knew better.

When they passed each other in public, the woman never acknowledged her unless she happened to be with someone of consequence. At the opera, Miss Harris had even heard Aunt Guthrie telling a gentleman that Susannah had no dowry to speak of. It was no wonder she'd had no interest from gentlemen these last few days, other than Mr. Wallace.

But as soon as she was in the company of someone with which her aunt wished to converse, she suddenly became her dear niece. The hypocrisy boggled

Susannah's mind, but propriety dictated she not cause offence in public, so she'd remained silent.

"Are you ready?" Lady Stanford asked from the door, interrupting her churning thoughts.

She stopped pacing and followed her into the vestibule. "I am. Where are Sir Nathaniel and Mr. Kendall?"

"Here," Mr. Kendall said, stepping out of the very parlor she'd just exited. "We've been waiting nigh on an hour for you both to finish prettying up."

"Liar," Lady Stanford said with a smirk. "You went down the back steps and came through the sliding door from the music room."

Sir Nathaniel descended the steps. "I told you she'd never fall for it."

Eddie chuckled. "Fine. I may have only arrived a minute or two before Mel, but I was here first."

"Again with the lies." Lady Stanford gave his ear a tweak.

"Ow!"

"You forget I can see into that entire room from the door. Besides, Miss Wayland only exited no more than a minute before you." She turned to Susannah. "Tell me Miss Wayland, was my brother waiting with you?"

Mr. Kendall cast her a look of pleading, his eyes growing droopy like a puppy begging for a treat.

She giggled, and Lady Stanford turned back to witness her brother's expression. "Oh, no you don't." She reached for his ear.

He skittered out of her reach, holding a hand over said ear. "I may not have been the first downstairs but at least I shall be the first to the carriage." Hat in hand, he escaped out the door.

Susannah laughed at the good-natured teasing between the siblings. It warmed her heart but also left it longing for her own brothers and sister.

Already Amanda had sent three letters begging her to find a husband quickly and quit London so she might return home. Finding the idea both humorous and heartbreaking, she'd not known what to write in return.

If she married, she would never return home to live. Her new position might even move her far away from them—unless she married John.

Why did everything circle back to John? If only she had a sizable dowry and as flattering a figure as her cousin. Maybe then he'd find her appealing. He certainly had not complained every time Miss Guthrie placed her hand on his arm or sat so close she might as well have been in his lap.

CHAPTER 18

"Are you well?" Lady Stanford asked as they made their way to the carriage.

"I am, why do you ask?"

"You looked like you wished to gouge someone's eyes out."

A surprised laugh bubbled out of her. "My face has a mind of its own apparently."

"Or your mind has more control than you'd like." Lady Stanford's blue eyes bore into hers. She lowered her voice. "You can tell me, Susannah. I will not divulge anything to anyone."

It would be nice to share her burdens, but they were just that—her burdens. Sharing only added to others' troubles and Lady Stanford had plenty of her own. No, she needed to be the strong one, like she always had been. Her family depended on her, if not to raise them financially, then to be the solid dependable one they could count on.

"I have no complaints; I am simply excited for the night and a little upset at my sister's letters."

Lady Stanford tipped her head slightly to the side. "Is she still begging you to return?"

"She is."

"Poor girl."

The ride to the Lincolnhurst townhouse was filled with lively banter and suppositions. Sir Nathaniel surmised that the countess only held this event to pressure her son, Lord Hamdon, into taking a wife, but Mr. Kendall insisted the woman hosted a great deal of parties with or without the incentive.

A pristinely dressed footman with a fine face and figure opened the door to the carriage when they arrived. To Susannah's delight, Miss Harris's carriage stopped behind theirs and the woman exited after her mother and father, two younger sisters on her heels.

"My, but you must have been crowded," Lady Stanford said softly to Miss Harris when she joined them.

"Yes. I cannot wait until Jenica's baronet takes her off, for then we might all fit nicely again."

Mr. Kendall sidled up to her. "Or you might consider marrying. Then you'd have your own carriage."

"Are you offering?" Miss Harris snickered at the look of horror on his face.

"I am not old enough for such an endeavor."

"But are you not the same age as Sir Nathaniel?" Susannah asked.

"No, thank heavens. I am a full half year younger."

The impish smile he cast her broke through her resolve not to laugh. Her hand flew to her mouth to cover the sound and she glanced around to see if anyone of importance had taken note. Too busy with their own arrivals, the other guests seemed not to notice.

After greeting the hostess and her dashing son, they made their way into one of the many rooms set aside for guests. A woman at the pianoforte played soft music as guests mingled or partook of the refreshments.

Susannah kept watch for John as she was again introduced to people whose names she was certain to forget, and finally she was rewarded for her vigil. Short-cropped yellow hair appeared above the crowd.

When the gathering parted, however, she found John with Miss Wallace on one arm and Miss Guthrie on the other.

To his credit, he appeared as if he'd like to hide under the furniture until there were no more people present, but the sight of so much attention being lavished on him nipped at Susannah's heart. Would she be afforded a single moment alone with him to offer her apology?

"Miss Wayland," a familiar masculine voice said. She turned to see the smiling face of Mr. Wallace. "Such a delight to see you again. Might I procure you some refreshment?"

"I—" She glanced at John, his focus taken up with the two pretty women who seemed to be vying for his attention. "Yes, refreshment would be nice."

Mr. Wallace disappeared for only a few moments then returned with tea and tarts. "Might we find a seat?" He gestured to a pair of unoccupied chairs.

She cast Lady Stanford a glance. Already in conversation with two older women, she gave her an encouraging nod.

"I would like that very much," she finally assented.

When they reached the spot, her eyes landed on her aunt who happened to occupy the seat across from them.

"Good evening Mr. Wallace," her aunt cooed. "Such a pleasure to see you here. I see you have found my dear niece."

Mr. Wallace looked between them. "Mrs. Guthrie is your aunt?"

She acknowledged the relationship.

"Really. How delightful? I am not sure if you know, but I have been acquainted with the Guthries for quite some time."

"Three years at least." Aunt Guthrie cast him a fond smile.

To Susannah's surprise, the expression seemed genuine. How irregular. Usually her aunt's expressions held a bit of artifice.

Her aunt continued on. "Miss Wayland is the eldest daughter of my brother. We quite adore her and try to help where we can. It is the least we can do, considering her family's situation."

"Oh?" Mr. Wallace glanced at Susannah and then leaned toward her aunt.

Aunt Guthrie lifted her chin, her eyes flashing. "Yes, but one does not speak of financial difficulties at a gathering such as this."

And there was the barb Susannah had expected, given in the sweetest tone with the most innocent expression, but with every bit of intent to injure.

Her aunt quickly changed the subject. "How is your family, Mr. Wallace?"

Susannah listened to their conversation for only a moment before her mind wandered. If Aunt Guthrie disliked her so much, why the act? There were plenty of families who lived separate and indifferent lives; something their two families had done for years. Why the false kindness now?

"Oh, look Miss Wallace, we have found your brother."

Miss Guthrie's voice pulled Susannah from her woolgathering. John and his two ladies stopped next to them.

Miss Wallace nodded to them before casting Miss Guthrie a tight smile. "Also your mother. Perhaps you would like to take a rest while Lord Newhurst and I take another turn about the room."

"No thank you, Miss Wallace. But you are welcome to retrieve some refreshment since you were complaining of a parched throat a few moments ago. Maybe your brother could escort you?"

John's attention bounced between the two ladies, his already confused expression growing more distressed by the minute. The man looked like he did not know what to do with himself as the two ladies continued to give excuses of why the other should leave their little grouping.

"Or perhaps you both should sit down," Mr. Roberts said, coming upon them from behind. "I am afraid I need to deprive you of your escort." He placed a hand on John's back and Susannah swore John breathed a sigh of relief although no sound came out.

"D-d-do excuse me, ladies." He shrugged off both their hands and stepped out of their reach.

Mr. Roberts put out a hand to her. "You as well, Miss Wayland. Lady Stanford has been looking for you."

She glanced at Mr. Wallace, not sure what to say. "Please excuse me."

He smiled at her. "By all means."

She handed her tea things to a passing servant and followed John and Mr. Roberts away from three frustrated looking women. And *if* a little cheer for her good fortune happened to bubble up within, she would not show it—no matter how much she wished to gloat over the others.

Mr. Roberts stopped when they reached the next room and took out his timepiece.

"Why did Lady Stanford need me?" she asked.

He glanced up at her as if surprised she still followed him. "She doesn't. I simply saw that a rescue mission was in order." He grinned at John. "I shall leave you two, for I have a baron's daughter to annoy." And with that he headed straight for Miss Harris who was deep in discussion with the son of their hostess, looking like she enjoyed the gentleman's company.

She looked after him for a moment, at odds with what to do next. John also seemed preoccupied with watching his friend. Then as if some invisible permission had been given, they both began to talk.

"Miss Wayland, I need to—"

"Lord Newhurst, I'm—"

They stopped.

He peered down at his feet and cleared his throat.

She looked away, her gaze catching on Lady Braithwaite clad in black with only white lace at her neck and sleeves to relieve it. The lady glanced her way and locked gazes with her, gave a subtle nod, and refocused on the two men who were speaking to her.

John's fingers lightly touched Susannah's sleeve. "I must ask your forgiveness, Miss Wayland. I had no right to lose my temper with you, especially as you were not to blame."

She shook her head. "Not so. It is I who must apologize. You had every right to defend your friend."

"Yes, but as you so keenly p-pointed out, Mr. Wallace was not to blame for the offense."

"But your sour mood was not the reason for my upset. I—" She quickly shut her mouth. Could she really admit to her jealousy over something as simple as a painting? It seemed silly now. Perhaps she had read too much into his reaction. What if he had no more interest than that of a devoted artist?

CHAPTER 18

"Susannah, dear," Aunt Guthrie said, taking hold of her arm. "Lady Stanford is this way."

She blinked at her aunt in confusion. "But I—"

"Do excuse us, Lord Newhurst." Aunt Guthrie tugged on her arm. "Harriet, will you be a dear and keep the gentleman company while I help your cousin find her friends?"

John stepped forward, his face set in a firm frown, but Miss Guthrie latched back onto his arm like a hungry leech.

Susannah wanted to object to her aunt's high-handed ways but she was already pulling her away.

"Do not make a fool of yourself," Aunt Guthrie hissed when they were out of hearing of the others. "Lord Newhurst is far above your station. You'd be better to assert your efforts with Mr. Wallace, if the man will have you. Even that is a stretch for someone like you."

Susannah stopped, the force of the larger woman's forward trajectory nearly pulling her off her feet.

Aunt Guthrie let go and turned to glare at her. "Do not be so stubborn, girl. I do not have to *lower* myself to help you."

A litany of arguments gathered in her mind, but she could not get any words past her lips. Her aunt's words held merit. John *was* above her station. Perhaps Mr. Wallace was as well, but she needed that status to relieve pressure off her own family.

Black swirled behind her aunt, and a silky-smooth voice said, "An offer of help from you might be considered lowering to anyone, Mrs. Guthrie."

Her aunt whirled about and for a moment Susannah saw Lady Braithwaite's chin tilted up and her eyes flashing.

Quietly she stepped to the side so she might see around her aunt. Aunt Guthrie scowled a moment before her face lifted into the false smile Susannah had come to expect from her.

"Lady Braithwaite, how are you this evening?"

"I have been better. Now do me the honor of introducing me to your niece."

How had she...

"But Your Ladyship—"

"That was not a request."

For a person so young and small, Lady Braithwaite spoke boldly, especially to a woman over twice her age. Those must be the rights of rank and money. Then again, that did not seem to apply to all. The Duchess of Bedford outranked Lady Braithwaite and yet she'd not spoken near so forcefully when in company with Aunt Guthrie.

Her aunt's jaw worked back and forth before she finally turned and gestured to Susannah. "Lady Braithwaite, may I present Miss Wayland."

The countess nodded, and Susannah curtsied. "I am pleased to make your acquaintance, Your Ladyship."

"And I yours. Miss Harris speaks highly of you and there are few opinions that I value higher than Miss Harris's. Let us take a turn about the room." Lady Braithwaite's attention returned to Aunt Guthrie. "Have a good evening, Mrs. Guthrie."

Aunt Guthrie's chest rose and fell several times, her lips pressed tightly together before she nodded. "And you, *Lady* Braithwaite."

Her Ladyship watched Aunt Guthrie closely as she stepped around her and crossed the room. A bit of the starch went out of Lady Braithwaite's spine, her shoulders relaxed and her fingers stretched before re-gripping her customary cane.

Susannah's eyes were drawn to the affectation: perfectly straight, a gray marble top, and the wood painted black. She'd seen her carry others, but this one seemed to be Her Ladyship's favorite. But why carry one at all? Lady Braithwaite had no apparent limp.

"Where are you on your way to, Miss Wayland? Perhaps I might accompany you."

She glanced over her shoulder, but John no longer stood where she'd left him. "I am on my way to find Lady Stanford."

Lady Braithwaite narrowed her eyes a fraction. "Are you sure you do not wish to return to your previous company?"

Heat crept onto Susannah's cheeks. Had she seen her look of longing?

"I will take that as a yes. Come." Lady Braithwaite motioned with her head, slowly making her way toward the door to the room she'd been in previously.

Susannah fell into step beside her waiting for the lady to speak, but they made it to the other room without a single word being uttered between them. Across the next room, she spotted John, his head bent as he listened intently to Miss Guthrie. She stopped and Lady Braithwaite followed her lead.

All the discomfort he'd displayed in the company of both women had vanished. She hesitated. He appeared to be quite content, even venturing to say

CHAPTER 18

something to her cousin. They'd not finished their conversation, but this was not the time. She'd not get involved in a tug of war. John deserved better.

He would visit Kendall House soon. No need to make a scene. They'd said the majority of what needed to be conveyed anyway. Perhaps providence had intervened so she would not make herself a fool in public.

"On second thought, I believe I will return to Lady Stanford."

Lady Braithwaite stared at her, her jade green eyes seemed to see directly into Susannah's soul, but she said nothing, only turned and gestured back the way they'd come. "She is in the red room. I will walk with you to the door, but no further. No need to incite your friend's ire."

The comment intrigued Susannah. It seemed Lady Braithwaite was as aware of Lady Stanford's dislike as Miss Harris had been.

"Please forgive my impertinence, but why are you and Lady Stanford at odds?"

The lady's eyes roamed the room, jumping from one person to another. Finally she spoke. "Have you not heard my infamy gossiped about in the drawing rooms of London?"

"Only of the existence of rumors, but no concrete proof that you have done anything untoward."

A self-satisfied smirk stole across Lady Braithwaite's face. "Then they are all too frightened to speak the worst of me. Just as it should be. As for your friend, Lady Stanford and I were acquainted in my first season. I was young and incredibly stupid. Lady Stanford thought much of her own consequence back then but took pity on me until I made a most advantageous match and so the friendship ended."

"Because you married?"

"Many relationships have ceased because of less. But I suspect the rumors are to blame. As you may know I have buried two husbands, one too many for London's superstitious nature. It is of no matter. I do not hold Lady Stanford in contempt for her caution. I might even applaud her wisdom."

A smirk stole across the tiny woman's angelic face, but it did not reach her eyes. There was heartache there, more than Susannah had witnessed in anyone other than her mother.

They were nearly to the red room when the subject of their conversation emerged, Sir Nathaniel supporting her.

"Miss Wayland, thank heavens you are here. Please fetch Eddie and meet us at the carriage."

Susannah's eyes widened. "Of course." She turned to excuse herself, but Lady Braithwaite was already gone as if she'd vanished into thin air.

It did not take long to find Mr. Kendall, for he came hurrying toward her the moment she entered the first room.

"What has happened?" He asked in low tones as he turned her about and headed for the door.

"How did you—"

"Lady Braithwaite. She said I was needed urgently."

"Your sister has taken ill. We are needed in the carriage."

He said no more as they collected their things at the front door and rushed down the steps. Susannah's thoughts were jumbled. Concern, disappointment, and confusion fought for precedence, but in the end amazement and gratitude won out.

Lady Braithwaite's quick action in finding Mr. Kendall had saved time and the upset of running into her aunt again. Or worse, seeing her cousin captivating John's attention.

Chapter 19

Johnathan took the steps of Kendall House two at a time, an easy feat for his long legs. To his surprise, Javenia passed him up and was in the house before he'd even reached the front door. He glanced over his shoulder to see where she'd come from and noticed her father motion from the open carriage door.

Retracing his steps, he approached the older gentleman, noting Javenia's mother and sisters within.

The man's face looked haggard. "Lord Newhurst, I am relieved to see you here. I need to return my wife and daughters to the house, but I will return for Javenia in an hour's time. Will you be so kind as to make sure she does not do anything brash such as hailing a hack and racing across town?" Lord Upton glanced at the door and sighed. "Again."

Johnathan bit back a smile. "I will do my best."

"That is all we can do where Javenia is concerned, is it not?"

"Indeed."

Lord Upton touched his hat, shut the door, and knocked on the roof. The carriage slowly pulled away, but Johnathan did not watch it go. Inside Kendall House he found Eddie pacing the front entry.

"What happened?" he asked.

Eddie stopped long enough to look at him and then motioned for him to follow him up to the second level where they found an empty sitting room. Johnathan took up the pink and cream brocade chair near the fire.

"I still cannot believe it, John." Eddie sat across from him in a matching chair and stared into the fire. "After all these years."

"I do not follow."

"She talked to me."

He squinted at Eddie, wondering if the stress had thoroughly stolen his senses. "I heard Melior was carried out of Lady Lincolnhurst's house."

Two slow blinks met his question, then Eddie's vision seemed to clear. "Oh, yes. Melior." He glanced down at his hands. "She is resting now. The doctor came and said her pain would pass. Nothing to worry about."

Johnathan leaned forward until he caught Eddie's gaze. "Then why are you so distressed? What are you not telling me, Eddie?"

His friend's attention drifted to the fire. "I am not unwell, only surprised."

"That Melior was injured?"

"No, Melior's complaints are of a natural source, it is only"—Eddie's voice dropped to a near whisper— "Lady Braithwaite spoke to me."

Johnathan wanted to breathe a sigh of relief at Melior's apparent health, laugh at Eddie for the moony way he'd spoken, and shake him all at once. By the way the man had been pacing, he'd expected to find that Melior had taken to her deathbed. Instead he'd found a lovesick fool.

Odd, he'd never even considered Lady Braithwaite to have any such effect on his friend. And yet here they sat, Eddie off in his own thoughts, a silly smile upon his lips.

Johnathan stared at him. It always surprised him how much the Kendall siblings shared in their appearances, from dark brown hair to bright blue eyes, and even their full pink lips. Each one of those features was accentuated in the firelight and for the first time, he wondered why his friend had not married before now.

Surely he would make some young lady very happy, but Lady Braithwaite? It was no wonder he remained unattached if she was his idea of a perfect woman. Not that Johnathan had anything against her, but she was as prickly as a cactus, and if rumors were true, about as dangerous as one.

He relaxed into his seat. "Well, I must say I am taken aback."

"I know. We have been acquainted all these years and not once has she approached me on her own."

"No, Eddie. I meant I was surprised to find you have a tendre for her."

Wide blue eyes met his. "You cannot tell Nate or Al. They would tease me to within an inch of my life. And if Lady Braithwaite found out, she'd have me drawn and quartered."

"She's not an executioner, but that sort of weariness is exactly why I am astonished. Other than her l-l-looks"—Johnathan took a deep breath, trying not to let his nervousness about ladies and relationships bind his tongue—"What can you possibly find attractive about such a woman?"

Eddie's eyes unfocused once again. "The woman can command a room with a mere glance, she is poised and controlled and puts up with nothing other than complete respect from her peers, but most of all, it is her fire that draws me in. It's not flamboyant or uncontrolled like other ladies. It simply exists in the containment she's built for it. It lights her jade-colored eyes whenever she finds a case of injustice, and I find myself wishing I held a singular gram of her conviction and strength."

Johnathan crossed his arms. It was even worse than he'd thought. Mere infatuation was one thing, but Eddie had grown poetic. His words showed he'd had ample time to consider her, years perhaps. He frowned. The lady had not always been *available*.

"And *how long* have you felt this way?"

His friend's gaze focused sharply on him. "I understand that tone; I am not unprincipled if that is what you think. I did not take note of her while she was married... at least not much," he muttered. "But she has been widowed for two years, is that not long enough?"

"Perhaps too long. You have nearly lost your senses over her. You must know she will never have you. She has no need to marry, not with the fortune Lord Braithwaite left her."

Eddie slumped. "I know."

The silence in the room became so thick one might cut it with a knife.

Finally, he said, "And that is why this secret must stay between the two of us. Nate and Al would not be so discreet as I know you will be."

Johnathan cut off a groan. Why was he always the keeper of everyone's secrets, especially when it came to women? He'd been sworn to secrecy by Nate several years ago when he'd admitted his attraction to Melior. And while Al and Javenia had never extracted such a promise from him, they both came to him when they had questions about each other.

"John? You will hold my secret, won't you?" Eddie's hands gripped the armrests of his chair as if ready to bolt if he did not get a satisfactory answer.

"You know I will." Johnathan leaned forward. "On one condition."

Eddie mimicked his position. "And what is that?"

"Answer a few questions I have about women without becoming a nuisance."

A bark of laughter disrupted the calmness of the room. "I am not sure I am the right man to ask about such things. More than once Nate has warned me from giving advice when I've never tried to woo a lady myself."

"But the women of the Ton flock to you."

"That's because I am the nephew of a generous duke and they hope for a piece of his wealth and consequence. I am a commodity to them, a means to a connection, nothing more."

"Even so, you hold their attention and what's more, you understand what they are saying... or more to the point, what they are not saying. For starters, I heard whispers between Javenia and Susannah about some fan language. Am I missing something?"

Eddie rubbed the top of his lip, but it did not hide his smile.

"You are laughing at me."

"No, I am not," Eddie choked out around a grin. "But it will take me some time to explain all the ins and outs of the fan. For now, just two of them will do. If a lady closes her fan, she wishes to talk to you."

Johnathan nodded.

"And if she flutters it slowly with her right hand, it means 'approach me.'"

"What if she flutters it quickly with her left?"

"She wants you to leave her alone."

Johnathan's brow scrunched. Susannah had done both flutters. Had she wanted him to leave at first, then changed her mind?

"And what does it mean if she blinks rapidly like she has something caught in her eye?"

This time Eddie did laugh.

"You promised not to laugh."

"No, you asked that I not be a nuisance, but I never promised anything."

Searching his mind, Johnathan realized Eddie had never made the requisite promise.

CHAPTER 19

"But to answer your question"—Eddie clasped his hands and leaned back into his chair—"Women bat their lashes because they think it makes them look alluring. Most of the time it just makes them appear ridiculous, but it is a clear indication of their interest."

A slow smile spread across Johnathan's face and he let his head fall back on the chair. Staring at the ceiling, he replayed his interactions with Susannah. She'd batted her lashes more than once at him.

Warmth spread from his chest through his entire body as he let hope take flight. There was a chance.

"Now who's the one mooning over a girl?"

Johnathan's attention snapped back to his friend. "Stop it, Eddie."

He held up his hands. "I'm not doing anything. Simply stating the truth."

A sigh broke through Johnathan's resolve. The sound encouraged his friend. "It's no secret anyway. You know that by now."

"I do, but it s-s-still m-makes m-m-me—"

"Nervous. Yes, I know." Eddie sobered. "I need to warn you, though. Melior has noticed a certain amount of affection between Miss Wayland and Mr. Wallace. It might be good to tread carefully until she has made it clear who she favors the most."

And like that, the hope he'd gathered like fallen leaves blew away on the wind of Eddie's words. Johnathan was beginning to despise Mr. Wallace. No, he was beyond beginning and well into actual loathing. And yet, from all he knew, the man would make a decent match for Susannah.

He shot to his feet. "I need to go. Please tell Melior I wish her well in her healing."

Eddie rose. "John, I—"

He held up a hand. "You spoke the truth. I would expect nothing less from a friend, but I promised Lord Upton that I'd not let Javenia hail a hack before he returned and yet I've been shut up here with you for nearly half an hour."

Eddie nodded and let his gaze drop to the floor. "And my secret?"

He stared at his friend silently, letting him grow restless in his seat. A little retribution for laughing at him. Then a slow smile formed. "Is safe with me."

Chapter 20

Javenia paced from one end of the room to the other but Johnathan did not know what to say or do. She'd come to his townhouse in high dudgeon complaining how Melior had been nearly carried out of Lady Lincolnhurst's on Friday only to attend the opera on Monday.

"Nate begged Melior to rest but she refused. I love her, but that woman is more stubborn than Prinny when he's found a new bobble he must have. What is she thinking?"

She passed by him again and he decided there was no use holding to propriety by standing. She'd pace herself out eventually. He lowered himself into his favorite chair near the fire. Large and sturdy, it fit his tall frame perfectly.

"And then if that was not enough, she accompanied Miss Wayland and the Wallaces to the menagerie on Tuesday. She is wearing herself thin and if she is not careful, she's going to hurt the baby."

His frustrated mind pondered her mention of the Wallaces when the second half of her sentence registered. He sat upright. "Baby?" As a man who prided himself on his attention to detail, it smarted that he'd somehow missed such a crucial piece of information.

Javenia stopped. "Nate did not tell you?"

He lifted his eyebrows and tipped his head to the side.

"I see." She sat in the chair across from him. "The day you left early, the one where we found you with Miss Wayland, he let us know of Melior's delicate condition."

He collapsed back in the chair. That was what Eddie meant by natural.

That Nate had not shared such private information with him would have been normal in any other part of Society, but it hurt knowing he'd been kept in the dark. They'd been the keepers of each other's secrets for years. Susannah's pretty face flashed in his mind—at least, he had been the keeper of Nate's secrets.

Johnathan had never told anyone of his attraction to Susannah.

Attraction was not a strong enough word. Not for the pull he felt whenever she was near. Like a bee to a flower, he was drawn to her, her very presence giving him a reason to live each day. Voicing any feeling was hard enough, but the intensity of his love for Susannah often overwhelmed his senses and made it difficult to articulate. So he'd stayed silent.

Then again, if Javenia was to be believed, they all knew. It was a secret no longer.

He laced his fingers together. "I s-suppose that is why she's been so ill of late."

Javenia nodded. "She should be resting, but she is so determined to find Miss Wayland a match this season that she's exhausting herself."

Johnathan stared out the window. "And is Mr. Wallace her choice?"

"Whose? Melior or Miss Wayland?"

Reluctantly he pulled his gaze away from the window. "Either one."

"I have seen that face before, John. Do not give up."

Closing his eyes, he focused on his next words. "I will not stand in the way of her happiness. No matter how painful it might be to s-see her married to someone else."

"Stop it!"

His eyes flew open. "What?"

"Stop playing the martyr. You need to fight for that girl, John. You love her like she needs to be loved, but she will never know if you do not tell her."

Leaning forward, he said, "And h-how am I-I-I supposed to d-do that? Y-y-you k-know b-b-better than anyone h-how h-hard it is for me to speak."

He gripped the arms of the chair. She leaned forward and placed her hand over his. "We all have mountains to climb. You will never know the wonders you will find at the top if you don't take the first step—or in your case, say the first word. You may find speaking far easier than you think."

Johnathan tucked his chin and tipped his head. "Really, Javenia? If I cannot speak to you about it, I hardly think my addlepated brain will be able to piece together enough words to the woman I love."

CHAPTER 20

She sat back with a satisfied smile. "And yet you said that entire sentence without one stutter."

"An anomaly."

"Hardly. You do well in Society when you are sure of your speaking material. Think of all the words you can spout off a definition for without a second thought. Do what you have with them; memorize what you wish to say."

He searched Javenia's familiar face, reviewing her advice. He supposed he could write something out and practice it, but what reason did Susannah have to choose him over Mr. Wallace? Only his title set him apart, but that would not sway her. She'd been raised with an example of the truest love. Money, status, even appearance would not sway her unless her heart were truly set on the person.

"I—"

The door to the sitting room opened and the butler announced, "Mr. Roberts to see you, my lord."

Javenia straightened in her chair, her hands smoothing her dress, then checking her curls. Johnathan smirked. She was quite talented at giving advice she herself did not take. When would she finally admit to Al that she saw him as more than a friend?

Al entered with all the swagger one could expect of him. "I thought I might find you at home."

Johnathan stood. "You thought correctly."

"I have a predicament and I think you might be the right person to help—"

Javenia stood, and Al's gaze snapped to her in surprise. He glanced around the room until he spied Javenia's maid in the corner. A small exhale escaped him, but his brow still furrowed.

"Why are you here, Javenia?"

The harshness of his tone would have made any other woman shrink, but Javenia only stood taller.

"I have as much right to visit a childhood friend as you do."

"Yes, but you are a lady visiting a single gentleman. Do you have no regard for your reputation?"

"And what of you? Do you have any regard for a lady's reputation? Or was it some other gentleman that I witnessed walking alone with Miss Giles in the garden behind Lady Lincolnhurst's house? In the freezing cold, no less."

Al opened his mouth, then clamped it shut.

"I thought so." She turned to Johnathan and took his hand. "Thank you for allowing me to visit. Please think on what I have shared." Then without warning, she stepped forward and kissed him on the cheek.

The action was so out of character that Johnathan hardly registered it before Javenia swept out of the room, not once glancing toward Al.

Silence settled in the room until the front door shut.

Al rounded on him. "What was that all about?"

"Pardon?"

"Why did Javenia kiss you?" Al's hands were clenched and his shoulders taut.

"Probably out of spite." Johnathan retook his seat. "There is nothing between us if that is what you are asking, but it seems there might be something between you and Miss Giles."

Al sighed, slumping into the chair that Javenia had vacated.

"I... that is, she... Oh, I do not know what there is or is not. She is pretty enough, I suppose, but she lacks..."

"Intelligence?" Johnathan slowly smirked. It was no secret that most young women of the Ton did not cultivate any decent amount of knowledge, but Miss Giles was especially lacking.

"I was going to say an interesting form of address, but I suppose that is from an absence of something. I hate to call a lady's intelligence into question, though."

"So you have come to me, a man of little experience with courtship, to ask if you should continue your pursuit of her?"

Al's head jerked back. "No. I already know she is not the woman I wish to shackle myself to."

"Then what?" Johnathan leaned forward.

When Al's gaze wandered to the door where Javenia had exited, he had his answer. But instead of voicing what was obviously on his mind, Al's head whipped back toward him.

"Lady Roberts gave birth last evening."

Johnathan's eyes widened. He knew Al's stepmother had begun her confinement, but it seemed awfully short. "I believe congratulations are in order." He stood to shake Al's hand, but his friend stared at the proffered appendage.

"I'm not sure congratulations are the correct sentiments in this situation. Condolences would be more to the point."

The wide smile Johnathan had sported slipped. "Was there a tragedy?"

CHAPTER 20

"Yes, the tragedy is that she gave birth to twins. Both girls." Al put a hand to his forehead. "That makes an even dozen, John. I have one dozen sisters."

A laugh burst out of him before he could hold it back. That the baby would be female had been a given, but that it should be two girls was simply too hilarious to withstand.

"It is not a laughing matter." The pull at the right side of Al's lips belied his words. "What's worse, he has named them Roberta and Richarda."

"You cannot be serious."

"I am in earnest."

"You mentioned the ridiculous name in hopes of dissuading him, didn't you?"

Al rubbed the back of his neck and unsuccessfully tried to rein in his smile but it burst forth. "I did. I am heartily ashamed of myself." He chuckled. "And yet Richarda might be my favorite name yet, born purely on the absurdity of it."

They both laughed. When the room quieted, Al asked, "Do you think if I'd have led with that news Javenia would not have buried me deep in her black books again?"

The comment, usually said with a bit of mirth, came out strained. Tension about Al's mouth and shoulders confirmed his true feelings.

Johnathan motioned for Al to follow him to the door. "Perhaps. But I believe it is jealousy that frightened her off."

"Javenia? Jealous of what? Miss Giles?" Al's expression lifted.

"Or you jealous of Javenia coming to visit me?"

Al sobered.

Johnathan locked gazes with him. "Perhaps one day you two will—"

"I need to be off." Al swept the door open in front of them and motioned to the footman in the hall. "My coat and hat, please." He turned back to Johnathan. "Thank you for commiserating with me on my acquisition of two more responsibilities after my father concedes defeat and gives up the ghost."

"Any time, my friend. Please send my congratulations to your family." Johnathan shook his head as Al sauntered out the door. He may be charming and handsome, but the man was an absolute dolt. If Susannah had given him half the indications of interest that Javenia gave Al, he'd be a happy man well on his way to the altar.

The knocker tapped on the front door and he wondered if Al might have forgotten something. When the door opened to reveal Miss Guthrie with her mother, he wished he'd had the forethought to make himself scarce. He could not refuse the visit now.

As he escorted the ladies to the parlor, he braced himself. His friend had made it out the door unscathed, not that Al would have minded small talk with ladies. But Johnathan dreaded it. Why did Al have all the luck?

Chapter 21

Today was the day. Only a few more minutes and they'd be leaving for Almack's. Susannah touched the curls at her temple, smiling at herself in the entryway mirror. Having a well-trained lady's maid was a luxury she did not have back in Kent.

She'd not been completely without help growing up. Her mother's maid had helped her and Amanda dress until their mother's passing, after which she retired from service, having served Susannah's mother for over twenty years. For the last nine months their housekeeper Mrs. Stone or their maid of all work had assisted her.

What would it be like to have her own help?

Miss Wallace had spoken openly of her own lady's maid, so she assumed the family was stable enough in their finances that should Mr. Wallace offer for her a lady's maid might be appointed.

She stopped fussing in the mirror, astonished at her own thoughts. It was one thing to enjoy Mr. Wallace's company, but quite another to consider him a candidate for marriage. He was a fine man to be sure, and his conversation delighted her at every turn.

This week alone they'd attended the opera, Vauxhall Gardens, and even driven out during the fashionable hour. Perhaps his fulfillment of her long-held dreams had somehow won him a small place in her heart.

"Are you ready?"

Susannah turned to see Lady Stanford in a white gown trimmed with silver beads and her signature blue ribbon woven in her dark hair, a matching blue ribbon tied about her waist. A subtle bulge poked out under the ribbon, one she would have missed if she'd not known of Her Ladyship's condition.

"You look lovely, Lady Stanford. How I wish my features were as striking as yours."

Lady Stanford waved her compliment away. "You are beautiful in your own right, Miss Wayland. Please do not compare us. And I must say pink is definitely your color. How your hair shines tonight. I am sure no man will be able to keep his eyes off you."

Susannah's cheeks warmed. "Thank you."

The butler helped them on with their cloaks and they were putting on gloves when Mr. Kendall entered from the back of the house, Sir Nathaniel following close behind. He stopped when he saw them both.

"Dear me, I forgot to attach my dress sword. Perhaps I should go retrieve it." Both ladies peered at him, perplexed. "With two ladies as lovely as you both I might be forced to beat the men off with it."

Lady Stanford swatted at his arm. "You have been taking too many lessons in flirtation from Al, I think. But I shall take it. As an old married woman, I am in need of a few compliments."

"Who are you calling old?" Sir Nathaniel took Lady Stanford's hand and pulled her toward him, wrapping an arm about her. "I won't have you speaking about my wife that way."

She smiled up at him and his head dipped toward hers.

"I believe we are intruding, Miss Wayland," Mr. Kendall said. "What say you to waiting in the carriage until they have finished their flirtation?"

Susannah, who had already averted her eyes, nodded. Mr. Kendall quickly snatched his coat and hat and they made their escape, titters of laughter chasing them out of the house.

"They are disgustingly happy, are they not?" Mr. Kendall said.

"Indeed, but I believe *delightfully* a better adjective."

"You sound like John." She peeked up at him and he smirked. "He always points out our fallacies in speech."

"I suppose years of friendship are wearing off on me." She tried to maintain her smile, but it faltered.

"You do not like that you sound like him?"

CHAPTER 21

Susannah glanced up at his concerned face. "Actually, I like it very much. Lord Newhurst and I have been friends for a long time. It is an honor to sound as educated as he is. It is just—"

How to finish? They reached the carriage and Mr. Kendall helped her up. When the door closed, he faced her.

"Just?" he encouraged.

"I am confused. You are his friend. Do you think... that is, do you know if..." She could not finish such an embarrassing question. What would Mr. Kendall think of her asking after his friend's affections?

He leaned forward, a twinkle in his eye. "I think you should ask John this question. If I am not wrong, it is one he wishes very much to hear."

The door to the carriage opened and Mr. Kendall leaned back against the squabs as the others entered. All the way to King Street she pondered his words, a bud of excitement blooming when she realized what he might have meant.

The chandeliers of Almack's drew Susannah's attention the moment they entered. Lit with hundreds of candles, their sparkle danced off of every wall. Ladies and gentlemen were already dancing a lively Scottish reel, their hands clapping and their feet skipping. Her eyes lifted to a magnificent balcony where the musicians played.

All the sights and sounds tickled her senses and left her toes tapping as she awaited her first opportunity to dance.

"Lady Stanford, what a pleasure to see you."

The grating sound of her aunt's greeting stole all the happy sensations and left her heart pounding. She'd known they were attending, but hoped with so many present she'd not be forced to spend much time with them.

Turning, she was surprised to find her uncle also present. She'd not seen him since that fateful day last spring. He nodded to her, a pleasant smile on his lips.

"Mrs. Guthrie," Lady Stanford acknowledged.

"Have you met my husband, Mr. Guthrie?"

"I have not."

Introductions were made and before long, Sir Nathaniel and Uncle Guthrie stepped away from the group, deep in a discussion about the merits of steam engines. The man intrigued her, his nature obviously more agreeable than his wife. But perhaps it was a persona he put on for show, much like Aunt Guthrie.

Miss Guthrie's head swiveled back and forth until her focus landed on Mr. Kendall. Target in sight, she advanced on him.

"Miss Wayland," he rushed to say, "Might I have this next set?"

Miss Martha snickered, and Susannah wondered if she might actually be opposed to her mother and sister's antics. She had insinuated her mother to be as annoying as a goose when they were last in company together.

Their eyes met, and Miss Martha gave a subtle nod. "Look, Harriet. Is that Lord Hamdon over there?"

Miss Guthrie spun. "I believe you are right. Come, Martha. Perhaps he has brought his handsome younger brother so we might both have partners."

Miss Martha gave a comical eye roll behind her sister's back.

"Will you survive?" Susannah asked near her ear.

"Is there any other choice?" Giving a jaunty salute, she followed her sister.

"Martha, do behave yourself," Aunt Guthrie called as the young woman walked away without a backward glance. "That girl," she muttered.

"Best make our break while she's still occupied," Mr. Kendall said quietly, offering Susannah his arm.

She gratefully took it, but not before her aunt turned back to her. "Susannah, I need to speak with you."

The music ended for the set and Mr. Kendall pulled her toward the floor.

"Perhaps after this set," he called back.

"But I—"

The rest of her aunt's words were swallowed up in the noise of the crowded room, and for the first time Susannah found she was thankful for chaos.

Two songs, when danced with a partner as agreeable as Mr. Kendall, were incredibly short. At least her mind believed so even if her feet disagreed. The moment the music ended, a familiar face emerged from the crowd and Mr. Wallace claimed the next two dances.

She smiled at his enthusiasm, but her parched throat and aching feet wished he'd have at least given her a set to rest. As usual, his conversation drew her in with stories of school larks and questions about her own education. When the songs came to an end, she found she regretted nothing of the last half hour.

He led her to the refreshment table where she obtained a glass of ratafia, drinking it far quicker than she probably ought.

"My, you were thirsty."

"I am indeed." She set down the cup and retrieved another, this one filled with lemonade. Less desperate than before, she sipped it as slowly as she could while Mr. Wallace pointed out different people he was acquainted with.

CHAPTER 21

"Bragging on all your *connections*, Henry?" Miss Wallace asked from behind them.

Mr. Wallace glanced over his shoulder. Susannah could not see his expression, but she could see Miss Wallace's. Her smile turned to a frown and she abruptly turned and walked to where a group of ladies were chatting.

"Please excuse my sister. It seems she's not quite learned that eavesdropping is rude."

The cheer that had marked his expression before had fled. His stance was stiff and his arms tucked against his side.

"I take no offense. It is a ballroom after all. Nothing said here is completely private and I am well aware of the good-natured teasing that exists between you and your sister."

He peered down at her and smiled. "Thank you. You are too generous. What might—"

"Susannah, there you are, my dear." Aunt Guthrie interrupted. Latching onto her other arm, she cast Mr. Wallace a bright smile. "Do excuse us. I have needed to speak to my niece on a matter of some import all evening."

Susannah tried to beg his intervention with pleading eyes and a subtle shake of her head, but Mr. Wallace was too much of a gentleman and immediately agreed to her aunt's proposition.

Aunt Guthrie pulled her toward the far rooms away from the music.

"Where are we going?"

"Never you mind." Aunt Guthrie's grip became painful. "You have far too much of your mother in you, I say, cavorting about like you come from good breeding. Why Lady Stanford brought you to London is beyond me. And how in the world did you receive a voucher for Almack's?" She shook her head, her jowls jiggling with the action. "The standards for entry are becoming dismally low indeed if they let chits of your standing attend."

When they reached a secluded alcove, Susannah dug in her heels, pulling her arm free. "Madam, you have said quite enough. I need to return to my party."

"Do not speak to me thus, you sniveling brat. You should be grateful that I have even noticed you at all this season. I could ruin you and your family in an instant, but I have chosen to be generous. In return, you *will* obey me."

"You can have nothing so serious to claim. My parents' reputation is unblemished."

"But it will not be when I have your father's debts called in and have him sent to debtor's prison."

Susannah sucked in her breath. "My father's debts?" The words were barely audible but must have been loud enough for Aunt Guthrie, for she smiled triumphantly.

"Yes, and if you do not want your brothers and sister to go there as well, you will stay away from Lord Newhurst. My Harriet has taken a liking to him, but you keep throwing yourself at him like a hussy. I have seen the way he looks at you."

"Like one looks after a sister. You must know we have been acquainted nearly all our lives."

"No, like one looks at a lover. Tell me, have you tried to seduce him much like your mother did my brother?"

"I beg your pardon." Red rushed to Susannah's cheeks at such an accusation, but another part of her heart beat out the same words over and over. *A lover, a lover, a lover.* Did he really look at her in such a manner? Had she been blind all this time? Mr. Kendall's words filled her mind.

"You heard me. I order you to stop your dalliances with Lord Newhurst or you shall force my hand."

"I've not—"

"I know what I see, Susannah. Now give me your word, or I shall go to Mr. Guthrie right away and have him contact your father's creditors."

She swallowed, tears burning in her eyes. "Lord Newhurst is an intimate friend of the Stanfords. I cannot simply avoid him."

"You can and you will. If he is over to the house, declare you have a headache."

John would never understand, but the thought of causing her family so much distress terrified her. There was no way around it. No one would want the contents of their home and they needed every bit of the land to live on. She had no doubt her father's debts were great indeed, for she'd witnessed the way her parents had economized over the years and Mama's doctor bills had been no small sum.

Perhaps she could petition her grandfather to intercede. He was not the kindest man, but when his own grandchildren's living was at risk, surely he'd help. Then again, he'd not even had the decency to attend her mother's funeral.

CHAPTER 21

She tried a different tactic. "If you ruin my family, it will reflect badly on yours. One knows that if one member falls the rest are found guilty as well."

The woman's dark eyes hardened. "I am willing to take that risk. Are you?"

Susannah hung her head.

Aunt Guthrie leaned in, her foul breath puffing in her face. "And do not dare speak a word of this to those friends of yours, nor your family, or I will make sure no man of good standing will ever want you again."

"That is not possible. I have done nothing worth censure."

"No, but a woman's reputation is very brittle. One wrong word from the right source can break it."

The steady click of a cane on tile brought Mrs. Guthrie's attention around. Susannah's eyes widened when Lady Braithwaite stepped out of a nearby alcove and approached.

Her appearance was a timely reminder of how ruthless the Ton could be. In all Susannah's experiences with the woman, she'd not uncovered any reason for Society's disdain. And yet, she'd heard whispers of intrigue, seductions, even murder connected to the lady's name these last few weeks. In Lady Braithwaite's case, she had enough money to ignore the gossip, but Susannah had none.

Ice formed around her heart.

When Lady Braithwaite stopped before them, gold flecked eyebrows rose over staggering green eyes. "Mrs. Guthrie." She gripped the top of a gold-handled walking stick. "What brings you to such a secluded area?"

"Nothing of consequence," Aunt Guthrie crooned. The change in her demeanor was so sudden that Susannah stared at her like she'd grown a second head. "I was merely having a word with my niece. We are incredibly close, as you must know, and I wanted to ascertain how she was enjoying the dancing."

The woman actually placed an arm around her back and Susannah had to clench her teeth until her jaw hurt to keep from pulling away. Frustration battled with fear. How could the woman claim such intimacy moments after threatening her?

"That must be nice to have such a *close family*. But you will have to excuse me, for I am come to collect Miss Wayland and return her to her party." The slow emphasis and almost imperceptible narrowing of Lady Braithwaite's eyes indicated she might not believe the woman.

What did Her Ladyship mean by collecting her? Knowing Lady Stanford's dislike of Lady Braithwaite, she highly doubted she'd employ her to seek her out. Susannah would not contradict Her Ladyship, though. Besides, the sooner she escaped her aunt, the sooner the threats would stop.

Aunt Guthrie threaded her arm through hers. "Do not trouble yourself, Lady Braithwaite. I can return my niece."

Was Susannah imagining things, or had Lady Braithwaite's nostrils flared?

"I think not." The tiny woman stretched to her full height, her eyes flashing with a warning no one could miss. "*I* have come for her, and *I* shall leave with her. Do not forget who I am, Mrs. Guthrie, for I have most definitely not forgotten who you are."

Aunt Guthrie shrunk back, her shoulders rounding, but her face grew hard. "I have not forgotten. You heard the woman, Susannah. Go find your friends. Only remember what we have spoken of and do behave yourself."

She'd probably meant the reproof to sound like a loving aunt looking out for her niece's reputation, but the threat carried far deeper. Susannah untangled her arm and followed Lady Braithwaite down the hall without glancing back.

Instead of returning her to the ballroom, however, Lady Braithwaite led her up the stairs. She said nothing, which suited Susannah after such a disagreeable encounter. On the second floor she stopped by a large multi-paned window.

"You associate with some very reprehensible individuals, Miss Wayland," she said softly, staring out the window.

"What do you mean?"

"Only that I have watched you since your arrival and you seem to be attracting all the wrong kinds of attention. Let me give you a word of wisdom. Sometimes snakes dress themselves up in gentlemen's and ladies' clothing, and parade about looking for their next victim."

"What am I supposed to gain from that?"

Lady Braithwaite finally turned to face her. "Be careful who you trust. It hurts to be bitten by a snake. I should know."

The beautiful woman returned her focus to the window. A crease in her brow and a shimmer in her eyes were the only indication of distress, otherwise she could have doubled for a statue. Perhaps a Grecian goddess, cold, distant, and unbreakable... or nearly unbreakable, as the presence of moisture proved her to be human.

As quickly as the look came, it was swept away under a polite smile. "I was once like you, young, beautiful... and incredibly stupid."

"Pardon?"

"Please take no offense. I pride myself on being frank and you must know you are a bit naive."

"I profess, I do not know a great deal about London or the world as a whole, but I would like to think I can be wise."

"Good. Then you will take my advice, for I will not always be around to rescue you from serpents."

"You do not like my aunt?"

"Not at all. She thinks too highly of her own importance and by the way she loomed over you, I would guess she is not as close a relative as she claims—at least, she is not as kind."

"You are correct on both accounts."

Again silence overtook them.

Finally Susannah asked, "Did Lady Stanford really send you for me?"

"Heavens no. You should know that. Lady Stanford worries my reputation will tarnish hers—not that it is as spotless as it once was. She would never have me fetch any ward of hers. I might taint them by association."

The way her lips curled at the edges belied her words. Her Ladyship held no distress at all about her blackened honor. Perhaps that was why she continued to wear shades of black even though her mourning period had passed long ago. The rebellion inherent in continuing to don the color even on the dance floors of London would be a statement indeed.

"In that case, I should probably return to my friends. I would not want to distress them."

"Yes, do." Lady Braithwaite's relaxed shoulders came up, as if she were putting on a shield. "We would not want them to think I have corrupted you."

There was pain behind the statement, although Her Ladyship tried to hide it.

Susannah stepped closer. "*I* am pleased with your acquaintance, Lady Braithwaite, and I look forward to advancing it."

Again those golden eyebrows rose and a tiny smile formed on the stunning woman's face. "As do I, Miss Wayland."

For the better part of an hour Johnathan searched for Susannah. He'd met with Nate and Melior moments after entering, but she'd been dancing with Mr. Wallace. He, in turn, had been dragged onto the floor by a very exuberant Miss Guthrie. He'd not been close to Susannah on the dance floor, but he had caught a glance of her every time the dancers returned to their starting positions.

Then she'd disappeared.

He supposed another gentleman had led her to the floor in a different part of the large room, so he waited. When that set finished, he was certain she must be somewhere else in the building, so he'd gone from room to room, even climbing the stairs to the second level.

How could one woman evade him so long? Was she in trouble? Was she doing it on purpose?

Near a window at the back, he came upon Lady Braithwaite. He nodded to her. She nodded back. He nearly passed without saying a word, then thought better of it.

Gathering all his courage, he asked, "H-have you, perchance, seen M-Miss Wayland?"

"I have, in fact. She left me not a quarter hour ago."

"Could you direct me to her?"

She indicated the stairs with her chin. "That way."

"I am much obliged."

He descended the stairs opposite of the ones he'd come up, re-entering the large assembly room. There, across the floor, was the vision he'd been seeking. He wove his way through the crowd, his eyes trained on Susannah, but another figure stepped in front of him.

"Lord Newhurst," Miss Wallace exclaimed. "I did not know you were coming this evening. What a pleasant surprise."

He nodded to her.

"I did not think you were fond enough of dancing to brave Almack's."

"I... do not mind dancing. It is a-a p-pleasant enough divertissement."

She tipped her head to the side at his choice of words. "Do you mean pursuit?"

"They are the same thing." He glanced across the room only to find Susannah had accepted a partner and taken a place in the dance. If she was to be there, so would he. "Would you like to dance, Miss Wallace?"

The woman's face lit with delight. "I would indeed."

CHAPTER 21

Taking his forearm, she followed him to the floor where he purposefully placed them so he'd come in contact with Susannah during the course of the dance. And if he were very lucky, he might be able to ask her for the next set at the end of this one.

"My brother tells me you enjoy painting, Lord Newhurst," Miss Wallace said when they met in the middle of the dance.

"Oh?" How had the man come by that information? Not many knew of his talents except those of his close acquaintance.

"Yes, he says you are quite proficient."

They separated and he glanced down the line at Susannah. The pieces clicked into place. Of course she would tell her new beau of his paintings. They'd talked about it quite often through the years.

"I would not say I am a master, b-but I do enjoy it." He took Miss Wallace's hands and led her in a promenade to the end of the line—where Susannah was positioned.

Her eyes met his as he passed and she immediately ducked her head. The action was so uncharacteristic of her buoyant nature. She must be cross with him. For what he was not sure.

He and Miss Wallace took their places to wait for the other couples in the set to complete their movements. Susannah's gaze rose when the call was given to circle with the corner neighbor. That was him.

They approached one another and he noted the tightness around her eyes and the shimmer of tears present. A plea lay in their depths, but for what? Back in his spot, he watched her smile at her partner, but it did not reach beyond her lips. Something was amiss.

When the music ended, she abruptly left the line of dancers before the second song of the set even started. Her partner rushed after her, his face a mask of concern. John was tempted to do the same. Miss Wallace frowned at him when he took a step in that direction, and he realized how rude it would be to leave her.

Melior appeared in the next instant and ushered Susannah out of the room. Perhaps she'd grown ill. Whatever the case, at least someone he trusted had come to rescue her.

When the set was completed, he went in search of her. At the doors he found Eddie collecting his greatcoat.

"Are you leaving already?"

"I believe we must. Melior and Mr. Wallace have already escorted Miss Wayland to the carriage on account of her feeling so poorly. Nate will be here momentarily and then we will be on our way."

Why did Mr. Wallace have to play the protector? Everywhere Johnathan wished to be Mr. Wallace already was, and it rankled.

"There you are, John," Nate said as he approached. "I hoped to find you. It seems Miss Wayland is ill."

He nodded. "That is what Eddie was telling me. Is there anything I might do to assist?"

"No, a little rest should do the trick. I believe she is simply worn down from Town hours. Melior voiced some of the same complaints moments before Miss Wayland left the dance floor, so an early removal is advantageous for both of them."

"May I call tomorrow?"

"Better not. I want the ladies to have ample time to rest. My wife overestimates her strength in going about in Society. The less people around, the less need she will have to entertain."

The refusal stung, not because Nate's reasoning wasn't sound, but because it added another day for Mr. Wallace to wheedle his way into Susannah's heart.

When Nate turned to put on his coat, he motioned to Eddie.

"I will be calling on the favor you offered to get a letter to Miss Wayland."

Eddie's face brightened. "Excellent. Do you have it now?"

"No, but I will soon."

Eddie glanced at the door, then back at him. "Don't take too long, John. You never know what might happen in the meantime."

The admonition was ominous and keenly felt.

Chapter 22

Tears trickled into Susannah's pillow. Her aunt had been right. Standing across the dance from John, she'd seen the love shining in his eyes. He *loved* her.

How had she been so blind? She knew him better than almost anyone, having watched him for years. He struggled to speak with others, especially women. He hated large gatherings. He loved painting and finding new words and spending time with his closest friends... and apparently her.

But it was too late. If he had spoken a few weeks ago, even a few days ago, perhaps her aunt would not have become so determined. It all came back to time. Why did it always have to come back to time?

The right time made all the difference. And now time had been stolen from her once again.

Tears continued to flow until sleep overtook her. It would have been a blessed relief if her dreams had not been filled with visions of being dragged off the dance floor. When she looked to see who pulled her, the face changed. It transformed from her aunt, to her cousin, to Miss Wallace, and even Mr. Wallace. When light began to filter into her room, she awoke with such a pounding in her head that she called for Cook to send up some willow bark tea.

She'd not have to claim a headache to avoid John today.

The bitter drink took the edge off the pain in her head, but not in her heart. How could she lie now that she recognized the truth? But how could she place her family into such a precarious position?

She did not know her aunt well enough to know whether she'd test her own fate out of spite for her brother's family. Aunt Guthrie's willingness to spread lies before the death of her mother seemed to prove that she'd go to no ends to tarnish the Wayland name.

Of course, those fabrications were different. They painted her mother as ill-tempered and a grasping social climber, but not morally corrupt. If Aunt Guthrie accused Susannah of unseemly behavior of an intimate nature... her cheeks heated at the mere thought. No one would want her after that, not with her meager dowry.

Her thoughts flitted to the Stanfords. She'd lose their friendship, possibly even John's if he thought she'd been immoral in any way. His upright nature would wither at the very thought.

And if her father were to go to debtors' prison she'd be her family's only hope of rescue. She needed to marry soon and marry well to keep that from ever being a possibility. With her aunt's threats, her choice had been made for her. As much as her heart rebelled against it, Mr. Wallace would be her future.

It was not *so* bad. She *had* considered his merits before they'd attended Almack's. Only now it stung, knowing what might have been had she only opened her eyes.

Thankfully, Sir Nathaniel had declared last night that they would dine in for at least three days. That would give time for her heart to come into alignment with her head, would it not?

When John was announced on the third day, however, the disobedient organ leapt in her chest. How would she ever face him?

He entered the sitting room, his complexion offset nicely by his fitted navy coat and snowy white cravat. His eyes met hers and a tentative smile full of hope pulled at his lips. It was too much.

She stood.

"Please forgive me for dashing off when you have just arrived, Lord Newhurst, but I have an urgent matter I must address."

She turned and nodded to Lady Stanford. "Do not wait on me for tea, it may take some time to settle." Rushing past him, she felt the tiniest graze of his fingers on her arm, but she did not stop. The gooseflesh he'd left would have to subside in private.

Once securely back in her room, she sat at her dressing table and stared absentmindedly at the correspondence she'd been planning to attend to. Not one ounce of her desired to take up the task, so she allowed each interaction over the last two years to play out in her mind like a puppet show. Two years of clues. Two years of tender words and gentle touches. Two years of blindness.

Lady Braithwaite was right. She was incredibly stupid.

How Johnathan had been convinced into taking Miss Guthrie for a drive, he still did not quite know. Spending any more time with her was the last thing on his mind, but it seemed she was everywhere he looked. And when she was not present, Miss Wallace managed to fill her place.

He gripped the reins as Miss Guthrie prattled on. Did she always speak so highly of her own abilities? It appeared to be the only topic she could converse on adequately. And when she was not extolling her own virtues, she was pointing out the faults of others.

Rotten Row was backed up as usual, carriages and riders moving slowly through the park as people came to see and be seen. Johnathan cared for none of it. Every once in a while Miss Guthrie called to the occupants of another conveyance and he was obligated to stop, but otherwise he'd not been required to say more than ten words the last half hour.

When a shiny yellow phaeton rounded the corner ahead of them, his jaw hung slack. It had been six days since Susannah had rushed out of the sitting room at Kendall House and even though he'd been by to visit four of those days, he'd not caught sight of her. To add to his concern, his friends had become increasingly quiet when the subject of Susannah's absence was brought up. He'd assumed she'd been indisposed, but her pink cheeks and bright smile were anything but sickly.

The wind whipped at the light pink strings of her bonnet, sunlight dancing off her enchanting golden curls. He could not pull his eyes from her. She was a masterpiece.

Miss Guthrie placed a hand on his arm, pulling him from his reverie. He glanced down at her.

She gazed back expectantly.

"I am s-sorry. I must have b-been woolgathering."

"I asked if you will be attending the Durhams' annual ball."

He pondered the question as the yellow phaeton driven by none other than Mr. Wallace neared their position. *Was* he going to attend the infamous ball that had been the ruining of Melior's reputation? Then again, it had been the making of Nate and Melior's happiness. Perhaps he should ask them their opinion on it.

"I have not yet decided."

"Please do," she begged. "It is always a splendid event."

CHAPTER 22

The tall conveyance was nearly upon them when Susannah finally pulled her eyes from the driver to look in his direction. She froze. Mr. Wallace, on the other hand, grinned broadly.

"Newhurst. What a pleasure meeting you here. My sister will be sorry she was not able to accompany us today. Thank you again for escorting her home from the tea shop on Monday last."

Johnathan's lips pulled down. He'd not wanted to play the gentleman as he'd been on his way to Kendall House, but Miss Wallace's maid had grown ill and far be it from him to leave a lady to walk home unattended.

"And is her maid recovered?"

"Maid?" Mr. Wallace's brow scrunched. "Oh, yes. Jones is quite recovered. She must have eaten something bad."

Johnathan adjusted the reins in his hands. The maid had claimed a headache, not a stomachache. He pressed his lips together to keep from saying something he'd regret. How had he been duped... again?

Glancing at Miss Guthrie, he wondered at his own gullibility. He'd prided himself on his powers of observation but lately life had proved him just as oblivious as the next fellow.

"I am glad she is recovering. And you, Miss Wayland, are you quite recovered from your illness?"

Susannah had sat with her head bowed, her attention completely on her clasped hands, but when he spoke she glanced up in confusion. "I am well, Your Lordship. Whatever gave you the impression I have been ill?"

Your Lordship? With two simple words the honorific placed so much distance between them that it might as well have been a chasm. He wanted to argue, to point out her absences at their gatherings at Kendall House, but then his eyes strayed to how near she sat to Mr. Wallace. Perhaps she'd truly been gone. A vice-like grip clawed at his throat.

Javenia had been conveniently absent as well, which meant that she and her mother might have been playing chaperone to Susannah. Had Susannah made her—he swallowed hard—choice?

No one had hinted at an impending engagement between Mr. Wallace and Susannah, but that did not mean it was not in the process.

"I am s-sorry," he finally choked out. "My information must have been faulty."

"It is nice to see you out enjoying the fresh air, cousin," Miss Guthrie said, slipping her arm through Johnathan's.

He glanced down at her, not sure why she'd taken such liberty. She maintained eye contact with Susannah.

"And you, Miss Guthrie." Susannah's words lacked enthusiasm. Johnathan studied her, noting a pinch at the corners of her eyes and the way she looked everywhere but at him.

He could stand it no longer. If his presence made her so uncomfortable, they would be on their way.

"Well, we m-must not h-hold up the others. Have a l-lovely day."

As their carriage pulled forward, Susannah's shoulders rose and fell as if she'd taken a deep breath. Like a knife stabbing through a painted canvas, her relief tore open his heart and ruined the future he'd painted for them. Perhaps Javenia had been wrong. Thoughts of the letters he'd begun and never found the words to finish came to mind. Letters that he would never finish now. Fighting for Susannah would only bring her pain. Why make them both suffer?

Chapter 23

The blasted clock ticked on the mantel as Lady Stanford awaited an answer Susannah did not want to give. To add to her discomfort, John's wounded face swam in her mind, heaping coals of guilt on her head. He did not deserve the distance she'd been forced to make between them. They were still friends after all, but she'd treated him no better than her maid.

"I will not question you further, Miss Wayland, but it really would help so I might provide a more comfortable environment for our dinner party. If you have set your sights on Mr. Wallace, I will adjust the invitations to make certain my guests"—she cleared her throat— "complement each other."

Susannah read between her words. Lady Stanford did not want to hurt John further. Of that they were of one mind.

"I do find Mr. Wallace's company to be most amiable." There. It was not a lie. She did enjoy spending time with him, but it did not answer Lady Stanford's first question. Did she care for Mr. Wallace?

What Lady Stanford had probably wished to ask was if she'd fallen in love. A lump formed in Susannah's throat. They'd fall in love in time, would they not? How could they not?

He was kind, diverting, and handsome. What more could a woman want?

Sparkling blue eyes lit with adoration filled her mind. The lump in her throat began to burn as she unsuccessfully tried to swallow. Lifting the rose-colored teacup from her lap, she took a big drink. The burn of the hot liquid filled her mouth with pain to rival that of her heart, but she swallowed it anyway.

John had always been her dream. She wanted to talk about paintings, show him her latest piece on the piano, pick cowslip in the churchyard, or watch her brothers crawl all over his lap. The vision filled her mind, but instead of her brothers, she saw little boys and girls with her golden curls and John's blue eyes. Her breath hitched and she fought back the urge to cry. Why was life so cruel?

"Susannah?" Lady Stanford said softly.

She glanced up, surprised at the familiarity.

"Are you well? I had not meant to distress you."

With steady movements she set the cup down, the time allowing her to breathe slowly and collect herself. A brief urge to lay her plight before Lady Stanford overcame her, but she pushed it back. This was her burden to carry. Besides, if she exposed her father's financial situation, the Stanfords might not look on her kindly. It was one thing to be poor and quite another to incur costly debts one could not pay.

"I think I need to lay down. I feel a headache coming on, but as for your dinner, you may invite whomever you choose. I would not want my preference for Mr. Wallace to change your plans in any way." She rose.

Lady Stanford compressed her lips, no doubt holding back further questions. Good. Susannah did not feel up to any more prying—not that she'd ever consider Her Ladyship nosy—only she did not wish to give way to any girlish sentiments when she knew exactly what she must do.

With a dip of her head, she bid Lady Stanford a good afternoon, promising to be ready to attend the theatre promptly at five.

The nap Susannah had hoped to take eluded her. No matter how she positioned herself she could not find comfort, not when her mind remained full of memories of John.

John, speaking of the latest innovations in papermaking with her father.

John, taking tea with Amanda when no one else was available.

John, bringing her flowers—

She bolted upright. The flowers. They'd all been meant for her. How had she not recognized it before?

No wonder he'd been so upset the day he'd come with the single pink rose. Jealousy had reared its ugly head for him much like it had for her when she'd thought about him painting another woman. She did not blame him either, for Mr. Wallace had been very forward that day with his glances, even kissing her hand.

CHAPTER 23

If ever a woman should feel of her own stupidity, she should. How blind could one be?

A soft knock at the door announced the maid's arrival and Susannah had to put away her soul crushing regret. It was too late to change things now.

After dressing in a fine cream gown with a light pink overlay, she donned her gloves and jewelry and joined the others in the vestibule. Lady Stanford had also chosen a cream gown, but hers was accented with several ruffles and tiny blue buds around the collar and hem.

They made their way to the carriage much the same as they'd done for the last several weeks, with Sir Nathaniel escorting his wife and Mr. Kendall lending his arm to Susannah. Inside the conveyance they chatted about the evening's entertainment.

At the theatre they exited much as they'd entered, but Susannah's excitement for the evening dimmed the moment Mr. Wallace took up his place by her side.

"Good evening, Miss Wayland. My, but you look resplendent this evening."

She smiled, a bit jaded by his compliments. John would have loved his use of the word resplendent. For her, it was the same as any other interaction they'd shared. He'd shower her with compliments, relate a few tales from his childhood, then find a time in the evening to sneak a kiss, which she'd only allowed to be on her cheek or hand.

The disappointment she'd witnessed at their last outing when she'd again turned her cheek to him had nearly made her rethink her stance, but she'd held firm. He'd not asked her for her hand and so she'd not give him her kisses.

It was all so... so... boring. And yet two weeks ago, before she'd known that John cared for her, she'd found great excitement in Mr. Wallace's attentions.

Mr. Kendall led the way to the duke's box, having received permission to use it for the evening. Three rows of chairs had been brought in, providing more seats than Susannah thought they would ever need. However, a few minutes before the curtain rose, Miss Harris joined them, accompanied by her mother and—

Susannah clamped her gaping jaw shut as John took up a seat behind her. His straight hair had been swept back with pomade, his dark coat and white cravat was accented with sapphires the color of his eyes. The man was devastatingly handsome. How was she ever to concentrate, knowing he sat within a few feet of her?

Johnathan swallowed hard. A curl rested ever so lightly on Susannah's neck and he could not pull his gaze from it. His fingers twitched with the itch to touch its softness. To wrap it about a single digit and let the others rest on the nape of her neck so he could—

He shook his head, dislodging the heady thought.

When Melior had suggested earlier today that he join them for the evening he'd not expected to be so overcome with desire. He was like a man who'd walked a hundred miles in the desert and now found himself at an oasis. It was not safe, but he could not help but drink in the sight of Susannah, from the top of her curls down to the toes of her satin shoes.

He missed her.

She sat close enough to touch and yet she was so far away. He missed listening to her play on the Kendall House grand piano. He missed her carefree chatter. But he especially missed the way she always knew what he wanted to say, how she made speaking easier with her intuition and her insight, and how she accepted him, flaws and all, as her friend.

Then Mr. Wallace had come along.

An unholy image of him throwing the man right off the balcony played across his mind. He'd never do such a thing, violence being against his very being, but he was not immune to his very humanity. If Mr. Wallace had never entered the picture, he and Susannah might have found happiness.

Mr. Wallace leaned in to say something to Susannah and she stiffened. He tried to pat her hand, but she pulled it away.

Odd. Johnathan had expected her to welcome Mr. Wallace's attention.

At intermission she rose, claiming a need to stretch her legs. Mr. Wallace offered to get her something and she gladly accepted. Javenia cast Johnathan a look, one that encouraged him to follow, but he would not. She obviously did not want to spend time with him. The last few weeks had made it abundantly clear who she favored.

Mr. Wallace and Susannah turned to leave, but Melior's hand stayed her. "Might I ask your assistance, Miss Wayland?"

"Of course."

Lady Stanford's gaze strayed to Mr. Wallace, then pinched. Was that pain?

Johnathan immediately stiffened.

Susannah must have noticed too, for she said, "Could you procure a drink for Lady Stanford, Mr. Wallace? I believe she could also use refreshment."

The man's easy smile faltered, but he answered in the affirmative. When he left the box, all pretense of bravery left Melior's face.

Nate stood. "We need to leave."

"Now?" Susannah asked. Her question, spoken a little too loud, echoed around the box.

"Steady, Miss Wayland, the people below are watching. We must keep up pretenses of calm." Melior rose unsteadily to her feet. "Please make your excuses to Mr. Walla—" She sucked in a breath.

Javenia swept up Melior's other arm, helping Nate hold her upright, but pretending it was the most natural thing. Dropping her voice, she said, "Mother, have our carriage called as well, please."

Lady Upton turned to leave and the door opened. Al, with a broad smile on his face and a pair of drinks in hand, entered, apparently ready to join the party. One look at all the worried faces, and his jovial expression faded to one of concern.

"What is happening?"

"Melior is unwell," Johnathan supplied.

Without a second thought, Al pushed the door back open and summoned a passing waiter. After relieving himself of the drinks and giving orders to have all their teams ready, he turned to escort Lady Upton to the carriages. Only it was not a simple exit as the hallways were teeming with gentlemen and ladies who wished to be noticed.

Javenia turned to him. "John, escort Miss Wayland as close behind us as you possibly can. With Mother and Algenon in front and you both behind, we will merely look like another group looking for refreshment."

He nodded, but when they took up their position, his heart thudded in his chest. A glance at the back of Melior's gown with a small red stain gave him all the information he needed.

Chapter 24

Lady Stanford's face was ashen when Susannah entered the carriage, her breathing labored. At the house, Sir Nathaniel swept his wife into his arms and carried her in.

Susannah followed Mr. Kendall to the front parlor where he dashed off a note to someone.

"Who is that for?" she asked, not having anything to occupy her time as she paced nervously in front of the fireplace.

"My uncle. He will want to know of the current situation."

She nodded and took another turn of the room. "Where are the others?"

"John will be here shortly, but Al accompanied Javenia and her mother to fetch the doctor."

Sir Nathaniel entered, panic in his eyes. "Miss Wayland, my wife insisted I call for you. She says you know some about birthing babies."

Susannah stopped, her eyes widening. It was too soon. "Only what little I remember from when my youngest brother was born, but that was six years ago." How much did they believe her thirteen-year-old mind retained?

"It will have to do." He grabbed her arm and pulled her out of the room.

"Sir Nathaniel, might you go to the housekeeper? She is sure to know more than I do."

"Mrs. Clark never had children."

Susannah wanted to name other servants that might have more experience, but they were already up the stairs and to the Stanfords' bedroom door. Inside, the room was stifling, the fire having been stoked higher than any other in the house. Lady Stanford lay on her side, sweat on her brow and a tear trickling down her cheek.

"I shall go await the doctor." Sir Nathaniel dashed from the room, leaving Susannah bewildered.

Slowly, she approached the bed. "Are you in much pain?"

"It is not the pain that distresses me so much as the knowledge that this baby will not—" her voice broke.

She did not need to finish her sentence. Susannah knew it was far too early for the child's survival. Kneeling down by the bed, she took Lady Stanford's hand.

"I am so sorry, Your Ladyship."

"Melior." She sniffled. "If you are going to share in my grief we might as well drop the formality. Besides, it is still odd to be called by my mother-in-law's title." A small smile broke through the grief on Melior's flawless face.

"And you must call me Susannah."

Melior nodded, then grimaced. Her features became taut, her hand tightening around Susannah's.

Panic filled Susannah's chest as the pain enveloped her friend. Thinking back to Michael's birth she pulled out the only bit of knowledge she had from her memory. "Breathe, Melior. In and out. Slowly."

She didn't know how much time passed in such a manner, but when the doctor finally arrived, she breathed a sigh of relief.

The man crossed to the bed and looked down on Melior, his face impassive. "How long since the pains started?"

"About two hours," Melior said through clenched teeth.

"Any more bleeding?"

More? Susannah's gaze flicked back and forth between the two. Melior had been bleeding and yet had still been up and about.

"Yes." Melior blew out a breath.

"More or less?"

"More."

"A lot more or only a little?"

"A moderate amount."

He clasped his hands behind his back. "Hmm... Well, I am sorry to inform you that this baby will not survive. Best to let your body take care of the process. It will probably take several hours, perhaps even days." He glanced at the drawn curtains while removing a handkerchief from his pocket. His bony fingers clutched the cloth as he first dabbed his forehead and then the tip of his nose. Last, he used the piece to wipe his hands.

Susannah cringed at the sight.

"Call me if the bleeding becomes too intense or you start to feel the need to push." And with that, he walked out, not once even touching Melior.

Susannah wanted to chase after him, to ask what he meant by too intense, to ask why he did not give her anything for the pain, but Melior's hand tightened around hers and she knew her place was here with her friend.

The housekeeper and a maid brought a basin of water, extra linens, and a cloth to wipe Melior's brow. They spoke in whispers as they moved about the room, but eventually were asked to leave, their motion and noise irritating Melior.

Sir Nathaniel stormed in twenty minutes later, his face darkening at his wife's prone form. "Mrs. Clark said the doctor left, and without talking to me. Did he do anything? What did he say?"

Melior listlessly turned her head to look at him. "He said to—" Her voice broke and another tear slipped down her cheek. The frustration on the baronet's face faded and, sitting gingerly on the other side of the bed, he took up her other hand.

"He said what, dearest?"

Melior cast Susannah a look of desperation.

"He said the baby will not survive," she said. "And to let Melior's body handle the process. We are to call him if the bleeding worsens or she feels it's time to push."

Sir Nathaniel's brows slammed down and he cursed under his breath. "And there was no other care given. What about draughts for the pain?"

Susannah shook her head, then returned her focus to Melior as another wave of pain hit her. When the pain passed, she glanced up at Sir Nathaniel. The desperation and fear in his face broke her heart.

Rushed footsteps echoed in the hall before the door flew open and Miss Harris appeared. She took in the room quickly.

"Nate, Al and John are downstairs with Mr. Kendall. You need to be with them."

"But my wife—"

"This is no place for a man, Nate." She crossed the room and took hold of his arm.

Another person stepped in but hung back, her dark gown nearly blending with the shadows. Susannah might have missed her had her halo of golden curls not shone in the dim candlelight.

Miss Harris pulled Sir Nathaniel to the door and pushed him out, shutting it firmly behind him.

"What are you doing here?" Melior hissed, her eyes locked on Lady Braithwaite.

"Mel, hear me out," Miss Harris said. "Livy has had far more experience than any of the rest of us in this. I know you worry about her reputation, but she can help you, unlike that devil of a doctor who has left you to suffer."

Melior's gaze shifted to Miss Harris, her eyes creased and her jaw locked. She began to squeeze Susannah's hand but it was the only outward sign of her pain. Her stoic expression was so different from how she'd handled the rest of her pains, as if she could not let down her guard around the new lady.

Lady Braithwaite stood straight; her hands clasped firmly in front of her. It was the first time Susannah had seen her without a cane of some sort. The lady's face held the same immovable expression that left no room for weakness, and yet in her eyes Susannah saw a flicker of uncertainty. "We were friends once, Lady Stanford. Or at least on cordial terms. Can we not be again?"

Melior did not answer. Was it from pain or an unwillingness to let go of the past?

Lady Braithwaite sighed. "This is a very private thing and I will not invade on your privacy if you do not wish it, but I *can* help you."

"How could you possibly know how to help me?" Melior said through gritted teeth. "For all I know you have come to gather gossip, much like you do with the rest of Society, only to wield it like a sword against me when the fancy suits you."

Susannah glanced between the pair, her brow furrowing. From the little she knew, gossip in Society was directed toward Lady Braithwaite, not coming from her.

The tiny lady stepped forward. "I never share things of a moral nature, Lady Stanford. You should know that by now. You and your husband have done nothing to be ashamed of, therefore there is no gossip to be had. I swear to you nothing that happens here shall pass through my lips."

CHAPTER 24

Melior's hand relaxed, and Susannah breathed a sigh of relief. Her grip had become increasingly painful.

"As to your question." Her Ladyship took another step toward the bed, her gaze wandering to the ceiling. "I have done this before... several times, in fact."

All eyes turned toward Lady Braithwaite, but she steadfastly gazed at the ceiling.

"You mean, you have helped people?" Melior asked.

"Yes. And I have done"—she waved her hand in a sweeping motion to indicate the bed— "this myself."

Something in the way the steadfast woman's voice cracked on the last word brought tears to Susannah's eyes. Lady Braithwaite carried herself as a goddess, far above the world she lived in, but in that moment she seemed almost human in her brokenness.

"But what can you do that the physician has not?" Melior's voice wavered and she let her head fall back on the pillow.

Lady Braithwaite snorted. "First lesson, Lady Stanford. Physicians are not your friend, at least not when it comes to female issues. Might I surmise that he entered, looked at you without even deigning to dirty his hands by touching you, then left with inane advice to 'let nature take its course.'"

Melior gave one sharp nod of her head, her jaw tightening.

"There are ways to speed this process along once it has started. Ones that I stumbled upon during my second and third experience." Lady Braithwaite approached the bed and peered down. "Let me help you."

More tears gathered in Melior's eyes. "I'm scared," she whispered.

Lady Braithwaite sat on the edge of the bed and ran a hand over Melior's sweaty brow, her face losing its reserve and her green eyes lighting with compassion. "I know," she said softly. "I know."

The empathy before her pushed the tears from Susannah's eyes and down her cheeks.

"What do we do first?" Melior finally said.

Lady Braithwaite's genuine smile surprised Susannah. Something as human as a smile seemed beyond her, but when it formed on her face the sight was glorious.

"Javenia, please summon the housekeeper," she ordered, then turned to Susannah. "Miss Wayland, help me get Lady Stanford to her feet."

"You want me to stand?" Panic laced Melior's voice.

The firm tone Lady Braithwaite had taken with the others immediately gentled. "Yes, it is necessary for the process. Please trust me."

Melior searched her face, then finally nodded.

When the housekeeper entered, Lady Braithwaite ordered her to bring the copper tub and fill it with hot water.

"But, my lady—" The housekeeper protested, her gaze sharpening on Melior supported between the two ladies.

"Do not question me, Mrs. Clark. Get it now. Can you not see that your mistress is in pain?"

The plain looking woman nodded, her hand nervously fluttering around her waist. Turning to a maid who had followed, she gave the orders and asked that a footman bring the tub.

When all was in place, Lady Braithwaite ordered everyone out of the room. Susannah stared at her, thinking she'd meant only the servants.

"You too Javenia, Miss Wayland. Lady Stanford needs quiet and calm. Squeamish misses will do her no good."

"Miss Wayland may go, but I am staying," Javenia protested.

Lady Braithwaite narrowed her eyes at her, but it was Melior who spoke.

"Please go, Javenia. I will have Lady Braithwaite call for you if you are needed."

A flash of hurt crossed Miss Harris's face and her shoulders dropped. "If that is what you wish, Mel."

"It is."

Miss Harris answered by linking arms with Susannah and turning to the door.

The last thing Susannah saw before leaving was Melior's dark head of hair, stringy with sweat, leaning on Lady Braithwaite's delicate shoulder as the other woman gently ushered her bent form toward the tub of steaming water.

Her heart ached for the pain and sorrow her friend must be experiencing. It must be agonizing to lose a child. Then fear crept in. Not all women made it through childbirth.

CHAPTER 24

John stood by the window watching the sun peek up over the buildings. They'd all stayed in the drawing room throughout the night, Nate and Eddie alternately pacing, Al making certain they did not run into each other at the center of the room.

For once Al and Javenia made no snide remarks at each other, working as a team to calm everyone while still checking on the situation upstairs.

The duke had arrived shortly after one, but had been so angry with the doctor's negligence that he'd left to track the man down. John had no doubt that the man of medicine would be hard pressed to find work after crossing His Grace.

Susannah had been the only one to say next to nothing all evening. She stared at the fire for the first couple of hours, then fell asleep somewhere near four in the morning, her head lulling against the side of the sofa. No one disturbed her nor asked if she'd like to retire.

John turned to look at her. She seemed so peaceful in light of the chaos that still played around her. He moved closer and noticed goosebumps on her arm. Moving to the chest in the corner, he removed a soft throw.

Gently he laid it over her, careful not to disturb her slumber. The way the morning light played off her lashes drew his attention and he leaned in for a better look. He drew so close that he could feel her breath on his neck. A wild urge to kiss her cheek overcame him and he would have followed through had Eddie not passed behind him on one of his many circuits of the room.

Instead he opted for sitting next to her. Perhaps it was too close for propriety, but no one would object, not with the turmoil they were all going through. To his surprise she readjusted, her head coming to rest on his shoulder. He stiffened.

It was not the first time Susannah had laid her head against him, but it had been years since they'd shared such intimacies. She was no longer a little girl and he was no longer a young man starving for a family.

He glanced around the room. This *was* his family. If his life had been in peril like Melior's, every last person in this room would be there for him too. Javenia had opened the idea to his mind weeks ago, but it had not taken root in his heart until this moment.

The door opened and a very haggard Mrs. Clark stepped in. "My lady is asking for you, Sir Nathaniel."

Nate bolted for the door with no more incentive. They all watched him go, then returned their attention to the housekeeper.

"Is she well?" Eddie asked.

"As well as can be expected."

"And the baby?" Javenia asked.

The housekeeper dropped her gaze to the floor. "She didn't make it, poor mite."

She. John's mind caught on the word. The baby had been a girl.

Al gravitated toward Javenia as the housekeeper left the room.

Javenia's arms were wrapped about her middle, head down, shoulders slumped. She turned away from the rest of the room. As much as she tried to hide it, no one missed the way her shoulders shook.

Al placed a gentle arm about her shoulders and she turned into his coat.

A quiet voice came from right by his ear. "We should leave them alone," Susannah whispered, her head still on his shoulder.

He saw the wisdom in it. Javenia never cried in front of them all, she'd likely be embarrassed to have them witness it. Eddie must have had the same idea, because he, too, quietly left.

Susannah rose and he followed, entering the hall and trailing behind her all the way to the music room. He glanced about, lost on why she'd chosen this place, then her hands gravitated to the keys of the grand piano. Of course. Music was to Susannah as water was to fish, at least it had been back in Maidstone. He'd had little chance to hear her play since coming to London.

A mournful tune filled the room, tugging at memories long since buried with his parents. Death was no respecter of persons, not young or old. It tore at all seams of Society.

When tears trickled down Susannah's cheeks, he moved to sit by her on the bench. He said nothing because there were no words sufficient enough. The song ended. She leaned into him and quietly wept. He placed a tentative arm about her. When she did not object, he pulled her close, hoping to offer a bit of comfort. A quarter hour passed in this way until her tears dried up, but she did not move.

For a moment he wondered if she'd fallen asleep tucked up against him, but when Eddie entered, she straightened. John lamented the loss of her warmth and the way she fit so perfectly in his arms. If only Eddie had chosen someone else to pester with his worries.

CHAPTER 24

Quickly he silenced his uncharitable and selfish thoughts. Eddie was one of his dearest friends. He would mourn with him in his time of grief.

Susannah rose and he cast a glance at her, worried the Susannah he'd always known would disappear again behind the mask she'd worn these last few weeks. The tremulous smile she bestowed upon him soothed his soul. Maybe he still held a little corner of her heart. One could only hope.

Chapter 25

The mourning of a child none of Society knew existed was an odd thing. Were they simply to just carry on? After a week's seclusion with only Sir Nathaniel's friends and Melior's family as visitors, Susannah was surprised to find little compassion from the Society of London. It was as if nothing had happened.

And yet something had, a very important something.

As difficult as it was to see her friend grieve, it had also been a week of relief for her. There were no visits from Mr. Wallace, nor her aunt, nor anyone who had taxed her energy over the last few weeks. Whether because the butler turned them away or because they'd not come, she did not know, nor did she care to find out.

The only other visitor that had been welcome was Lady Braithwaite. She came once a day to check on Melior to make sure she healed properly.

Something had changed in the way the two ladies interacted. No more tension emanated between them, only a deep understanding that could be witnessed in the way they spoke of their shared experience. Susannah had not been allowed to stay for a majority of the discussions, but she'd heard enough to know that the two women had more in common than she'd originally supposed.

There were other enlightening moments she kept to herself. Like the day she'd caught Mr. Kendall standing beyond Melior's private parlor door with a clear view of one of the room's occupants. At first she thought she'd imagined the look of adoration on his face since he'd swept it away quickly and kept walking. But when she'd caught him glancing in on the countess multiple times with much the same expression, she no longer doubted his affection. Mr. Kendall it seemed, had fallen head over heels for Lady Braithwaite.

Even now, as they all took tea with Melior on her first visit outside her own rooms, his gaze still gravitated to the tiny, fierce blonde across from Susannah. She smiled into her teacup, the secret tucked safely in her heart. If Lady Braithwaite could not see it, Susannah would not give him away.

Her gaze shifted, taking in John's profile as he spoke to Sir Nathaniel. How she'd loved being able to be in company with him nearly every day this week. They'd not spoken much, their time being spent in company with others, but he'd sat with her several times at the piano and she had in turn taken time to watch him paint a little miniature of tiny footprints. In those moments, it was almost as if they'd turned back the clocks to a time when things had been simple.

She read him Michael's latest attempt at a letter, he told her about a new invention he'd discovered, and they both had sat quietly for minutes at a time in comfortable silence.

Melior set her teacup down with a rattle, pulling Susannah from her woolgathering. "I am fatigued, please excuse me."

Sir Nathaniel shot to his feet to help his wife, but she waved him away. "Do not trouble yourself."

There was an unusual snip in her words. Sir Nathaniel's brow creased and he looked to Lady Braithwaite after his wife left.

"It is to be expected," she said. "Her body is not the only thing that needs time to heal."

He nodded and began to sit.

She let out a huff. "Go after her, you dolt. She is hurting and will need that broad shoulder of yours to cry on."

He straightened and made for the door, completely amenable to being ordered around. No doubt he wished to be out of company just as much as his wife.

Lady Braithwaite shook her head, a trace of a smile on her pert lips. "If only all men were as easily compelled as that one," she murmured.

Susannah smiled into her teacup.

"Is everything all right?" A male voice asked from the door.

She turned to see a very concerned Mr. Roberts glancing back into the hall.

"I just saw Nate taking the stairs two at a time. When I tried to ask, he waved me off."

Mr. Kendall crossed to him. "Nothing we can help with. What brings you to Kendall House? I thought you were engaged for the afternoon."

Mr. Roberts's gaze swept the room, his shoulders tense. He must have concluded there was no need for concern, for he relaxed. "I have a problem."

"What sort of problem?" Mr. Kendall asked.

"The kind in skirts with a very determined mother."

Lady Braithwaite leaned forward. "Does this lady happen to have the surname of Giles?"

"She does."

A smile, much like Susannah imagined a cat might sport before pouncing on a mouse, bloomed on Lady Braithwaite's face.

"Allow me to be of some assistance." Her Ladyship rose gracefully from her seat and fairly floated across the room. "I am especially adept at dealing with menacing machinations from that quarter." She took gentle hold of each man's arm without slowing and guided them from the room.

A moment's disappointment overcame Susannah at not being privy to their conversation, then her eyes met John's. It was the first time they'd been alone together in weeks.

Her insides quivered, excitement mixing with fear muddling her thoughts. If she'd been given this chance before her aunt had made her threat, she'd have taken the opportunity to move closer in order to explore the newfound knowledge she had. Then again, she'd not realized how much John felt for her until her aunt had opened her eyes.

"Machinations is a marvelous word," he said somewhat to himself as he rose and paced to the window.

She took in his slender athletic form. Once, before her mother passed, she'd seen him in only his shirt sleeves, rolled to expose his sculpted forearms. He'd been teaching her brothers to fence behind the stables and thought no ladies were in view of him. Her mind conjured the way his muscles had bunched and extended with each position he'd demonstrated.

Her mouth had gone dry watching him, but she recognized that it was not only his exterior that had attracted her. He'd been patient and kind with her brothers; teaching them slowly and carefully without derision when they'd accidentally dropped a foil in the mud. The moment had solidified his place in her heart.

He stared out the window a moment, then turned to face her. She waited, knowing he had something he wished to say.

"Are—" He stopped, his gaze straying to the door.

She glanced at the opening. The others had left without shutting it. She focused back on John, who looked to be fighting with himself.

His fisted hands opened, then closed at his sides, then slowly opened again. "Are you attending the Durhams' ball this evening?"

"I am. Miss Harris invited me to attend with her. Lady Upton shall be our chaperone."

He nodded. "And will Mr. W-Wallace be there?"

A weight settled in the pit of her stomach as the threats and restraints her aunt had set in place fell back on her shoulders. "Yes, he will."

She hated the way John's face contorted in pain. Why could they not talk of other things? Painting, music, flowers, anything. Couldn't she avoid speaking of her future for a few more days?

John crossed to the settee. "I must know. Do you c-care for him?"

The weight in her middle rolled over, causing a wave of nausea. She hated the answer she was required to give him, hated her aunt for putting her in this position, hated herself for being so blind.

"He is a fine man. How could I not care for him?"

John's eyes briefly closed. When they opened, a look of resolution replaced the agony she'd witnessed.

She opened her mouth to speak, to try to smooth over her words, but he spoke first.

"I wish you much felicity and prosperity."

He turned to leave.

"We are not promised yet." She blurted out, a small part of her wishing John would fight for her. That he would somehow be able to fix everything her aunt had threatened. In truth, if she did marry John, it might be possible.

Realization struck and horror nearly made her cast up her accounts. What if her father had ruined John's finances as well? Papa had been helping him run his estates for years.

CHAPTER 25

If John learned of her father's situation, and if her father had led him astray when acting privately as his steward, it would crush him. He might never forgive any of them. John could never know of any of this.

She clamped her mouth shut, her heart warring with her head.

John's gaze filled with compassion. "Anyone who knows you cannot help but love you, Susannah. I am certain you will receive the proposal you wish for very soon."

Tears gathered in her eyes. Mr. Wallace was not the man she wished for.

"I need to be going." John gave her an abbreviated bow and crossed to the open door.

Susannah's heart screamed out from within and she could not help calling out, "Is there any reason I should not accept his proposal?"

John turned. The clock ticked on the mantel. One, two, three, four, five times.

"No."

Susannah sighed inwardly. Could this day get any worse?

Her ears were still ringing with John's final word when the butler announced her aunt. Why, after a whole week's peace, had he let the woman in now? She supposed her intention to go out tonight made it seem she was available to visitors, but not this one. Anyone but this one.

Her presence was like pouring salt into an open wound, with angry glares and her impertinent questions.

"Answer me, girl. I know you have more insight into Lord Newhurst's comings and goings than you have admitted."

Susannah clamped her teeth shut, not willing to give away any of John's secrets for this woman to use against him. If her aunt wanted to force John into a marriage she'd have to find her information elsewhere. Susannah was done causing him pain.

Her aunt leaned forward. "Fine, but Lord Newhurst did not arrive this morning for the ride he'd planned with Harriet. If you have done anything to dissuade him from seeking her out..."

The threat hung in the air.

Susannah's eyes smarted. Why did Melior have to still be abed? If she was in the room, or anyone for that matter, her aunt would not stoop to threatening her. *Please someone interrupt us*, she thought.

As if he'd heard her very wish, the butler arrived at the door again and announced a pair of visitors.

"Lady Plum and Mrs. Cline."

Not the visitors she had hoped for, but she'd take any distraction at this moment. The two women, complete opposites in appearance, entered the room and stopped.

"Where is Lady Stanford?" Mrs. Cline asked, her hand coming to rest over her ample bosom.

"Yes, we have come to commiserate with her." Lady Plum's stony face looked anything but compassionate.

More likely they had come for a bit of gossip. Over the weeks she'd been in London it had not been hard to see where the majority of rumors spread from.

Susannah stood. "Might I offer you some tea? You find only me"—she glanced at Aunt Guthrie and swallowed the bile rising in her throat— "and my aunt today."

CHAPTER 25

Aunt Guthrie smiled and gestured to a few open seats as if she were the hostess. "What a lovely thing to meet you both here. Do sit down."

The matrons readily agreed. Tea was brought and conversation passed easily among the older women. Susannah, however, chose to remain silent.

Her mind wandered as the ladies traversed the usual polite topics. In the half hour she'd sat alone after John's removal a letter had come for her. One she was even now hiding on her person, knowing if any of these ladies knew an unmarried man had written to her, their wagging tongues would have no restraint.

That Mr. Wallace had written, implied the intimacy that he believed existed between them—a closeness she now regretted. He'd asked her to meet him on the balcony at nine, only one hour after the ball began. She could think of no other reason for his request but that of a proposal. Her stomach still churned at the thought. Yes, it had been the direction she'd expected their relationship to progress, but she wasn't ready.

Would she ever be ready?

Talk turned to how often her cousin had been seen with a certain lord and her attention snapped back to the conversation. The way her aunt gushed about her happiness and hinted at her expectations nearly drove Susannah to walk out. But the last thing she needed was to have two of London's biggest busybodies spreading rumors of her rude behavior.

The door opened again and she expected to see the butler with another announcement. Instead Mr. Kendall entered with Mr. Roberts close behind, but Lady Braithwaite was nowhere to be seen. Had she left already?

Mr. Kendall and Mr. Roberts greeted the older women in a friendly manner and took up seats about the room, asking after their health. When everyone had answered with positive reports, Aunt Guthrie resumed her earlier topic.

"Lady Plum, did I tell you how kind Lord Newhurst has been to my girls, especially my Harriet? He's taken them driving several times these last few weeks. Is that not good of him?"

Susannah fought to keep a scowl off her face. So her aunt would try to force John to propose by subterfuge, creating such an expectation that he'd be labeled a rake for not offering for Miss Guthrie's hand.

"I had heard rumors," Lady Plum said.

Mr. Roberts leaned back. "Yes, Newhurst extends his kindness to many young ladies. Why, just last week I saw him walking Miss Wallace home from the shops when her maid grew ill."

Aunt Guthrie frowned, but Susannah cast Mr. Roberts a grateful smile. He gave a subtle nod in return. Thank heavens she was not the only one who had seen her aunt's intentions.

Five minutes later, Lady Plum and Mrs. Cline stood. Mr. Kendall and Mr. Roberts did as well and Susannah glanced at the clock to see it had been exactly fifteen minutes since the women had entered.

She rose to her feet and bid them a good day, hoping her aunt would also take her leave, but she made no move to go. When she tried to return to her seat after, however, Mr. Kendall stepped close enough to impede her.

"I am sorry to imposition you, Mrs. Guthrie, but visiting hours are over and Miss Wayland is needed upstairs. You are welcome, however, to stay and finish your tea. Our butler will show you the way out when you are ready."

Susannah fought back a grin. Her aunt was being thrown out in the kindest way possible.

Aunt Guthrie looked first at Mr. Kendall and then at Mr. Roberts. They smiled. She cast Susannah a subtle glare of warning.

"No need," she finally said. "I have had my fill and am ready to leave."

"Very good," Mr. Roberts said. "Might I have the pleasure of escorting you to the door? It is not often I get the opportunity to walk with a lady such as yourself."

Pink touched Aunt Guthrie's cheeks and she preened a bit, but Susannah had read between the words. Mr. Roberts had not given her a compliment. The pleasure was in seeing her leave.

Once they were out of earshot, Mr. Kendall leaned in. "Is something amiss?"

"What do you mean?"

"When John left earlier, he seemed… distressed."

He searched her face, but she could not look at him. Her gaze dropped to her hands, and she tried to cover the sudden urge to cry, or scream… or something. "If he is distressed, he did not share why with me."

Again his brilliant blue eyes studied her.

"Well, then"—he glanced up at the clock— "perhaps John will enlighten us this evening. Al needs me elsewhere this afternoon, but I will see you at the ball, will I not?"

CHAPTER 25

"Indeed. I am to attend with the Harrises."

"Will there be enough room? I could return and escort you and Javenia in the Kendall carriage if you wish."

"No, I am fine. Lord Upton is already taking his other daughters in their chaise so they might leave the landau to accommodate me. No use in giving them more passengers."

"But that leaves one more seat."

Mr. Roberts re-entered the room. "No, it does not."

Mr. Kendall glanced at him.

"I promised Upton I would escort the ladies tonight."

A grin broke out on Mr. Kendall's face. "That should discourage Miss Giles quite nicely if Lady Braithwaite cannot dissuade her from her plight."

"Plight?" Susannah had been so caught up in her own troubles she'd nearly forgotten about Mr. Roberts's distress.

Mr. Roberts clasped his hands behind his back and tipped his chin up, no doubt trying to appear calm and collected. It only succeeded in making him look like a boy who'd been caught stealing biscuits.

"It seems the lady has taken my kindness to mean far more than it ought and has once or twice tried to encourage me into a *situation*."

Mr. Kendall burst out laughing. "What you call kindness is shamelessly flirting. Come now man, you know you shower your compliments too liberally for anyone to imbibe. It is no wonder she is trying to coerce a proposal out of you."

For the first time ever, Susannah witnessed Mr. Roberts blush. She'd thought the man incapable of being embarrassed as he always put up a front of looking completely collected.

"Might I assume," she said slowly, "that the situation you speak of is not one of an upright nature?"

"You would be correct, but I have not encouraged her for nigh unto a fortnight."

Mr. Kendall grinned. "You have not discouraged her either."

Mr. Roberts glared back. "I'll not be rude. No lady deserves unkindness."

"I think all those sisters of yours are going to your head. You have a backbone, man. Use it. Tell your hoard of admirers no for once."

"Easily said by a man who is completely oblivious to the ways of women."

Mr. Kendall's easy smile disappeared and he crossed his arms over his chest. "Are you calling me stupid?"

"No, just naive."

For a moment Susannah thought Mr. Kendall would dispute the claim, but he uncrossed his arms and shrugged.

"You have me there, but at least I know when to put my foot down."

Chapter 26

Johnathan stared at the fire in his bedchamber. That one word had taken all his willpower to say. He wanted to scream his objections, to beg her to reconsider, but he was a gentleman. When a lady had made her choice, it was not his place to interfere.

The fire popped in the grate at the same time something inside him snapped. Sometimes he hated being the gentleman his father had raised him to be. Snatching the nearest thing to him, he hurled it at the wall. The expensive vase shattered against the stonework of the hearth.

He sucked in a breath as tears pooled in his eyes, but he refused to let them fall.

He abruptly stood and rang for his valet. What was the use of staying home to lick his wounds alone? As much as he hated people, he needed a distraction. Might as well dress for the Durhams' ball. He'd not dance, but perhaps a game of cards and a stiff drink would help distract him.

Lost in thought, he allowed his man to choose whatever ensemble suited him best. When the man finished, he looked in the mirror. Hair perfectly styled, cravat tied in a crisp mathematical, and his black jacket in place, he wondered what the night would bring. Most likely Susannah's ultimate happiness, and his lifelong torture.

He scowled at himself. Might as well get on with it then.

Even though the sun had long since set, the streets of London bustled with fancy carriages carrying wealthy passengers to various parties. Dogs barked, and somewhere in the distance, music played. Life carried on, much to Johnathan's dismay.

Did the world have no respect for his pain?

He could have ridden in his own carriage, but the walk had served its purpose and cleared his mind. Inside, people waited in line, each taking their turn to greet the host and hostess. It was strange to think that just one year ago, Nate and Melior had been caught in the cloakroom of this very house. So much had happened since that fateful evening.

So much could yet happen. Would Mr. Wallace choose to offer for Susannah this evening?

After making it through the line, Johnathan entered the crowded ballroom. He had been one of the last guests to arrive, so when the music began a few moments later, he was not surprised. Couples gathered in the center of the room and one person in particular drew his attention.

Susannah, bedecked in the softest of pink gowns, ribbons and pearls gracing every inch of her, stared back at her dance partner. He did not need to look to see who accompanied her. In fact, he refused to.

Why had he come? Did he enjoy having his heart ripped out and danced upon like the chalk outlines on the floor?

He took a glass off the tray of a passing waiter and let his gaze travel to the ceiling. Paintings of cherubs and clouds filled the sections between the gold beams that lined it. How had the painter spent so much time perfecting each image? He slowly sipped the champagne he held. If he could lose himself in questions of art, perhaps he'd be able to make it through this evening.

When he lifted his glass to take another sip, someone bumped into him, spilling the contents of his drink all over his nicely pressed cravat.

"Lord Newhurst, do forgive me," a feminine voice said, as he tried to look down at the damage. He recognized the owner of the voice but did not glance up. He'd been hounded by Miss Guthrie nearly day and night for weeks, and while he'd once thought her interest might be sincere, he no longer wished to connect himself with her. Distance was what he needed. Space from Susannah and all who were connected to her.

Maybe he would go abroad. He'd always wanted to see Africa and the Americas.

"Here, let me help you."

Miss Guthrie wiped at his cravat with her handkerchief.

Johnathan jerked back. "No, thank you. I will attend to it myself." What was the woman thinking, allowing such intimacies, and in a ballroom no less?

He spun on his heel and exited, finding his way to the men's retiring room. Glancing in a mirror, he assessed the damage. Thankfully it had been champagne and not ratafia. While the white cloth had taken on a dingy hue it would not be entirely ruined.

After several dabs with his own linen and a quarter hour's time for it to dry, he deemed the neckcloth recovered enough to hide away in the card room for the rest of the night. He'd not planned on dancing anyway.

In the card room, he took up an unoccupied table near the back, pouring himself a glass of brandy from the decanter that sat in the middle. Conversation swirled around him and men at a nearby card table laughed. Johnathan's eyes drifted down and he pulled out his reading glasses to examine the grains of wood in the tabletop in front of him, letting time slip by in an achingly slow fashion.

Mr. Wallace would be a fool if he did not use tonight to offer for Susannah, especially with the way other gentlemen had begun to take note of her. Who would not notice her? She was everything a man could hope for. Everything *he* had ever hoped for: kind, talented, dedicated to her family, generous and thoughtful with her friends, talented at speaking—something he'd never be—but mostly he'd always just hoped for *her*. He realized he'd always loved Susannah, and probably always would.

"She is a pretty thing," someone said from the card table. "Have you managed to finagle a kiss out of her yet?"

"No, but she won't be able to resist much longer. I'm not one to lavish compliments for nothing."

Johnathan's head came up. He recognized the second man's voice. Glancing over his shoulder he saw three men, two with dark hair and one with blond. He removed his glasses and placed them back in his pocket so he could get a better look.

The blond spoke. "Never has been a lady you couldn't charm, Wallace. You must be losing your touch."

"No, just enjoying the challenge."

Johnathan could only see Mr. Wallace's profile as he turned to one of his friends, but his smile screamed rake of the worst kind. His gut churned. Susannah trusted this man, no doubt even loved him. How could he speak so vulgarly of her in front of other men?

"Besides, it can't be too much longer before Newhurst proposes to her cousin. Once he's out of the way, there will be no more strings attached. Might as well get what I can while I can. Then I'll take the money and a few kisses for the road." Mr. Wallace took a sip from his drink.

"She seems a bit missish. What makes you think you can get anything at all?"

"Because," he drew out, "she's already agreed to meet me *alone* tonight."

Johnathan's jaw clenched and he moved to stand but the first man said something that froze him in his seat.

"I don't envy Newhurst his soon to be mother-in-law. That woman is a harpy of the worst sort. What woman would pay..."

A burst of raucous laughter drowned out the end of his sentence, but the other men nodded in agreement. Johnathan leaned forward to hear them better.

"But she pays well," Wallace said. "Both in money"—he paused and waggled his eyebrows— "and with the goods she's offered up. Curls, curves, and innocence. How could I resist?"

Bawdy laughter filled the room and Johnathan had heard enough. His long legs ate up the distance between himself and the men. For whatever reason they had not noticed him, but he was grateful, for it gave him the element of surprise.

Mr. Wallace caught sight of his angry face and stood moments before Johnathan reached the table. Much shorter than himself, it made it easy to wrap a hand about his throat and push him up against a nearby wall.

Several men skittered out of the way, snatching their drinks and rescuing them from certain demise.

Johnathan lifted upward until Mr. Wallace's feet barely touched the floor. It seemed he was not as opposed to violence as he'd previously thought, especially when a snake had been lying in wait for the woman he loved.

Mr. Wallace grabbed at the hand about his throat, but when Johnathan retracted his fist to punch him, he held up his hands in defense. The fear on his face was a heady reward.

Johnathan stopped. "How dare you," he growled.

The men in the room seemed to collectively lean in waiting to hear why the otherwise silent Lord Newhurst had suddenly become a charging bull.

CHAPTER 26

Lowering his voice in hopes of keeping at least a small amount of information private, he said, "You are nothing more than a sniveling snake. I'll have you know that I never intend to offer for the woman you implied, so any payment you hope to receive will never happen. As for the other young lady, if you so much as say her name or breathe in her direction again"—he leaned to within a few inches of his face— "I *will* ruin you."

Mr. Wallace's brown eyes widened, and he swallowed under Johnathan's grasp.

"Might I suggest," Johnathan continued in a conversational tone, "a trip to your family's county seat. Your younger siblings are probably in desperate need of you this time of year, don't you think?"

It was not a suggestion and Mr. Wallace wisely did not protest. Or perhaps he couldn't, for when he tried to nod his assent, he found his chin trapped above the hand about his throat.

Slowly, Johnathan released him.

Taking a step back, he noted the silence. Gentlemen all over the room stared at him, some with admiration but most with astonishment. He had no doubt they had all considered him a pacifist, his show of force rendering them speechless. Well, let that be a revelation to all, including himself.

He would never allow anyone to mistreat Susannah ever again. Not Mr. Wallace and most definitely not her deceitful aunt.

Mr. Wallace rubbed at his neck, a wary look on his far too handsome face, but he did not move.

"Do not push me, Wallace. It is time for you to leave."

With one sharp nod, he trudged out of the room, Johnathan close behind him.

He'd not risk Mr. Wallace defying his orders. He was not sure when or where Susannah had agreed to meet him, but he'd not let the man stay in the house to hurt her.

"I need to collect my sister," Mr. Wallace muttered when he stopped at the ballroom doors. "You cannot expect me to leave her unprotected."

Johnathan glanced into the open room, searching the crowd for Miss Wallace. Unfortunately the young woman danced in the middle of the ballroom with a gentleman he did not recognize. They would have to wait. No need causing a bigger scene than the one he'd already made in the card room.

"What time had you planned to meet Miss Wayland?" he asked.

No reply came.

He turned, but Mr. Wallace no longer stood next to him. A curse escaped his lips. He should have known he would use any excuse to his advantage. Taking a quick perusal of the hall he realized Wallace had either left or slipped into the crowd while he'd been searching for Miss Wallace.

"There you are," Eddie said, coming up from behind. "I have been searching for you all evening. Where have you—"

"I don't have time for pleasantries, Eddie. Tell me you've seen Susannah."

Eddie's dark eyebrows crept up at his use of Susannah's Christian name. "Not since the last set. Why?"

"Is she in the ballroom?"

"I think she left for the retiring room."

Johnathan shifted directions. Eddie caught up to him. "What is the matter?"

"Find Mr. Wallace and whatever you do, do not let him near Susannah. I'll explain later."

The cloakroom where Nate and Melior had been found last year was the first place he checked. He breathed a sigh of relief when he found it empty. Perhaps she really had only gone to the women's retiring room. He retraced his steps and followed the hall toward the room as far as he was comfortable, waiting where the door was visible.

He shifted from foot to foot, hoping a woman would come out, any woman, so he might ask if Susannah was within. When Miss Martha Guthrie exited with a shorter woman, he cursed his bad luck. Then he remembered her goose description of her mother and all the times she'd rolled her eyes at something Miss Guthrie had said. Taking his chances, he lifted a hand to stop her.

"Miss Martha, might I have a word with you?" He glanced at the other woman wearily. No use having anyone else questioning Susannah's reputation.

Miss Martha tipped her head to the side but complied. "Of course."

They took a few steps away from the other woman, and dropping his voice he asked, "Was Miss Wayland in the retiring room?"

Her head jerked back. "That is not something I should be answering, Lord Newhurst. It is her private business if she is or is not."

"Please, I have reason to believe she may be in some danger and I only need to know if she is safe in the ladies' retiring room."

She glanced back at the room and frowned. "Would this happen to be concerning Mr. Wallace?"

CHAPTER 26

"It is."

"The scoundrel," she muttered. "I do not even know why my mother keeps him around, but he is not good company. Then again, my mother does a lot of questionable things." Her attention returned to him. "To answer your question, she is not, but I am happy to help you find her." Then her eyes widened. "Have you tried the balcony?"

His eyes narrowed. "No, but I will if you believe that is where she is."

"I only say so because I heard Mr. Wallace commenting about the view from that very spot a few nights ago."

He reached out and grasped her hand, relief washing over him. "Thank you, thank you very much." He turned and sped away as quickly as he could without drawing too much attention.

Chapter 27

Susannah pulled her cloak tighter around herself. Thank goodness she'd thought to retrieve it before leaving the warmth of the stuffy ballroom. The cold March air nipped at her nose and made her wonder why she'd even come to this place.

She no longer wanted a proposal from Mr. Wallace, but she was trapped. If John loved her as she knew he did, he'd not offer for anyone else. And if he didn't offer for her cousin, she'd find herself and her family in dire straits. No one would want her, not even John if he thought her immoral and unprincipled.

And what if her father had accrued as many debts for the Newhurst holdings? John would feel betrayed as he ought.

She stared at the star-covered sky. No, she would sacrifice herself for her family's security. Perhaps Mr. Wallace could help her find a way to pay her father's debts.

The squeal of the door drew her attention and she turned to meet her fate.

Light spilled onto the dim balcony, blinding her for a moment as a man stepped out then quickly shut the door behind him. Her heart beat wildly in her chest as fear clawed at her throat. Nothing in her wanted this moment. She reached behind her to steady herself on the stone balustrade.

"Susannah?"

The voice that met her ears made her freeze. "John?" she whispered.

An audible sigh was the only answer that met her ears. Her eyes adjusted and she took in his wonderfully tall form. How had she confused him for

Mr. Wallace? They were nothing alike. The dread that had built in her chest loosened.

"You m-must be freezing out here," he finally said.

"It is a bit cold."

Several seconds of silence beat between them. She should probably hurry him along but she didn't want to.

"Why are you outside?" he asked.

What should she tell him? He needed to leave before Mr. Wallace came, or before they were discovered by someone else. Her aunt had been angry enough knowing she'd seen John on several occasions this last week while Melior healed. She would be livid to know she was in such a compromising situation with him.

Then again, no one was here to witness it. What would one last moment hurt? A tingle of warmth budded in her chest. She'd come early and Mr. Wallace would not arrive for several minutes yet; why not enjoy John's presence?

"Susannah, I—"

The hesitancy in John's voice drew her in and she stepped closer. He, in turn, moved forward as well.

"I need to, that is, I want…"

He wanted? So did she. She wanted to run away with him and pretend that none of the chaos that had enveloped her life had ever existed. If only she'd never come to London. If she'd been happy to stay in Maidstone, maybe eventually they'd have found their way to one another.

"What do you want, John?" she asked softly.

He exhaled. She could not help herself. She reached out to touch his arm, but in the darkness she missed, settling her hand at his waist. He shivered and her hand flexed, feeling the muscles beneath his jacket.

Her other hand came up of its own accord and placed itself on the other side of his waist. Warning bells rang in her head, but she ignored them. This was her chance to have one last moment with him, a sort of goodbye.

"D-do y-y-you know what you are doing t-to me? I-I can h-hardly s-s-speak."

"Then don't," she whispered. They didn't need to talk. If only he'd hold her and give her something to remember for the rest of her life. One moment to cherish and carry with her in the dark days ahead.

"But I—"

CHAPTER 27

She laid a finger over his lips, bravery or perhaps desperation motivating her actions. The soft skin below her fingertip was warm and tempting. She allowed her finger to move the slightest bit, enjoying the feeling a moment longer.

John inhaled and leaned into her touch, his lips pursing and gently kissing the tip of her finger. It was her turn to shudder. What would it be like to kiss those lips?

Silence met her thoughts. No footsteps, no impending doom, only John holding his breath as if waiting for her to act.

The temptation was too much. Her left hand slid up his torso to meet her right hand behind his neck as she raised up on tiptoes. He did not resist, meeting her halfway. His lips were as delicious as she'd once imagined, and she lost herself in the kiss.

The leash that had held John's feelings bound snapped when Susannah pressed her lips to his. There was nothing stopping him. No Mr. Wallace, no deceitful aunt, and not even Susannah herself stopped him. *She* had come to *him*.

All this time he'd thought her heart entangled with Mr. Wallace's, but the moment her hand had settled on his waist he'd known. She would never have allowed such intimacy if she'd not felt something for him. Mr. Wallace himself had admitted that she'd not allowed him to kiss her.

And yet here he was kissing Susannah, holding her close and sharing her warmth. His lips explored each crease of hers, deepening the kiss until he worried he'd suffocate her. He pulled back, but she followed, her lips hungrily searching for his. The little restraint he'd gathered fled and he gave into her kiss, body and soul.

Light burst upon them, and he wondered if they'd stepped into a corner of heaven.

"What in the world?" Someone screeched.

"My goodness," another woman said.

Susannah jerked back, pulling out of his grasp. John opened his eyes to see a plump woman fanning herself.

A tall, slender woman clucked. "My, my Lord Newhurst, but you shall have to marry her now after such a display."

He recognized the voice as Lady Plum, but it was the rotund woman at the front, her eyes shooting daggers at Susannah who worried him most.

"How dare you, Susannah!" She hissed.

Susannah shrank back against the stone edge. "I... I..."

He needed to speak, to claim her as his own right now before all these ladies, to let them know he had every intention of marrying her, but his tongue stuck to the roof of his mouth. He'd ruined her. How could he have been so foolish?

Mrs. Guthrie turned to the other ladies. "I told you she was a hussy. We need not tie Lord Newhurst to such an unprincipled girl. I am ashamed to call her family."

Mrs. Cline's nasally whine filled the air. "Hussy or not, he has ruined her and he must be held accountable."

"But—"

Lady Plum held up a hand. "Mrs. Cline is right. We do not hold for such behavior, and in such a secluded place. Who knows what they were doing

CHAPTER 27

before we came upon them." She glanced pointedly at John out of the corner of her eye.

Heavy footfalls gained volume as a man burst onto the balcony. John's eyes had adjusted enough to recognize Mr. Wallace before Eddie rushed out the doors. Sliding to a stop, he grabbed Mr. Wallace by the sleeve. Then his eyes widened when he took in the scene on the balcony.

Lady Plum with her hands on her hips. Mrs. Cline with her hand still fanning herself, and Mrs. Guthrie glaring at Susannah who cowered behind John.

He let go of Mr. Wallace. "I suppose I can let this cad go since it seems you have things under control."

Al strode onto the balcony at a much more appropriate pace. "Care to share why we need to remove a certain piece of rubbish from the ball, Newhurst?"

Johnathan opened his mouth, but nothing came out. He swallowed hard. Of all the times for his mind to play tricks on his mouth, this had to be the worst. He took a deep breath.

"Not here," was all he could say.

Susannah had been through enough. He needed to get her away from the ball, needed to protect her from the ire Mrs. Guthrie had not ceased to cast her way with her glares. They could figure this out later, then confront the Guthries.

He grabbed Susannah's hand and pulled her past the staring matrons.

Mrs. Guthrie's hand shot out and latched onto her arm. "Leave her with me; I am her closest kin."

Anger bubbled hot and ruthless in his chest. He grabbed the woman's hand and yanked it from Susannah's arm.

"No. And you'd do well to watch yourself, Mrs. Guthrie. I will be meeting with your husband in the morning."

She shrunk back, her eyes widening. Her mouth opened and closed several times, but nothing came out.

John pointed at Mr. Wallace. "I told you to leave town. You dare to disobey a peer?"

Wallace glanced at Mrs. Guthrie and then at Susannah. "N-no," he stammered. "I am leaving." He warily watched Al and Eddie as he passed them, probably expecting them to pounce on him at any moment. Once far enough away, he straightened his jacket and raised his chin. "She's too missish for me anyway."

Al lunged toward him and Mr. Wallace ran away like the coward he was.

"I will make sure he gets all the way out of town," Al called over his shoulder as he followed after.

"Take my horse," Eddie called. Al lifted a hand in acknowledgement. Turning to Johnathan he said, "Do you want me to get the Harrises?"

"Yes, have them meet me at the front of the house."

"We'll expect that announcement by morning, Lord Newhurst," Lady Plum said.

"Consider it announced," he bit out, then led Susannah away.

Chapter 28

Susannah followed without saying a word. Anger radiated off John like steam off boiling water. She'd forced his hand, brought shame to him and his name. If she had only controlled herself. If she'd not been so willing to throw all her inhibitions over the edge of the balcony, for she was certain someone would find them splattered on the ground below.

But, oh, how she'd wanted his kiss. Craved it even.

And what had her selfishness gotten her?

Even if he married her, he'd probably hate her forever for such a disgrace. One thing was certain. It had not taken Aunt Guthrie's meddling to ruin her reputation. She'd done that all on her own.

And what of her family?

Would John save them from debtor's prison when Uncle Guthrie had her father's debts called in? Or would he be so upset to find out he'd trusted his own finances to an irresponsible steward that he'd refuse?

Miss Harris met them at the door, her mother and Mr. Kendall following close behind. "What happened?"

John said nothing as he took his coat from a footman.

Already dressed in her warm outerwear, Susannah found her voice. "Can we talk about it in the carriage?"

Miss Harris took in her disheveled state and her face relaxed into a look of concern. "Of course."

The women's things were fetched, as well as Mr. Kendall's and only then did Miss Harris ask, "Where is Algenon?" Deep grooves formed in her forehead as she glanced back in the direction of the ballroom.

"He had something to attend to," Mr. Kendall said, his hand coming up to cup Miss Harris's elbow and turn her toward the door.

"But he is our escort. How will he get home?"

"He took my horse. Would you mind if I took his place?"

Miss Harris met Mr. Kendall's gaze and some silent communication happened between them, for she nodded and allowed him to escort her out.

Susannah trailed after them, not wanting to cause John more trouble than she already had. When they reached the carriage, Mr. Kendall helped each lady in. Only after she was seated did she see John waiting not far away.

Mr. Kendall stepped away from the conveyance to speak with him in hushed tones. She could not hear their words, but the myriad of emotions that played across Mr. Kendall's face left her in no doubt of his displeasure. Embarrassment washed over her once again.

"Care to share why they are gesticulating so wildly?" Miss Harris asked.

A tear slipped past Susannah's defenses, then another. "I ruined him." Her shoulders began to shake and large sobs racked her body. She tried to hold them in, but shame and remorse overpowered her.

A hand patted her knee. "We can fix this, Miss Wayland. Please take heart."

Kindness from Miss Harris she could understand, but Lady Upton's sweet words were completely unexpected. A new wave of tears struck. No one should be kind to her. She'd brought this upon herself.

The 'we' in Lady Upton's words slowly squirmed its way into her heart. She'd always tried to lighten everyone else's burdens by shouldering her own, but this was one thing she could not carry. Her hand found the older woman's and she squeezed while the tears fell down her cheeks.

Miss Harris switched sides of the carriage and slipped an arm about her shoulders. "Mother's right. We will find a way."

The last of her resolve to stay strong on her own slipped away and she melted into Miss Harris's side, wishing to disappear forever as grief racked her body.

CHAPTER 28

Johnathan stared in the direction the carriage had gone long after it had pulled away from the Durhams' townhouse. An image of Susannah's face, covered in tears as she sobbed, burned in his mind.

He'd stolen her choice. Not that Mr. Wallace had been a choice at all, but Susannah did not know that. When she'd reached for him, he thought she wanted his attentions. Now he wondered if his desire had painted the desperation in their kisses. Maybe he'd simply overcome her good senses in a fit of passion, and now she would suffer for it for the rest of her life.

Even worse, in the time he'd needed to speak, when he could have calmed her fears and confessed his undying love, he'd choked. His disobedient tongue had refused to share the feelings he held so close to his heart. *If* there was a place for him in Susannah's heart, he'd not claimed it. He'd left her in doubt of her own future.

What if her tears were out of fear that he'd not offer for her?

His feet moved with the thought, eating up the distance that now separated him from Susannah.

Of all the days to have chosen to walk, this had to be the worst. Kendall House was a much longer distance from the Durham residence than his own place. It would take him at least a half hour, and all that time Susannah would be living in fear, a fear that he had caused.

He was no better than Mr. Wallace.

His hands curled into fists. Not true. That man would have taken what he wanted and left Susannah to face Society's wrath alone. He wouldn't. He'd voice his feelings for her if it was the last thing he did on God's green earth.

Beads of sweat gathered on his forehead by the time he reached Kendall House, even though his breath clouded in the cold night air. Taking the steps two at a time, he was startled when the door opened before he knocked, the butler ushering him in and to the study.

"What the devil happened tonight?" Nate asked before Johnathan was even fully in the room. "I trusted you, John."

"Where is Susannah?"

Nate crossed his arms, his wide stance appearing as immovable as a wall. "With Javenia and Melior... and Lady Upton," he added as an afterthought. "But by the state she was in when she entered the house, I should call you out. I could not get one word out of her. Eddie was no help either, only dashing in, saying I should talk to you, and something about needing to borrow my horse."

Good, then Eddie had already gone to do his bidding. It was late, but hopefully early enough to deliver the message and get a response.

"I need answers, John."

"Susannah and I were caught together... alone... on the balcony tonight." He cleared his throat. "I-in an"—he swallowed—"intimate embrace."

Nate's arms dropped to his side and his face went slack, then without warning he laughed. Not a short burst, but a long guffaw. "You are joking."

"No, I am quite serious."

"That's not what I meant. All this time we have been trying to gently nudge you toward Susannah and all it took was a few moments alone on a balcony."

Johnathan stomped toward his friend. "This is no laughing matter, Nate. I ruined Susannah's reputation this evening. Can you not understand the gravity of the situation?"

Nate sobered. "Of all of us, you know I understand better than anyone what a marriage begun on a ruined reputation looks like. But at least for you, the lady returns your feelings."

Johnathan stopped, rocking back on his heels. "What did you say?"

"Susannah loves you. Melior and I have suspected it since long before we came to London. We'd hoped that by offering her a season, the competition would compel you to find your voice and speak up."

"That was cruel, Nate."

Confusion crossed over his friend's face. "How so? It helped, did it not?"

"At what expense? Do you know that her aunt paid to have Mr. Wallace pretend interest in her in order to keep her away from me? Or that Mr. Wallace intended to use Susannah for his own purposes, then take the money and leave her with heartache? If you'd not brought her to London, none of this would have happened. She'd still be safely tucked away in Kent in a loving home with a family who adores her, instead of here with that despicable woman who claims a kinship with her."

Nate crossed to the seat at the desk and melted into it. Staring vacantly at the far wall he said, "I had no idea."

"Neither did I until tonight. And as for me, I am a grown man. I no longer need my friends to speak for me or fight my battles. I am grateful to you, Eddie, and Al for standing by me and defending me through my Harrow days, but I'm old enough to speak for myself."

Nate lowered his head into his hands, allowing silence to envelop the room. The only sound was that of the tick of the longcase clock.

Time ticked by slowly as Johnathan's frustration cooled. Melior and Nate had meant well. There was only love in their desire to help him and Susannah find happiness. His heart softened. Crossing to the desk, he laid a hand on Nate's shoulder.

Nate lifted his head. Moisture shimmered in his eyes, but he blinked it away quickly. "Did we make this trip for nothing? Endanger my wife and lose my daughter for nothing?"

Johnathan's hand tightened on Nate's shoulder. How could he have forgotten their recent heartache? They had sacrificed time, money, and even Melior's health in an effort to help him find happiness. While misguided, it was a true sign of their loyal friendship.

And what had he done in return? Laid a heavy accusation at Nate's door, one he held little blame for. No, blame for Susannah's situation lay squarely on her aunt, cousin, and Mr. Wallace.

Memories of Miss Wallace showing up at inconvenient times led him to wonder who else had been involved in the scheme.

Nate sniffed.

"Some good might still come out of this," Johnathan finally said. "As the vicar back home might say, 'God in his infinite mercy has brought goodness out of the dark.' As much as I am loath to admit it, I have found more courage these last few weeks than I'd previously exercised."

Nate picked up his letter opener and fiddled with it. "I suppose that is a comfort," he said rather flatly.

"It is a good thing Mr. Wallace is a pompous idiot prone to boasting."

That pulled a chuckle out of his friend. "There is a story behind that."

"Indeed. The man could not help but brag to his friends in the card room. Thank God I heard it before anything unrepairable happened to Susannah. And thanks to his loose tongue, I have evidence that can be held against Mrs. Guthrie, should she try to make more trouble for Susannah—something I suspect she has been doing for several weeks now."

Nate sat up straight, his gaze alert. "How so?"

Johnathan took up the seat across the desk and crossed his ankle over his knee. "There have been too many instances where either Miss Guthrie or Miss Wallace have crossed my path and wheedled out invitations. It has been positively uncanny. And then Susannah suddenly withdrew from me after the ball at Almack's. Why? It made no sense until tonight."

"You think her aunt has threatened her?"

"I do."

Nate's nostrils flared. "And under my roof, for I know the woman came for a visit this very day. Why did Miss Wayland not tell us? Did she really think we'd leave her to such mistreatment?"

Johnathan crossed his arms. "In all the time you have been acquainted with Miss Wayland, have you ever known her to complain or make requests for her own comfort?"

A shake of the head answered his question.

"Neither have I. Even after her mother died, she consistently thought of others, sacrificed for her father and siblings even at the expense of her own comfort. I suspect that independence runs far deeper than any of us realized and it seems her aunt capitalized on it. But I aim to see her threats stop. Eddie has delivered a message to Mr. Guthrie to meet me in the morning or face formal charges against him."

Nate leaned over the desk. "On what? Do you think he has been a party to his wife's dealings? Even then, how could you prove such a thing and what crime could you possibly charge him with?"

"Nothing. But I am banking on the fact that he is a man who conducts his fair share of business. Hopefully his conscience will convict him, if nothing else. I only need to warn the man to keep his wife and daughter in check."

"And what about Miss Wayland? What are your plans where she is concerned?"

"I plan on marrying her... as soon as time permits."

A slow smile spread across Nate's face. "Good. It is about time you both came to an understanding."

"About that." Johnathan fiddled with the ring on his finger, tracing the seal it carried. "H-how do you know Susannah loves me?"

"No one who has seen you two together could ever doubt it. In the days before our loss, she'd become quiet and reserved. Then afterward, when we stayed at home and you came frequently, she lightened. There was relief in her expression and she returned to her easy, chatty nature. The only explanation for the change was you."

Johnathan stopped fidgeting and glanced up at his friend.

CHAPTER 28

"You bring her comfort, John. And that, my friend, is a treasure to have in a marriage. Take heart, for you are about to embark upon the greatest experience of your life, and there is no other woman better suited for you than Miss Wayland."

He nodded, too choked up to reply. All these years he'd wondered, second guessed his own eyes, and battled his tongue for control. In a few reassuring words, his friend had lightened his load considerably.

If Susannah loved him, she could not possibly regret the incredible experience they'd shared. She'd *meant* every kiss and every caress. After a few deep breaths he asked, "Will you see if she will come down and speak with me?"

"She cannot," Melior said softly from the doorway.

Johnathan jerked to the side, surprised by her silent arrival, but he should not have been. He'd been the one who had forgotten to close the door.

She stepped in. "Poor thing cried herself to sleep. I think it would be best to leave and come back in the morning. Or, if you'd rather, we can make up a room for you? I am sure your valet could bring over clothes in the morning."

He weighed the options in his mind. Mr. Guthrie had been instructed to go to his residence, but perhaps a servant could be sent early enough to redirect him here. It would be nice not to embark on another long walk.

"A room would be appreciated. Thank you."

Chapter 29

Somewhere in the house, a clock chimed midnight. Johnathan hoped Susannah was sleeping well, for he'd yet to settle his mind enough to rest. Neither Al nor Eddie had returned, but Javenia and her mother had left over an hour before with a promise to visit in the morning.

The way she had placed a hand on his arm and promised him all would be well should have comforted him, but there was sadness behind her gaze. Where had it stemmed from? Had Susannah said something that led Javenia to pity him? Had Nate been wrong?

He paced in front of the dying fire of the sitting room. It was not good for him to be left with his own thoughts. Without someone to reassure him he'd convince himself it was all a lie. That Susannah didn't love him. And if his fears collided with his overpowering love for her, he'd not be able to voice all the beautiful thoughts inside his head. Ones filled with hope for the future and undying love for the girl who had grown into an extraordinary woman.

The front door opened and male voices filtered in from the hall. Johnathan moved to intercept them.

"John," Eddie said in surprise. "I'd not expected to see you here. I wish I'd known or I would not have roused a messenger to take the note I sent round to Newhurst House."

Johnathan's gaze moved to a rumpled looking Al. His appearance gave far more answers to the unasked questions between them than anything else. That Al had allowed himself to become anything less than completely presentable meant he'd had a rough time of chasing Mr. Wallace out of the city.

"Is he gone?"

Al nodded. "Thanks to a little help from a certain lady, I doubt he'll be back."

"Lady?" John asked.

"Yes." Al motioned for them to follow him back into the sitting room Johnathan had just exited. "Javenia always says when you need information on unsavory characters, consult with Lady Braithwaite, who I had the unprecedented luck of meeting with while I waited for Mr. Wallace to pack his things. It seems she hears and knows most everything that goes on. She arrived at his door escorting Miss Wallace, whom he'd left to her own devices at the ball. Needless to say, their father was livid at his son's oversight."

"I knew the search for his sister was a ruse." Johnathan took a seat on the plush blue settee. "So not only is he a cad, but a dissolute brother. I am not surprised."

Eddie, who had taken up one of the embroidered chairs, spoke up. "I am. For my part, I'm aghast at all that has transpired. He seemed so sincere." He turned to Al. "What time did you say Lady Braithwaite arrived with Miss Wallace?"

"I did not note the hour, but probably right before eleven."

"Interesting. She must have made good time, for I saw her carriage on Margaret Street on my way to the Guthries. That's in the complete opposite direction from the Wallaces. How could she be there, and yet know of Miss Wallace's situation?"

Al straightened. "To tell the truth, I do not know how Lady Braithwaite came to know. Perhaps she came upon the lady walking home. But leaving his sister is not all the sins I have to lay at Mr. Wallace's door. You should have seen the man's face when Lady Braithwaite came in and pulled a jade comb from her hair. Poor man went whiter than a sheet. I'm not sure of the significance but he did not put up a single protest after that."

"Was not that the comb he claimed to have purchased for his sister?" Johnathan asked.

Al shrugged.

Gripping the arms of his chair, he asked, "Was it carved in the shape of lotus flowers?"

"I believe it was."

"That is the very comb he showed us on Bond Street, proudly declaring his intention to give it to his sister."

CHAPTER 29

Eddie leaned forward. "Are you in earnest?" Then he flopped back. "What a lout. This man gets filthier the more I learn about him." Then his face froze. "You do not think Lady Braithwaite and Mr. Wallace..."

Al chuckled. "Not likely. That lady is more likely to fight a duel with the scoundrel than enter an understanding with him. No, I suspect it came from some mistress or another. But there is more."

Johnathan and Eddie waited for Al to continue, the crackle of the fire punctuating their interest.

"It seems last season Mr. Wallace had to leave for nearly the same reason he now faces. Apparently he'd been keeping company with Lord Ansley's cousin, a Miss West, who had a rather significant dowry. When Ansley learned of Mr. Wallace's dissolute manners, as well as a scheme for the couple to elope to Scotland, he put an end to the matter, paying Mr. Wallace a hundred pounds to keep silent and leave London. Ever since, our Mr. Wallace has found a way to make quite a tidy sum. It seems Ansley is not the only one who will pay for him to disappear."

"Or in the case of Mrs. Guthrie," Johnathan said, "To appear where he was not wanted."

"Exactly," Al said.

"So how do we keep him from reappearing?"

"We don't." Al grinned. "When his father learned of his dealings, he swore to ship him off to India. With the elder Mr. Wallace's place in the House of Commons, he cannot have any scandal connected to his name. Either Mr. Wallace goes to India as his father directs or risk losing his meager inheritance as a second son."

"Meager?" Eddie glanced at Johnathan, then back at Al. "He'd led Susannah to believe he had substantial holdings separate from his father's estate."

"It seems there were many things he led everyone to believe," Johnathan muttered. "At least he is gone. Did you find out any more information about his agreement with Mrs. Guthrie?"

Al shook his head. "No more than you probably already know. He was promised a large sum—a number he refused to reveal—to keep Susannah out of the way until you were married to Mrs. Guthrie's oldest daughter."

"And was Mr. Guthrie involved?"

"He only mentioned the mother."

Silence punctuated the statement. Johnathan rubbed the back of his neck, trying to put the pieces together. He could understand Mrs. Guthrie wanting to raise her daughter to a title, but why not see her niece happily married and then use the connection to grant both her daughters more opportunities?

After several minutes, Al yawned. "Well, my friends, thank you for giving me a most diverting way of avoiding Miss Giles tonight."

Eddie chuckled. "Thank John. He's the one who not only foiled a plot but created a scandal to add a little excitement to our evening."

Johnathan sighed. "Do not remind me." Clasping his hands together, he stared at the fire.

Eddie sobered. "Have you and Susannah come to an agreement?"

He shook his head. "Melior said she cried herself to sleep before I had a chance to talk to her."

The fire crackled and Al stepped back from the grate, a frown creasing his face. "Maybe sleep will make the conversation a little easier."

"F-for whom?" Johnathan stood and began to pace. "I can talk to you both about paintings, and words, and inventions, even diabolical plots, without much trouble. But place a lady before me and mix in my f-f-feelings…"

"And your words shut down," Eddie filled in.

A curt nod was all Johnathan could manage.

"Then write it."

Johnathan stared at him.

"He's right," Al agreed. "Your issue does not extend to your fingers, only your mouth. Write out your feelings. Tell her how long you have admired her, adored her, even loved her. You could even read it, if you find you have the clarity to do so."

The idea took root in his head. It was so simple and brilliant. Why had he not thought of it himself?

Eddie leaned forward, lacing his fingers together. "I once said I'd be your messenger, John. I could do so now."

"No. I want to give it to her myself."

"Probably the best option." Al's eyes twinkled in the firelight. "Then you will be present to receive her many thanks."

Johnathan swiped a decorative pillow from the edge of the settee and lobbed it at Al.

CHAPTER 29

He caught it without trouble and laughed. "What? You cannot claim it did not at least cross your mind."

The reminder of Susannah's arms wrapped around him, her kisses filling his whole soul brought warmth to every inch of him. It would be a lie to say he did not want to be near her when she read his words, but there was more to it. He wanted to stand before her when he offered everything he was or would ever be, to be hers for the rest of their days.

"I think," Johnathan said slowly, "the two of you need to leave me alone and get some sleep. I have a declaration to write."

Chapter 30

Susannah woke with a start, blinking into the dark room. Confusion enveloped her. What time was it? Why had she woken so early? She probed around her eyes. Why were they so puffy?

Then it all came rushing back to her.

The ball. Those glorious minutes on the balcony. Then John's anger.

Would he leave her to suffer her fate alone? She would not blame him if he did. After she'd practically forced herself on him, why should he carry the consequences? But, oh, how wonderful it had been when she'd not only seen but felt his love in his kisses. Mr. Wallace and all her fears for the future had been forgotten for that one moment, that brief space of time.

Time. It always came back to that measurement of life.

Over the last year she'd learned just how much could change in a single moment. Losing her mother, gaining a season, realizing John's love, and then losing it had all been brief glimmers in the grand scheme of life. But they had changed everything.

She sat up in bed. It was time to face each of those moments.

Last night Miss Harris had stroked her hair and promised her that all would be well and Melior had tucked her in as she'd blubbered out all her troubles. She'd laid every burden down at their feet and Lady Upton had listened from a nearby chair.

Her fear of disappointing her family and adding to their financial burden, her aunt's threats and the worry that she'd carry through with them, even her concern that John would never be able to forgive her for forcing him into a marriage—that if he married her, he'd grow to hate her so much that he'd banish her to one of his other estates.

The last thing she remembered was Melior promising that she'd feel better in the morning, to forget her troubles, and rest. Her soothing alto voice had lulled her to sleep.

If only she could feel that peace now.

Half an hour later, a little maid crept in to stir her fire and Susannah sat up. The maid let out a squeak of surprise.

"Sorry, miss. I'm only here to fix your fire. I'd not meant to wake you."

"It's not your fault. I was already awake."

"I see. Can I get you anything?"

"I know it is early, but is there someone who might be available to help me dress?"

"Yes, miss. Lady Stanford's maid is already up and breaking her fast. I'll send her up."

"Thank you."

True to her word, the maid finished the fire and had Baylor up to help Susannah in less than ten minutes. However, after dressing in her morning gown and sitting for her hair to be styled, Susannah wondered what to do next. It was not even seven in the morning.

Baylor straightened the dressing table in front of her.

"Is it too early for a breakfast tray?"

"No, miss. What would you like?"

"Some toast and an egg would be nice."

"Coffee or tea?"

"Tea, please."

At a quarter past seven, the tray arrived and Susannah nibbled on toast as her mind continued to spit out scenarios of doom. Eventually she gave up on breakfast, her stomach churning too much to swallow another bite.

A light knock sounded on her door and she answered it.

"A visitor to see you, miss," the housekeeper said.

Susannah glanced at the clock. Eight o'clock. "At this hour?"

"Yes. Do you want me to send her away?"

Fear crept up her spine. Had her aunt come to fulfill her promises? She could not ruin her much more than she already was, so only her father's debts hung in the balance.

CHAPTER 30

"W-who is it?"

"Miss Martha Guthrie."

Miss Martha? "Anyone else?"

"No, miss."

That her cousin had come to see her this early in the morning intrigued her. "I will come."

Carefully she shut the door behind her and followed the housekeeper to a small morning room. Inside she found Martha at a window, wringing her hands together. The young woman's head whipped around the moment she entered.

"Miss Martha, what a surprise," Susannah said.

She smiled at the greeting. "You can drop the miss, we are cousins after all."

Susannah nodded and gestured to the sofa. "It is a bit early for tea, but I can ring for some if you wish."

"No, thank you. I came this morning on a matter of urgent business. Is it true that you are to marry Lord Newhurst?"

"I... that is..." He had not declared himself to her, but he had told the ladies last evening to consider the matter settled. Then a second thought struck. Had Martha been sent to ruin her life further? She'd never seemed a party to her mother's schemes before.

"If so, I am happy for you."

Susannah relaxed.

"I never did like how my mother treated you or any of your family. Do you remember when we were eight and you came to stay with us for a time?"

An easy smile bloomed on her face. "I do. It was my last visit."

Martha leaned forward. "Why was it your last visit?"

"Because your mother told us it would be better if our mother died."

The horror that crossed Martha's face had been exactly how Susannah had felt as a girl of eight.

"That's terrible. I knew my mother disliked yours, but to wish her dead? To even tell her children such a thing."

"But why did she hate my mother? I know my parents' marriage was not conventional, but is connection really the only reason she refused to mend the break?"

Martha's eyes widened. "You do not know?"

She shook her head.

"When your father declared his intention to marry your mother, my mother was on her sixth season. She was desperate to marry a man of means, as they had grown up comfortable but not with the affluence some of her friends had. Lord Upton had begun to court her that season and she was certain she'd finally get the title she'd always desired. But within days of your father's announcement, Lord Upton stopped coming to visit and by the end of the season he had taken a wife. She believes he ceased his attentions because of your mother. Since then, she has not been able to stand the sight of your mother or the Harris family."

That explained her firm dislike of Javenia. "But your mother married nearly a year before my parents."

"Yes, because your father wanted to be certain he had the means to support a family without the use of your mother's large dowry. It was quite romantic, if you ask me. I wish some man would go to such lengths to show he loved me and not my money."

Susannah blinked at her. "Money?"

"Yes, your grandfather placed a large dowry in hopes of luring a gentleman into an arrangement. My mother claims he was disappointed when he only got your father, a country gentleman, and not a knight or a baronet. Either way, she thought the action quite vulgar."

"To place a large dowry on my mother? But it is a standard practice in the gentry."

"I never said it made sense." Martha smiled. "Most of my mother's anger makes little sense. Even so, it is how she views life and why it was so important to her to ruin yours."

"Mine? What have I done to her?"

"Nothing. I believe she only wanted to get revenge on you because of your mother. You look like her, you know. You are both very pretty."

Susannah cupped the curls near her face. "Thank you."

Silence settled between them; the tick of a clock the only sound in the room.

"I am confused. If my mother had a great dowry, what happened to it? Aunt Guthrie insisted my father had accrued enough debt to send him to prison. Even now, she is probably going to your father to have my father's debts called in."

Martha let out a short laugh. "It will not work."

"What do you mean?"

CHAPTER 30

"I came this morning because I overheard my father arguing with my mother last night. We had several late evening visitors that were quite enlightening." She smirked. "As well as a threatening note."

"From whom?"

"Your Lord Newhurst."

Her Lord Newhurst? She liked the sound of it, but John was more to her liking. Her John.

"From what I could gather, my father is to meet with him this morning. It seems my mother paid to have Mr. Wallace 'entertain you' until Harriet convinced Lord Newhurst to marry her—among other things. Lady Braithwaite divulged other information, but I'd rather not speak of it. Because of it, my father is removing us to the country and refuses to give Harriet another season. It seems my sister knew what was afoot this whole time."

Susannah's heart tripped over itself, the information not quite sinking in. The realization that her family was free from Aunt Guthrie's threats finally struck and she melted into her seat. Tears formed in her eyes, but she did not let them fall.

"Thank you. You have relieved my mind of a great burden." Then Martha's words caught up with her. "Paid Mr. Wallace?"

She nodded. "It must have been significant too, for my father blustered about how she could promise so much. I could not hear the amount through the door, but I would say it was probably in the thousands."

Susannah's mouth fell open. Her aunt must have harbored an inordinate amount of hatred to go to such lengths for revenge.

And Mr. Wallace... The compliments, the blatant stares, all a lie.

"Did Mr. Wallace ever intend to offer marriage?" she blurted out before she could think better of it.

"No." Martha clasped her hands in her lap. "His intentions were not at all honorable. Harriet even complained about how he'd ruined everything by not compromising you before Lord Newhurst did."

Susannah gasped.

"Sorry, I probably should not have repeated her words. Harriet and my mother are of like minds; she takes after her in more ways than one."

"And you, do you agree?"

"No. I am my father's daughter, as much as my mother detests it. She never wanted to marry my father anyway, but he was the quickest way to cover her embarrassment after Lord Upton removed his attentions." Martha untangled her fingers and gazed at the window. With a sigh, she said, "Some days I wish he was my only parent because now I am guilty by association."

Susannah leaned forward and placed a hand over Martha's. "It is not your fault. None of this is your fault."

"Society will not see it that way if any of this ever gets out."

"Then we shall see that it does not. I am certain my uncle has enough sway that he can keep things quiet."

Martha smiled. "Perhaps. Do you know, last evening was the first time I have ever heard him stand up to my mother? It was a thing to see... er... hear." She dropped her head. "You must think me an awful person for eavesdropping."

Susannah laughed. "Not at all. For once, I am grateful for a little bit of underhandedness."

Martha covered Susannah's hand where it still lay over hers.

"We were good friends as little girls. Can we not be again?"

Susannah placed her other hand over Martha's so their hands intertwined. "I would like that very much."

Chapter 31

Johnathan lifted his sleepy head and glanced around the paneled room lined with books. Why was he in the study?

Running a hand through his rumpled blond hair, he stared down at the desk. Crumpled papers littered its surface, but in the middle under his spectacles was one nicely folded square.

He'd only meant to lay his head on the desk for a moment after he'd finished, but apparently he'd fallen asleep.

Gathering the remains of his late-night writing into a pile, he vowed to replace all the paper he'd wasted, or perhaps he could repurpose these pieces. He'd seen paper made often enough in Maidstone. It could not be too difficult to soak and re-screen old pieces.

The door opened and Johnathan straightened.

"You look terrible," Nate said as he took in his appearance. "Did you stay up all night? You are still in your evening wear."

"Not all night. I had a letter to write."

"And you could not wait until morning?"

"No." Not wanting to answer any more questions, he quickly tucked the finished square into his jacket pocket. Fishing out a coin, he set it on the desk. "For all the paper."

Nate grabbed up one of the crumpled pieces that had fallen to the floor. "My dearest Susannah—"

Johnathan yanked it out of his hands before he could read another word, but not before a huge grin spread across Nate's face.

"Best clean up before you deliver the finished product." He slapped Johnathan on the back, then sniffed. "Make sure to wash well."

With a roll of his eyes, Johnathan left to the sound of Nate's soft chuckles.

A half hour later, washed, shaved, and redressed, he returned downstairs. He was too nervous to eat breakfast and he had no idea where to find Susannah, but he could wait no longer.

Someone cleared their throat and he glanced up.

Mr. Guthrie stood alone in the entryway. "I believe the footman went in search of you."

"Ah, yes." He stared at the pudgy man, his mind going to his letter. He didn't want to have an interview with Mr. Guthrie just now, but it would probably be best to do so before speaking with Susannah. He needed to clear the way so there would be no more obstacles.

"This way." He gestured down the hall to the study he'd left only a half hour ago. They passed the footman on their way and he nodded in acknowledgement, releasing the man to see to other duties.

When they entered, Johnathan found Nate, Al, and Eddie seated near the fire. He stopped. Perhaps another room would be better for this discussion.

"Come in," Eddie said. "We have been waiting for you, Mr. Guthrie."

The man visibly swallowed. It was one thing to have to face a viscount, but quite another to also face a baronet, a future baron, and the nephew of a duke. Johnathan noted the extra chairs that had been brought in. It seemed his friends were here to provide added incentive for the man to hold his ground against his wife.

Once they were all seated, Johnathan shared what he knew.

Mr. Guthrie listened quietly, not contesting or denying anything he said.

"Is this true, Mr. Guthrie? Did your wife pay Mr. Wallace to pretend interest in Miss Wayland?"

"Yes." He shook his balding head. "It is all true. And sorry I am to admit it. I first received knowledge of it from Lady Braithwaite who arrived at my house, a sniffling Miss Wallace with her. The young lady told of her brother's arrangement, and I immediately left to collect my wife from the Durhams' ball." He cast a glance at all of them. "Please know that I had nothing to do with this. My wife acted of her own volition and I do not condone her behavior."

"And what was Miss Wallace's part in all of this?" Johnathan had to know. If the plan had been to point him in Miss Guthrie's direction, why have another contender?

Wrinkles formed on Mr. Guthrie's forehead. "As I said, she revealed her brother's dealings."

But not her own. Had she acted alone hoping that by exposing Miss Guthrie she'd be able to somehow catch him for herself? If so, she'd be sorely disappointed. With the way swept clear, there was nothing holding him back from Susannah.

Except Susannah herself.

"How did your wife control your niece?"

"I beg your pardon?"

"Miss Wayland and I have been friends for quite some time, then suddenly she became cold and distant. What threat did your wife use to keep her away?"

The man's bushy eyebrows furrowed. "I know nothing of that. Only my wife's dealings with Mr. Wallace."

A light tap at the door announced the butler before he opened it. "Excuse me, but Lady Stanford has sent me to fetch Sir Nathaniel." Then taking in the room's occupants, the man said, "Mr. Guthrie. I had not realized you had attended your daughter here. Would you like her to await you in the vestibule?"

"My daughter?"

"Yes, she is nearly finished speaking with Miss Wayland and asked that her things be fetched."

Johnathan stood, anxiety clawing at his throat. If Miss Guthrie had come to cause any more harm to Susannah... He marched out of the room, Mr. Guthrie struggling to follow.

"Where are they?" he asked the butler who scurried to keep up.

"In the sitting room. I am sorry, my lord, I had not thought it—"

"Never mind your apologies."

Johnathan turned briskly into the indicated room and pulled up short. Susannah sat on the settee, smiling. Across from her was not Miss Guthrie, but Miss Martha.

"Martha?" Mr. Guthrie asked from behind him.

The woman's blue eyes widened. "Father?" She pulled a timepiece from her pocket and gasped. "I have been here far longer than I intended."

"Do not trouble yourself," Susannah said. "I have enjoyed our visit. It has been very enlightening."

Miss Martha glanced at her father. "Even so, I have been saying I am on my way out for quite some time. I should hold through with my promise."

Both women rose and briefly embraced. The sight caught Johnathan so off guard that no words would form. No malice remained in the air, something he'd not expected to find when he'd charged down the hall.

Miss Martha crossed to her father and Johnathan moved close to Susannah.

"Are you alright?" he whispered.

Her warm brown eyes sparkled in the morning light and she nodded.

Mr. Guthrie cleared his throat. "Lord Newhurst, I want you to know that no more ill shall come your way, at least not from the women in my household. As for myself, please accept my apologies and well wishes for your future."

Then the man unexpectedly turned to Susannah. "I am sorry, my dear, for the harm my wife has caused you. I am not as aware as I should be of her comings and goings, but I promise to be more watchful."

Susannah cast him a gentle smile. "Thank you, Uncle Guthrie." She shifted from one foot to the other and Johnathan felt the awkwardness of the moment. He'd expected to have to threaten the man and perhaps demand an apology, but Mr. Guthrie had offered his help without reservation.

"I do have one question," Susannah finally said.

"What is that?"

"How much are my father's debts?"

"Your father's debts?" Johnathan echoed Mr. Guthrie's question.

The man looked to him in confusion and then as if the sun had risen in his mind, his eyes widened. Johnathan's realization took a moment longer, but when it struck a slow smile formed on his face.

Mr. Guthrie spoke first. "Am I to assume that my wife indicated your father had many debts?"

Susannah nodded. "She threatened to have them called up."

Johnathan rubbed his upper lip to cover his smile. "It is difficult to call up debts a man does not have."

"But, our house. You have seen the furniture. And the lack of proper servants."

CHAPTER 31

Susannah's doe-like eyes burrowed into him and the concern and disbelief he saw there tamped down his amusement. She'd truly thought her father one step from social ruin.

"Y-your father is a frugal man, wise with his money and careful in his costs. That is why I turned to him for help with my own properties. He has no debts. And with your mother's dowry, he has enough to give your brothers a decent start in life."

"But my dowry?"

"Is s-set to avoid fortune hunters but is sufficient for your needs." He lowered his voice. "Especially now."

Pink touched her round cheeks and the moisture in his throat grew thick.

"It seems I have more apologies to make on my wife's behalf," Mr. Guthrie said, breaking Johnathan's focus and reminding him that others were still in the room.

Susannah shook her head. "It is not for you to take on all your wife's misdeeds. She is a grown woman and can carry them herself. Think no more of it, Uncle Guthrie. I do not hold you accountable."

The man's shoulders relaxed. "You are very generous. Thank you." He reached out and placed a hand lightly at Miss Martha's back. "Shall we go?"

She nodded. "Good day, Susannah, Lord Newhurst."

"Good day, Martha." Susannah said. "And a good day to you, Uncle Guthrie."

Johnathan nodded to them both but said nothing. In a few moments they would be gone and the time would come for him to speak. And if the words would not come... he patted the letter in his pocket. He'd repeated the words so many times to himself last night that they burned brightly in his mind. If his mouth failed him at least his letter would convey all the elegance of thought his heart wished to shout to the world.

Chapter 32

When Martha and Uncle Guthrie turned to leave the sitting room, Susannah caught sight of boot tips showing at the bottom of the doorway. They quickly pulled back at the sound of footsteps, but not soon enough.

"Good day Mr. Roberts, Sir Nathaniel, Mr. Kendall," Uncle Guthrie said, not at all surprised at their presence in the hall.

Susannah waited for the men to enter after her uncle and cousin left, but instead Mr. Kendall reached in and pulled the door shut, a cheeky smile on his lips. She was alone with John. Her heart pounded, memories of last evening swirling in her mind and warming her cheeks.

Slowly she turned to him. He stared at the closed door, his face unreadable.

Fear crept in where excitement had been, stealing her thoughts away to a dark place. She had been the one to instigate the kiss that caused the scandal. The relief of her uncle declaring her father solvent had swept up her thoughts and carried them into a fairytale world where John would automatically forgive her and confess his love.

But this was real life.

She had forced his hand, and he might never forgive her for that.

John's gaze slowly met hers and his hand came up to pull something from his pocket. A letter if she was not mistaken. He held the corners of the paper gingerly with his fingertips, spinning it in his hands.

"S-s-sus-s-sannah." He swallowed. "I-I..." He shook his head, then meticulously opened the paper.

What was it? An explanation for why he could not rescue her, or a reason he would, but why he held her responsible? The distance he kept between them seemed to indicate his distress.

He cleared his throat as he pulled his reading spectacles from his pocket and settled them on his nose. His stance was all business.

Taking a deep breath, he said, *"M-m-most b-beloved Susannah."*

Her heart tripped in her chest. He still loved her? She did not need any more words to confirm it, but she listened all the same, tears rolling down her cheeks.

"F-from our childhoods y-y-you have been one of my d-dearest f-f-friends." He took a deep breath. "I reverence each experience of loss that we surmounted together and cherish each joy we shared. Never, in those early years, would I have imagined those experiences would lead me to an unutterable love and longing for you that has blossomed since my return from the continent." With every word John's gaze moved less and less to the paper he held.

"I cursed my mouth daily for the words it refused to say and the feelings it kept locked inside my lungs." His deep blue eyes rose and locked on hers. "But it holds me captive no longer. I stand before you in agony, praying I am not too late."

He stepped forward, pulling Susannah from her reverie. She mimicked his movement, bringing them closer.

Johnathan dropped the letter to the floor. "I love you with all my body and soul. You fill my life with the words I struggle to grasp, with music to lighten my darkest days, and with a generosity of spirit that looks over my inadequacies." He extended his hand and she took it. "Can that generosity forgive me now as I beg for your hand in marriage? For it is my dearest desire to traverse each season of life with you, to love you, and build a family with you. To give myself to you body, mind, and soul."

Susannah sniffled and he pulled a handkerchief from his pocket and handed it to her. If only she could get ahold of her emotions. How the tables had turned. He was pouring out his heart and she was the one who could find no words. She dabbed at her face.

He lowered his head, spectacles now removed, to look into her eyes. "Please relieve my suffering and say you will be mine."

Grinning, she threw her arms about John's neck, knocking him off balance. He stumbled back a step but caught her about the waist. Laughter bubbled up from within her and spilled out.

CHAPTER 32

"I-is that a yes?"

She placed a hand on each side of his face so she could look him in the eyes. "Yes, without a single reservation in my heart. You have been my dream for as long as I can remember. It grew slowly, a girlish admiration, but these last two years it has blossomed into a womanly desire. You are the kindest, most honorable man I know and it would be my honor to become your wife."

He pulled a hand away from where his arms had encircled her waist and gently caressed her cheek with his knuckles.

"I... love you... Susannah."

"And I love you, John."

He buried his hand into the golden curls at the back of her head and captured her lips with his own. The kiss was gentle at first, warm and sweet, but it was not enough. She leaned into him, her arms encircling his neck, her mouth hungrily meeting his kisses with fervor.

He pulled back and gasped for air, then leaned his head against hers. "W-what do you say to a common license?"

Susannah giggled. "A wise choice after the scandal we've created."

"Not to mention the amount of kissing going on behind this door," Mr. Kendall called.

Surprise sent Susannah skittering back before they both burst into laughter.

"I should have known they'd not leave even after the door was closed," John whispered. "They are worse than Lady Plum and Mrs. Cline."

"I heard that," Mr. Roberts called. "I suppose I should be the one compared to Lady Plum since she is the finer dressed of the two."

Another round of laughter ensued from both sides of the door.

Susannah stepped back into John's embrace and said, "Might you all give us a moment? We are planning the rest of our lives in here."

"I thought we *were* giving you a moment," Sir Nathaniel said.

"What are you three doing?" Melior's voice joined those in the hall.

"Eavesdropping," Susannah called, then giggled. "Would you kindly remove them?"

Melior cracked the door open and a broad smile spread over her face, flashing her nearly perfect teeth. "Of course I will. Take your time."

Then the door shut and a chorus of complaints faded as Melior no doubt ushered their audience back down the hall.

John cupped her face. "Run away with me."

Her eyes widened. "Where to?"

"Anywhere but London. At least for a few weeks. My responsibilities will no doubt pull us back."

"Maidstone?"

He gathered her hands and tipped his forehead to touch hers. "I like the way you think. Tomorrow?"

"Today."

He pulled back. "Are you certain?"

"Absolutely. I want to be married with our family surrounding us."

"Our family?"

"You have always been one of us, John, only now it will be legal."

He smiled, a contented warm smile that reached all the way to his eyes. "Your wish is my command, my lady."

"Your lady. I like the sound of that."

CHAPTER 32

The moment they stepped down from the carriage, Michael flung himself at their legs. They'd not had time to send word of their coming, but it seemed he'd seen their carriage from his window and roused the rest of the house to their coming, for Terrance was already on the drive, Amanda running down the steps behind him.

They all began talking at once, each asking how they were and why they'd come. When Susannah turned to show their other surprise, they gasped. "Andrew!"

"How?"

"Why?"

Susannah held up her hands as her father joined them and the Stanford carriage pulled up behind theirs. "I will explain once we all are in out of the cold, but first Lord Newhurst needs to meet with Papa."

Her father's gaze turned to John and a slow smile spread across his face. Stepping forward, he gave Susannah a kiss on the cheek and shook John's hand. "Well, let us proceed." He gestured toward the house, making sure to include the Stanfords and Mr. Kendall.

It took all of Susannah's willpower to keep from blurting her news to her siblings the moment they were in the parlor, but she refrained, allowing her father to meet with John upstairs to receive the happy news and grant his blessing. When they finally returned, her brothers and sister suddenly ceased speaking.

The clock on the mantel ticked, time slowed, and for once Susannah was grateful for time, grateful for the joy it had brought and the lessons she'd learned. Looking at the expectant faces, she realized how wrong she'd been to try to carry life's burdens on her own when the rest of her family had learned to share them. To lighten the load where it was heaviest, much as Lady Braithwaite had done for Melior, and then Melior and Miss Harris had done for her.

"Well," Michael said impatiently. "Tell us. Did you come because you are getting married?"

Soft, nervous laughter erupted around the room.

"Yes, Michael," Susannah said, "Lord Newhurst has asked me to be his bride."

A loud whoop filled the small space as Michael leapt into the air, fist high. Susannah smiled. She felt much the same.

"Now you'll never have to leave home," Michael said.

John looked at her over the boy's head, mirth dancing in his soft blue eyes. "Would you like to tell him or should I?"

Epilogue

The last few weeks had been the most glorious of Susannah's life. Who knew time spent with the right person could hold such joy? Nervousness filled her, though, at the thought of returning to London. But she would not stand in the way of her husband's parliamentary duties.

Her husband. Lord Johnathan Newhurst. The Right Honorable The Viscount Newhurst. She could hardly believe it. Some mornings she had to pinch herself to make certain it was not a dream.

She speared an egg on her plate and glanced up at him across the breakfast table. "I would like to accept a few invitations that have been forwarded from London. Would you like to attend with me or would you rather remain at Newhurst House?"

John glanced up from his food. "Wherever you are is where I wish to be."

"But you hate social gatherings."

He nodded. "But I love you."

She smiled. It had gotten easier for him to speak his mind these last few weeks and she adored it. Never had she imagined how poetic he could be.

"There is one in May that will take us out of the city for a few days. Is that acceptable?"

He grinned. "Absolutely. I'd much prefer gatherings in the country. Larger gardens to get lost in if the crowd is especially exhausting."

She raised her eyebrows. "Are you getting lost in these gardens alone?"

"Not a chance. I have it on good authority that a certain lady likes flowers a great deal, especially pink roses."

Susannah's eyes strayed to a side table where a huge arrangement rested, one John had given her to celebrate their first month together. "I suppose I could be convinced to wander about a secluded garden path."

He chuckled and returned to eating. After a few bites he asked, "Where is this country gathering?"

"Eastley End House. Mrs. Hardy is feeling particularly lonely since her husband went on his last voyage and has decided to have a grand gathering to lift her spirits."

"And how do we know Mrs. Hardy?"

"We don't." She cast him a cheeky grin. "But Lady Braithwaite does. Apparently the woman showed her some kindness several years ago and she wants to return the favor by having several notable guests attend."

"Like a viscount and his wife?"

"Exactly. And perhaps a duke's nephew?"

"You wish to include Eddie in our party?"

"I do. I witnessed something at Kendall House that leads me to believe an invitation to attend such a gathering would be welcome."

His head began to shake. "No, no, no. I will not fall into this trap. Did you learn nothing from Melior and Nate's attempt at matchmaking?"

"I did." She leaned forward and placed a hand over his. "I learned it works." She smirked. He rolled his eyes but could not argue the point.

Setting his utensils down, he dabbed at his mouth with a napkin. "I am not opposed to having Eddie along for the duration of the party, but that is it. Neither of us will meddle in his affairs. He is a grown man who can make decisions for himself and does not need us pushing him into trouble."

"A marriage is not trouble."

"It would be if the other person is Lady Braithwaite. I know she has been very helpful, but by what means? There is deception and intrigue surrounding that woman at every turn. Eddie's infatuation will pass. We simply need to give him time."

Susannah was unconvinced, but she made no protest. "Alright, only the gathering at Eastley End House. Then I shall leave him to his own devices."

John pushed back from the table. "Good. Now if you are finished, I have something to show you."

She took one more drink of her tea and allowed him to help her up. Hand in hand, he led her to the second story of Gimly Hall. It had taken some time for her to get used to the large, drafty home. Its stately grey stone was nothing like the warm brown brick home she'd grown up in, but it had its benefits.

New furniture being one of those. John had allowed her to choose the colors she wished to finish her favorite rooms in and then ordered furniture to suit her liking. It was strange to think a month ago she'd worried her father would be thrown in debtor's prison, only to learn he was far better situated than most of the families in Maidstone.

After witnessing the artifice of London, she was grateful for his frugal disposition. It had taught her to appreciate what she had, great or small, and it had allowed all of them to benefit. Her dowry, which had been a few hundred pounds, was not the only money given upon her marriage. It seemed another sum had been set aside from the money her mother brought into the marriage. One ten times the size of what she'd expected to receive.

She saw the wisdom in her father's financial management, for if Mr. Wallace had known her fortune, he may have been tempted to forgo Aunt Guthrie's offering and press her into a marriage.

"Where are we going?" she asked John when they did not stop at any of their usual rooms.

"I have a surprise for you."

She grasped their conjoined hands with her other hand. "A surprise? Is it a new dress?"

He shook his head.

"Another dozen roses?"

"No."

"Did the furniture for your painting room arrive?"

"Not yet."

They stopped at a door she'd not yet entered. In their tour of the house the day after they married, John had said this room needed some work and was not quite ready. So she had not questioned it.

"Is the room fixed?"

He smiled. "It is. Now close your eyes."

"What?"

"You heard me. It is a surprise." He placed his hands over her eyes and a servant opened the door.

They stepped in slowly as he guided her around something, then asked her to sit. Her seat was soft, the fabric velvety to the touch. His hands fell away from her face.

"Can I open my eyes now?" She asked.

His breath tickled her ear as he whispered, "Yes."

She opened her eyes, and her mouth went slack. The long room held dozens of portraits and paintings, but it was the one directly in front of her that captured her attention.

"That's... me." She stared at the large canvas, her profile obvious with curls that came alive. They were piled on her head and draped over her neck. The light caught on each one and seemed to shimmer across her jaw. Then it struck her.

She turned to gaze into John's smiling face. "It was *me* you painted?"

"It was," he said softly, then played with a few of the curls at her nape. "You have no idea how long it took me to catch the essence of your beauty."

Tingles danced up her neck at his touch, then he stood straight and gestured behind her. "It took a great deal of practice."

She glanced over her shoulder and then stood. The wall behind her was covered in paintings of different sizes and at different ages, but all of them were of her. A laugh bubbled in her chest.

"I am not sure how I feel looking at dozens of pictures of me. Visitors might think I'm excessively vain and demand a portrait every year."

He laughed. "No, they will think the painter is madly"—he stepped forward and took up her hand— "wildly"—he clasped her waist with his other hand— "And completely in love with you."

She leaned in close enough to kiss. "You certainly know how to propitiate your wife."

His eyes lit up. "Propitiate, now that is a fine word. Did you know it originated—"

She covered his mouth with hers. They could discuss the etymology of words later. For now she had a husband to thank, and she wished to do it properly.

Also By

Harrowed Hearts

Rescued from Betrayal

Pursued beyond Treachery

Coming soon

Saved Through Deception

Merry Men of Eton

Secrets of a Baron's Daughter
Secret to an Earls Heart
Secrets of Fallow Hall
Secrets a Captain Keeps

Newsletter subscribers only

Secret Love at Eton

Men, Mistletoe, and Marriage

A Lovely White Christmastide

Hearts of Somerset

An Unclaimed Heart

Author's Notes

In researching this book, I first drew upon my life experiences. Children often have speech patterns that resolve over time, but sometimes those impediments draw criticism that initiates mental health struggles. As a child, I had a very hard time pronouncing the s, r, and th sounds. Because of this, I attended speech therapy once a week at school. If you know anything about growing up in a small town in the 80s, this was the perfect fodder for children to make fun of me. Not that they really needed any more reasons as I often arrived unkempt to school because my family was large and I had a disabled sister that needed a great deal of my parents' attention. This teasing made learning and growing up hard and sensitized me to this type of injustice.

So when my youngest child was recently called out for his stutter, it really got under my skin. Yes, it takes him some time to express himself when he's excited. Yes, he's now developed the tendency to avoid eye contact because it makes him more nervous to see others' expectations and, therefore, short circuits his brain. But the last thing he needs is for people to pick him apart for it. He is extremely intelligent; one of the top in his class, and he is the most giving and loving six-year-old I have ever met. So why not write a character with the same struggles and strengths; with a talent for words and a heart of gold.

Additionally, I added social anxiety to John's character profile as it seems to run hand in hand with speech difficulties. I no longer struggle with pronunciation and can speak in public with little to no problem, but fear of social backlash is still real. While my insecurity does not center around the opposite gender, I know people whose anxiety does. So naturally I paired these together for a more dynamic character.

As I am not a trained painter, I contacted a close friend to help with the painting scenes. Thankfully she was able to correct what I had wrong and suggest other options. I enjoyed learning something new and maybe some day I will try my hand at what she taught me.

When it comes to the cacophony of big words, I simply draw from my husband's vocabulary. Well, not completely. I came across some of those words myself, and then, like the word nerd I am, I went down the rabbit hole of research to find each word's origin and how best to use it. I never thought I'd be able to use this specific idiosyncrasy in a book, but then John just fell right into the role.

There are several places that I describe in London that took a great deal of research to portray accurately, such as the layout of various buildings and how and when they were used. Almack's did indeed have a balcony for the orchestra and Carlton House had the fantastic staircase I described. Some of these details were difficult to locate as several buildings do not exist anymore. For example, Almack's was destroyed during WWII. I did my best, however, to remain true to the time period.

During the Georgian period, women's medical needs took a sharp decline. Previously midwives had been employed and taught by generations of women. But with the introduction of modern scientific medicine, male intervention became more socially expected. Unfortunately with it came a dark period of obstetric history when approximately one third of women and half of all infants died in childbirth. This was due to a lack of respect for the knowledge and understanding that midwives had already gained. In addition, physicians of this time period were often gentlemen who did not want to dirty their hands if they could help it. Hence the scene where the doctor speaks with Melior, but does not physically check anything is historically accurate.

Last, I dove into several laws that John might have felt compelled to fight for, which I mention in the chimney-sweep scene. By this time it was illegal to employ a boy under the age of 8, but that did not stop it from happening. In 1834 parliament went on to raise the age again to ten with a stipulation that the child had to be 14 to actually enter the chimney. In 1840 the Chimney Sweep Act was passed raising the age to 16. My fictional character would have worked hard for the rest of his life to bring about these changes after his interaction with the young boy on the street.

As usual, there is a reference to a cat somewhere in this book. But I have resorted to subtlety after my last *CATastrophe* with fictional felines led to demands for reparations. Enjoy the search.

About the Author

Teah Kemp Weight

Greetings reader! I am so honored that you took time to read my book. It has been a true labor of love. There will be many other books to come. I would love to share them with you! Please sign up for my newsletter where you will find sales, giveaways, and special offers like a free novella. Links can be found on Facebook and Instagram where you can find me under the name Teah the Writer.

A little about me, I grew up on a ranch in eastern Utah changing sprinkler lines, herding cattle, training horses and bailing hay. In high school I participated in choir, drama and dance. It was during this time I won my first award for writing.

I had always planned on a career in English literature, but life threw me a curve ball and I found myself raising a large family as I followed the love of my life through several states as he pursued a doctorate in history and began teaching.

Twenty plus years, four states, seven children, and multiple universities later, I have put pen to paper—actually fingers to keys—and started writing again.

I am an avid reader of historical romance, but I also enjoy a good romantic comedy. I hope to create many more stories set in various time periods of history. Currently, most of my stories are set in the Regency period of the Georgian era.

I live in South Texas with my very own Prince Charming. We have seven children and far too many pets. When not writing, you can generally find me being a mother, such is life with so many children. But I also enjoy horses, mountains, fall foliage and chocolate.

Acknowledgements

I want to thank my editor, Julia Allen, for always believing in me and helping me to get better with each book. If you would have seen the draft of the first book I sent her, you'd understand how much she's had to put up with for these last few years. Thankfully, she didn't just look at my mess and run screaming in the other direction.

To Johanna, Brooke, Molly, and my daughter. Your the best team of readers, writers, and friends I could ever ask for.

And to my honey, I made it through another one! Thanks for pulling me back together when I fall apart, and cheering me on when I soar.

Last I want to thank my sister-in-law Shimayne for not only boosting my ego by raving about my books, but also opening your home to me so I can attend writing conferences and book signings without breaking the bank. Love you lots.

Made in the USA
Middletown, DE
01 April 2025

73517224R10151